We declare and we hold as firmly established
that love cannot exert its powers
between two people who are married to each other,
for lovers give each other everything freely,
under no compulsion or necessity,
but married people are in duty bound
to give in to each other's desires
and deny themselves to each other in nothing.

Marie, Countess of Champagne 1174 A.D.[1]

osamund's ower

By Susan McGeown

Published by
Faith Inspired Books

Magnificent Cover Art courtesy of Laury Vaden
magentaswan@patmedia.net

Published By Faith Inspired Books
3 Kathleen Place, Bridgewater, New Jersey 08807
www.FaithInspiredBooks.com

Footnote credits appear at the end of this work.

Cover Art Credit: Queen Eleanor and Fair Rosamund (WDM27988)
by Morgan, Evelyn De (1855-1919)
© The De Morgan Centre, London/ The Bridgeman Art Library
Nationality/copyright status: English/out of copyright
Used by permission.

The beautiful decorative font on the cover and throughout this book is
courtesy of the stunning talents of Rudolf Koch; "Initialen" font.
http://www.moorstation.org/Koch_Memorial/dl/index.htm

**To all Women of Faith
who have made God smile
through the best and worst of times…**

*The Lord announces victory,
and throngs of women shout the happy news.*

Psalm 68:11 (NLT)

Table of Contents

Mistresses we keep for pleasure, concubines for daily attendance upon our persons, wives to bear us legitimate children and to be our faithful housekeepers.

Demosthenes, 4th Century B.C.[2]

Current Time
Warwick Castle
Home of Bartholomew Beauchamp, Earl of Warwick and
       Maud Fitzjohn, Countess of Warwick
Warwickshire, England
14 August 1161 A.D.

Chapter One

Thomas sat with his back guarded against the stone of the castle wall. His position, though relaxed, was calculated and precise. He felt light without his armor, so accustomed was he to wearing it, often even as he slept. The grim reality of life had taught him the necessity of always being careful and on guard. Even at a wedding. The festivities below had warranted a less threatening attire, however, and he had complied. To some extent. His sword was still strapped to his side, his dagger was still in his boot, and another knife was tucked at the base of his back, all nestled against him like the comfortable companions they were. Besides his horse, they were the most reliable associates he had. He straddled the castle parapet, negligently dangling one leg over to the sheer drop below, eyes closed, all other senses alert. It was the closest he came to being at ease. He let the beauty and delight of the night seep into his bones; the smooth aroma of warm earth baked by the summer sun, the flutter of bat wings and songs of night bird calls, the utter stillness of the brilliant array of stars and brightness of the half moon. This was where he needed to be to relax.

Not down in the great hall. Festivities or no, more food and drink than a body could imagine, the fetid smell of bodies in close proximity, so many unwashed, made him loose his appetite. And that was no small feat, for he was always hungry. It was a standing joke among the other young knights that no matter how much he ate he could always, happily, eat a bit more. He was often the first to arrive in the morning when they broke their fast and when dinner was served in the evening. He sighed and rubbed the back of his neck and then tucked his finger in the collar of his tunic and pulled. It was tight. Again. Another collection of clothes he would be forced to discard. Another collection of new gear for which he would be forced to work off the purchase. He had so many other more permanent things he wished to purchase with his meager salary such as land; a place to call home. Just when would this growing cease? At a score and eight, most of the other young men of his company had settled comfortably into the size and stature they were destined to be. But not him. It sometimes seemed that overnight he outgrew his clothes, his shoes… God, please not his armor. Again …

Thomas knew, suddenly, that very shortly he would no longer be alone. With senses alert he gauged the person's approach up the nearby stairs while he silently lifted his leg back over the parapet in a more defensive stance. He leaned back into the shadows of the wall behind him and waited.

It was a woman, a young one, dressed in a splendid gown, her hair piled stylishly about her head. Jewels glittered at her ears, neck, wrists, and hair. She was quite lovely, he thought in a distracted sort of way. He had no time for women, although certainly was willing to appreciate a beautiful one if she came into his view.

Thomas watched her for a long while. She seemed, he thought, almost to be seeking exactly what he had come into the night for. Peace. Renewal. She was completely unaware of him. She clasped her arms about her in the chill night air, closed her eyes, and took a huge breath, held it, and then let it out slowly. She looked up at the moon and the stars, smiled for a brief moment and then said quietly, "Hello."

He made no sound and yet, all of a sudden, Thomas knew she was conscious of him for her stance changed; relaxed turned tense, peaceful turned alert. Slowly she turned and looked at him, still concealed in the shadows. For a brief moment, she said nothing, but seemed to try to decide who he was and, perhaps, if she should know him.

"Should I fear you, sir?" she asked after a time.

"No," Thomas said and stepped back into the moonlight and resumed his precarious perch straddling the castle wall. "You have no need to fear."

"I see that you seem to be enjoying the festivities as much as I," she said with a small smile.

"Yes, it would seem so."

"Should I know you? I have been introduced to so many people this evening that I am afraid I will not be able to remember my own name. Please accept my apologies if we have already been formally introduced."

Thomas shook his head. "No, we've not been formally introduced. I will not overload you with another meaningless name, either. I leave on the morrow with the rest of William FitzRobert's knights who are a part of King Henry's forces." He shrugged. "There are so many of us here at this celebration I knew I would not be missed should I choose to leave early."

She smiled. "Were you at the festivities at all?"

He grinned then. "I walked past an alcove opening and peered in at the crush. Does that count?"

She shook her head. "I think not. You must truly experience the entire, stifling ordeal in order to say that you were *there*." She smiled again, and looked out at the night.

"You are not enjoying the festivities?"

"No."

"I would think a beautiful young woman would be dazzled with all of the pomp and circumstance a wedding between two highly placed families would offer."

She looked at him. "You know much of beautiful young women then?"

"No," he conceded. "I probably know almost nothing."

"Well, let me give you some much needed information, then," she began briskly. "Young women," she glanced at Thomas, "beautiful or no," and then looked back out into the night, "in the case of wedding festivities, are usually filled with absolute terror. The bride is at the mercy of the men in her life who have made choices for her in which she has had no say. She is expected to go off with the groom of her family's choosing with her head held high, a smile on her face, and her decorum at its most perfect. She goes off to a life that, should she be lucky, will place on it a value at least equal to her husband's horse." She looked at him again, "But that is doubtful." She looked away from him out onto the dark horizon, "and she must then begin the only real task that anyone cares about: producing a healthy heir to the family dynasty. Should she be successful and produce this heir – and live - she may achieve some level of prestige and honor. Should she fail, her life will be a misery that cannot be imagined unless lived. For those young women at the wedding who are not the bride, those destined for the same fate, they watch with fear and trembling *and pray*."

"Does it work?"

She looked puzzled at Thomas' question so he explained himself. "The praying."

"Yes," she nodded emphatically. "It does. I would not be what you see before you had it not."

"How old are you?"

"I will be fourteen years in a month."

"You don't seem to be fearful and trembling to me," Thomas observed.

"It is a skill I have mastered," she said and closed her eyes, "*through prayer.*" She took another deep breath, held it, and then let it out slowly.

"I am impressed."

"Are you fearful and trembling when you go into battle?" She looked at Thomas again as she spoke and he struggled unsuccessfully to determine the colors of her hair and eyes.

"No," and then he conceded, "not anymore."

She smiled at him, almost in a tolerant fashion he thought. *Could she only be thirteen?* "I am impressed," she said giving his words back to him.

He smiled back, understanding her point. "It is a skill I have mastered."

"Without prayer," she qualified.

"Yes," he acknowledged. In a teasing tone he said, "Perhaps I would have acquired the skill sooner had I tried it your way, however."

She smiled but did not respond. They stood in silence for a period of time. "I know of the groom," Thomas said at last.

"Yes, I do, too. He is an acquaintance of my father's. Sir Humphrey and my father grew up together, studied together, fought together …"

He studied her in the moonlight. "Sir Humphrey is considered an honorable man." It was the highest compliment Thomas could offer.

She sighed. "Yes, he is an honorable man. I do not think that I have ever heard a harsh word out of his mouth to his men, to women, or to the servants. I do not believe that he will be cruel to his wife, and that should give her some small comfort."

She turned to him, reluctantly he thought. "I must go back," she said finally. "Someone is bound to have missed me already." She looked at him then. "Thank you for letting me intrude on your solitude." She had a thought. "Where do you head tomorrow?"

"The Marches," He gave her a wry grin. "to follow King Henry's orders. We join with the King when we leave from here. He seems to have a standing date with a few mad Welshmen. There is always training, preparing, and fighting."

"I would know your name so that I can remember you in my prayers."

"Do not trouble yourself," Thomas said dismissively. "My sword, dagger, and horse are all I need."

"Then you are a fool," she said with absolute certainty. "Prayer protects you in places where nothing else can." She closed her eyes, took a deep breath, held it, and then let it out slowly. One single tear escaped from her closed eyes and she brushed it away impatiently. She turned to go.

"By some, I am known as Thomas," he said to her retreating back.

She turned and looked at him, now composed and serene. She inclined her head like a queen. "Whether you wish it or not Sir Thomas, I shall remember you nightly in my prayers. I will seek to secure your safety and continued health and happiness." She smiled at him then. "Whether you attribute those things to your horse, your sword, your dagger, or God is entirely up to you." And then she was gone.

He managed to find a meal for himself late into the night. There was no possible way he would have been able to sleep otherwise, for his stomach would not have allowed it. He slept with his horse, washed in the early hours at the water trough, dressed in full armor and readied his possessions to ride out immediately after dawn with the rest of the men after breaking his fast.

Thomas had not exaggerated when he had spoken last night and said that there was always training, preparing, and fighting. Even with the civil war effectively over there never ceased to be minor skirmishes no matter where they traveled. And now with Henry's all consuming determination to demolish every single baronial castle that had been erected without royal license, well ... Thomas had participated in more castle sieges than he could count.

He liked the new King though, truth be told. King Henry was a fighter and a thinker, a good combination in a leader in Thomas' opinion. He agreed with the King's desire to obliterate the rebel castles built during the civil war under King Stephen's rule, for their loyalty would always be questioned. In establishing a clear base, a definitive standard, King Henry showed one and all what was required and who would be making the rules. Thomas' only concern in the systematic destruction of the castles was the weakening of the western border defenses from the Welsh. The mad Welsh.

Just the thought of them sent a chill up his spine, still, now. God, Thomas could still remember the wild Welsh army standing bare chested, with little armor and fewer weapons on that cold January day in Lincoln so many years ago. He had been just a child then and on the *opposite* side of the fighting to where he was now. Just a lowly page for one of King Stephen's trusted knights, standing on the parapets of the castle wall witnessing his first battle. He remembered, too, the way King Stephen's men had said, *"Welshmen."* At that time, Thomas had thought it was said with contempt; but now he realized what it had truly been: awe and fear. No, it had not been King Henry's attacking knights that had caused the initial tightening of King Stephen's gut, it had been the *Welshmen* accompanying them.

Those Welshmen had been helpful in the Lincoln battle only because it had suited them. They had felt no binding loyalty to Henry, the new King then nor did they now. Earl Robert, King Henry's most senior man at the time, had been able to control the Welsh, but he had been dead these past ten years. Earl Robert's son, William, while a powerful and confident man in his own right, could not command the same respect with the Welsh that his father had. Thomas chuckled to himself, for truth be told, he did not think that Earl Robert had ever *really* controlled the Welsh, but more likely they had respected him enough simply to listen to him.

Like the march barons, the Welsh had taken advantage of England's preoccupation with its lengthy civil war. The Welsh had plundered, conquered, captured, terrorized, and reclaimed. When it suited them they joined forces with others for a time, such as at the Battle of Lincoln as allies to King Henry. But now, in present day, the Welsh blatantly challenged King Henry with their military tactics. Despite the fact that the civil war was now over, King Henry, with the aid of his knights, needed to continually remind both the march barons *and* the Welsh who, indeed, was Sovereign. It was a never ending duty.

Not that he was complaining. All this fighting was certainly good for Thomas. He had nowhere to go, no home to return to, no place to long to get back to. The average knight's duty was for forty days a year and then he was free to tend to his own personal life. But Thomas had no personal life. He had his horse, his armor, his shield, and his sword. That was it. So he continued to serve and to fight, growing stronger and more experienced. He was pleased to be part of the close circle of knights that now rode exclusively where King Henry rode. It was an honor and a privilege. Considering his beginning, he had certainly come far.

Achieving glory and fame was not what he sought, however. Thomas never had. Anything and everything he did had one means to an end. To own - outright, free and clear - his own place. He cared not whether it was a farm, a small cottage, or a castle. Having never had *anything* but the clothes on his back and the necessary materials to continue on with his profession, the concept of owning a place that one could call home was nigh onto staggering. The reality was that even working year round he had little coin saved and certainly not enough to purchase anything in which he could eek out a comfortable living. The other knights joked continually about finding a rich heiress, marrying well, and acquiring lands and title, but Thomas was more of a realist. His life had taught him thus. What titled heiress would set her sights on him, a lowly knight – without status and family - and a bastard to boot? Nay, he was not foolish enough to delude himself with dreams that would never be. He would continue to serve King Henry faithfully, working year round and carefully saving as much as he could. Perhaps when he was a score and ten he would have enough to purchase a small plot of land. The idea of a wife and family were so far on the distant horizon that it did not even register in his thoughts. But a place to call home, now *that* was something to dream about.

Thomas decided to try the hall that morning, hopeful that the majority of the people still present after the celebrations were sleeping off the results of their revelry. He found the place relatively quiet and secured a seat at the large table next to other of King Henry's knights.

"Where were you last night, Thomas?" Brian, a knight to his left said. Of all the knights, Brian was one of the few he considered friend. "With all that food around, I thought for sure you'd be right in the thick of things." Brian grinned at his own humor.

"Found yourself something better than food?" The knight to his right, Gavin, said in a disbelieving tone. Another man whom Thomas counted as friend. Gavin looked around at the others feigning absolute puzzlement. "For the rest of us a beautiful woman, a glass of fine port –

well then I would understand – but everyone knows that nothing gets in the way of your meals." He clapped Thomas on the back. "Were you ill?"

Thomas was used to their ribbing. He would have felt left out without it as a matter of fact. "I got my meal," he said between mouthfuls, and then couldn't help himself, "and had a lengthy conversation with a beautiful woman as well." There, let them stew on that for a while he thought as he reached for another hunk of bread and cheese.

There were loud wolf whistles and catcalls around the table, and Thomas received some good-natured shoving. He purposely let them think anything they wanted and made no effort to provide more information. He just kept eating. God knew when he was going to get another full meal again once they were traveling.

The mood changed when Sir Humphrey, Earl William, and the other nobles strode into the hall. The volume of conversation dropped, the general ribald humor disappeared, and an air of controlled behavior permeated the table. The new arrivals were seated at the raised dais, at a table set aside for those of elevated social standing.

"The groom looks happy enough," Brian mumbled under his breath. Thomas spared Sir Humphrey a brief glance while reaching for a leg of mutton.

"You wouldn't see me at this hour of the morning after my wedding night, I'll tell you," Gavin said. "I'd be …" He sighed a great sigh and then grinned. Thomas chuckled and shook his head.

"They're up early because they're leaving early," volunteered Robert, another knight at the table. Robert envisioned himself – in Thomas' opinion – as superior to the other young knights. He made it his concerted effort to be the first and foremost with every piece of new information. "They will travel to Sir Humphrey's holdings in Herefordshire – Goodrich Castle. I know, too, that Sir Humphrey will mix business with his pleasure." He gave them a knowing smirk.

"Thank you for your efforts to inform," Gavin said sarcastically. Robert frowned. Others around them snickered at Robert's expense.

In order to live a relatively peaceful existence among the knights, a man needed three things: a good sense of humor, a thick skin, and a strong right hook.   Most of them had at least two, but Robert had none. Consequently, he bore the brunt of most of the jests, most of the insults, and most of the misery the men could force on one another.   It was often a riding bet how far Robert could be pushed and prodded until he lost control. And once that happened, then the fun really started.

Before Robert could respond and before his baiting could truly begin the women began to arrive. As befitted ladies of rank, the knights stood in deference.

"Were you here at all last night?" Brian mumbled to Thomas under his breath as the women appeared in the upper hallway and began to make their way down the staircase.   Brian, as his closest friend in the group, would have been surprised if Thomas had said that he'd been present.

"No," Thomas admitted.

"That's Countess Maud," he said as the first richly garbed woman descended the stairs. "She's married to Earl Bartholomew. You *do* know that they own this castle, do you not?"

Thomas gave him an impatient glare.

"That's Lady Margaret, she's the mother of the bride. That's -"

Thomas interrupted him. "I *know* who that is." Earl Williams' wife, Lady Hawise, was a diminutive woman with a temper that could set your hair on fire should she choose. Everyone knew who Hawise was, or found out in a rather painful and immediate fashion.

Thomas saw her then, at the top of the stairs, just as serene and composed as she had been the night before. *Ginger hair,* Thomas thought. She was dressed regally and carried herself with a quiet dignity.

"And that," Brian said, "is the bride, Lady Rosamund. She doesn't look that much the worse for wear having endured a night of raging passion with Sir Humphrey, do you think Thomas?"

Thomas heard her voice from last night then, watching as she elegantly descended the stairs. *'She is expected to go off with the groom of her family's choosing with her head held high, a smile on her face, and her decorum at its most perfect.'* He watched her as she walked past him, smiling placidly, nodding attentively to Lady Hawise's whispered conversation. He searched her face and her movements, looking for a crack in the façade that he knew she had built around herself. There was none. Only he had seen the crack last night, he realized then, in the form of one solitary tear. But only one.

Sir Humphrey came down from the dais as she approached and kissed her chastely on the cheek before putting his arm around her and escorting her to her seat beside him. Once the ladies were all seated, the knights sat as well and resumed their meal. For the second time in less than a day Thomas found that he had lost his appetite and set his uneaten leg of mutton down.

He felt Brian's eyes on him. In a low tone Brian spoke so that only Thomas could hear, "That's the beautiful woman you spoke with last night."

It was said as a statement, rather than a question. Thomas looked at him but said nothing.

Brian grinned and then nodded with his own certainty. "Lady Rosamund. That's who you spoke with. You look like you've just been hit in the back of the head with a sword." But still Thomas did not answer him. He looked at her sitting, smiling, nodding, responding.

Let me give you some much needed information.

He heard Earl William shout loudly with laughter along with Sir Humphrey while Lady Rosamund smiled shyly and the women around them tittered daintily behind their handkerchiefs.

He felt as if someone had just lit a candle in a dark room. He, who had worked and fought and laughed and lived considerably in his score and eight years thought he knew quite a bit about life and the world in general. Thought he had most of the answers to the puzzles of life. Knew what was important, what was worth fighting for and dying for. But as Thomas sat there with his meal slowly congealing on his plate he realized what a narrow view he truly had had.

Thomas let his mind remember what had brought him to this exact point in his life, experienced and yet so shockingly ill informed. He had learned how to survive. Knew with complete certainty that anything of real importance could be acquired with hard work and determination. Believed that life was what you made of it and how you chose to deal with it, be it with sword or fist.

Riding out with the King's men, lost in thought remembering his sorry past where he had honed these beliefs, he heard her say, *Prayer protects you in places where nothing else can.*

And at last he understood what she meant.

Men's courage is shown in commanding and women's in obeying.
Aristotle, 4th Century B.C.[3]

Almost twenty years prior …
Battlefield of Lincoln, England
Lincoln Castle
Camp of King Stephen de Blois, Count of Mortain,
    Duke of Normandy, King of England
6th January 1141 A.D.

Chapter Two

Thomas would see to his obligations. Not the bitter cold, not the stench of death, not the screams of those who lay dying on the battlefield, not even his own all-consuming horror would keep him from it. He would see to his obligations or die trying.

"You watch my possessions, boy, or you will regret it for the rest of your life," Sir Robert FitzUrse had said to him as he had stalked off to battle, and foremost over everything Robert FitzUrse was a man of his word. Thomas, having been in his service as a page for more than two years, had learned through first hand experience that even the horrors of the battle he was witnessing were not as terrifying as the punishment Sir Robert could mete out should he become displeased. Even with the frigid cold, numbing his bare hands and toes, he could still feel the places on his body where Sir Robert's feet and fists had last beat him. Oh yes, Thomas knew how to prioritize his fears, and the battle before him came second to the punishment he would endure should he not see to his obligations.

Though this was the first battle he was to serve as squire, it was not a privilege he had earned. Rather, Sir Robert's squire, Martin, had fallen fatally ill not one week prior. Thomas' dreams these past few nights had been haunted with nightmares having watched the young squire writhe in agony on his pallet as he burned with fever, too fearful to cry out for help or comfort. But at least in death, Martin had at last found peace.

Thomas was not ready to be a battle squire. He knew it and Sir Robert definitely knew it. It was not for lack of knowledge, but more for lack of size. The job of a squire was strenuous work, lifting and carrying a knight's equipment: swords, shields, lances, body armor, not to mention all the armor required for the knight's horse. Thomas had the awareness of what needed to be done but not yet the muscle to do it. Even at seven years he was small for his age. He was, after all, only a *puny, good-for-nothing little bastard*, as Sir Robert liked to call him.

King Stephen had been at Lincoln castle for the past two months, four weeks outside the castle wall during the siege and four weeks inside as the victorious army. Earlier today, standing on the battlements of Lincoln Castle, they had listened to the speech made by the leader of the besieging army below. Thomas was fascinated to witness the utter gall – and sheer bravery – of a man who had lost possession of the very same castle not one month prior. King Stephen's siege, in which they had burned every bit of ground and structure surrounding the castle, had been a basic military maneuver. The only fault in the otherwise brilliant execution had been the failure to capture the Earl of Chester, defeated owner of the castle. Now the castle belonged to King Stephen of England.

But here was the Earl of Chester, outside the gates of what had once been his own castle, surrounded by a massive army of knights and men, shouting insults at the top of his lungs to the King and the King's men gathered above. The Earl was surrounded by the most vicious collection of men Thomas had ever seen, some (he had heard Stephen's men mutter *'Welshmen'* as if a curse) appearing to be unarmed and unarmored but for their ferocious glares and sharp daggers clasped in their hands.

Thomas heard the Earl of Chester begin to describe the Earl William, one of King Stephen's most trusted men, as, "… slothful in deeds; presumptuous in heart; magnanimous in words; pusillanimous in acting; the last to attack, the first to run away, tardy in battle, swift in flight …" Thomas risked a glance at the man currently being described to the delight of the surrounding enemy army below. Judging by the Earl William's near purple countenance, his fury was barely contained.

"Earl William! Can you hear me?" the Earl of Chester shouted once again, grinning despite the cold wind and the impending battle. Why he could be seated in a great hall enjoying a mug of ale for all the concern he seemed to exhibit. "Earl William, a man of singular constancy in crime, abandoned by his wife by reason of his intolerable filthiness!" The enemy army laughed uproariously. Thomas stood fascinated on the battlements watching the scene unfold before his eyes. The provocative banter was something he was accustomed to – in the dining hall, on the training field, and in the knight's quarters. But he had never realized until today it could be a part of the battlefield as well.

King Stephen's army was larger, better equipped, and better trained. The outcome of the battle was a foregone conclusion. "Let him have his fun," Sir Robert had growled under his breath to Lord Baldwin Claire, King Stephen's favorite noble, "and then I will cut his tongue out of his head myself." Thomas looked down at the Earl of Chester still grinning and shouting insults. Did he know how close to death he was? Thomas had never known Sir Robert to make an idle threat. Never.

And that's why he stood, slowly freezing to death, fulfilling his squire' obligations while the battle swirled around him. King Stephen had had such confidence in his own knights' and army's skill that he had abandoned the superior defensive position of the castle to rout the enemy army on the battlefield below. Thomas had followed as was befitting his duties, staying on the edge of the battlefield, yet in sight of Sir Robert. He had Sir Robert's spare horse, as well as his spare shield and spare sword. Managing the prancing mount and holding on to Sir Robert's weaponry had begun to make the muscles in his arms and back scream with the prolonged effort. Factor in the cold and what his eyes were witnessing for the first time, and he could not control his trembling. The thought of Sir Robert striding off the battlefield filled with the lust from fighting to find him shivering and quaking uncontrollably caused Thomas even greater fear. Obligations met or not, should he appear weak or afraid before the other knights, Sir Robert would likely kill him just for that.

Thomas' senses became overloaded with the battle that stretched out before him as far as his eyes could see. Swords clashed and sparked as steel hit steel, battle axes swung and whirred overhead to be embedded into any skull that was nearby, and men and horses screamed in the agony of injuries too great for Thomas' eyes to truly process. There was a smell to a battlefield he realized, one he had never, ever known. It was fear and blood and sweat and excrement all mixed together …

Turning, Thomas saw King Stephen to his far left, his back guarded by Sir Robert. They fought like madmen. Thomas had never seen anything like it and thought he would never again witness anything equal to their skill. Suddenly, King Stephen's battleaxe broke, but before Thomas could even locate one of the royal squires King Stephen's sword had been drawn and was clashing and sparking against his enemy. There was a high-pitched scream and a thud at Thomas' feet. As he looked down a hand and forearm clad in a battle glove lay at his feet. Thomas could not help himself and he felt the bile roll up from his stomach and spew from his mouth and down his chin.

The tone of the battle changed. King Stephen still fought like a man possessed but the enemy seemed to surge with fury and suddenly Thomas saw Sir Robert drop to his knees. He had a moment's panicked confusion wondering what he was required to do, what he would be expected to bring to him. And then Thomas watched Sir Robert topple forward on his face while an enemy knight in full battle frenzy screamed and speared his sword into his back. There was a cracking sound and Thomas watched King Stephen's sword break across the back of the man who had just felled Sir Robert.

Slowly the action of the battle slowed as King Stephen raised his hands, still clutching the broken sword shaft, above his head. One enemy knight, two, three, … five all pointed their swords at the King, but none made a move to kill him. Over the noise of the continuing battle one knight threw back his head and let out a chilling victory cry, "Come! All of you see what I have! I HAVE TAKEN THE KING!!!"

Thomas did not know how long he stood still meeting his obligations. The field, only long moments before loud and filled with the sounds of hatred and death, gradually quieted and slowed so that only the moans of the wounded and voices of the victorious could be heard. What was one to do when one's knight was killed in battle? Was Thomas meant to die as well? Was he meant to turn and run? He had no idea. He knew simply what he had been told to do and could think of no way to release himself from the job. *"You watch my possessions, boy, or you will regret it for the rest of your life."* Thomas took the horse's reins and stood on them. He laid the shield to the side; he could barely lift it let alone use it to defend himself. He drew Sir Robert's second sword from its scabbard and with all his might, using both hands, raised it so that it rested on his right shoulder. Should anyone seek to relieve him of his obligations they'd die … or he would. He looked around at the men capturing and surrendering … and prepared for his life to end.

Time ceased to exist. The cold stopped bothering him. His shivering ceased. He drew inside himself and waited, feeling surprisingly invisible - alone on the edge of the battlefield that was victorious to his enemy. The sound of footsteps gradually entered his consciousness, followed by a loud snort of laughter. "What ho? Look what we have here! A brave and fearsome knight from King Stephen's army still ready to do battle!"

There was a second voice that also spoke with laughter. "Why, based on the way most of de Bloise's men fought today, I'm surprised the whole army didn't look like this one." The knight, his helm removed and his dark hair plastered to his head with sweat, made a motion toward Thomas. "Hey boy, hand me the sword before you hurt yourself."

Thomas swung the sword using the downward momentum from its resting place on his shoulder and all the strength he still had left in his weary arms. He swung in a haphazard arc towards the knight's outstretched hand. It missed wildly but he'd made a statement.

"Why you little-!"

"What goes on here?" It was a voice of authority, drawing the attention of the knights surrounding Thomas away from his feeble attempts to get the sword back up on his shoulder ready for yet another attack.

"The little bugger just tried to take my hand off, that's what goes on here, Your Grace. I'm just about to teach him a lesson about respecting his *victorious* superiors." There were some chuckles and murmured comments in agreement. A crowd was beginning to gather.

"Do you know who he is?"

"No, Your Grace. I'll venture a guess though that it isn't his horse, shield or sword." More laughter.

"We would know your name, boy," said the voice of authority.

Thomas swallowed and looked up but did not speak. He did not trust his voice.

"Watch out, Your Grace. Seems beside his obvious weapons he has at least one hidden one."

The noble turned a questioning expression toward the taunting knight who grinned at him and said, "Vomit."

The humiliation welled up in Thomas as he remembered the stained front of his tunic. It was one more emotion in a day like no other, and in a fury he had never felt he screamed his own newly discovered battle cry and swung the sword once again.

The noble easily side stepped the swing, moving back and to the side, and in short order Thomas was dangling like a limp puppy from the scruff of the back of the neck of his tunic. He lost his hold on the sword and the horse – now free – began to move away towards better graze. He fought like a wild thing, kicking and struggling and screaming and thrashing about. After a moment the noble shook him. Like a wet rag.

"Cease your struggles. You are a captive but alive, unlike many of the men in your army. I admire your courage but have little patience beyond that. Decide now: struggle and die or be still and live. I have many things I must see to."

Suddenly, Thomas was too tired to move. Truth be told, had he been told to struggle and *live* he probably would have stayed still and died. "Good," the voice of authority said, "let this choice be the start of many more wise decisions for you. What name are you called?"

Thomas lifted his head, the muscles in his neck straining with the effort. The eyes he looked into were hard, unyielding, seasoned. The man's dark hair was liberally sprinkled with gray. His eyes were the eyes of a man whose life had been nothing but war. But they were not brutal eyes like Sir Robert's. "Thomas," he managed to say.

"Have you no other names?"

Thomas hesitated, conscious of the crowd of knights who stood and stared at him dangling like a trapped sparrow in a net. "Thomas," he said and let his head drop from exhaustion and mortification, "*The Bastard.*"

The noble lowered Thomas so that his feet touched the ground, but seemed to sense that were he to let go he would have crumbled like a piece of dirty linen. Still clutching the back of Thomas' tunic, with his other hand, the noble forced Thomas' chin up so that he again looked directly into his fierce eyes. They stared at each other for a space of a moment and then the voice of authority said, "So you are in excellent company, then."

There is a good principle which created order, light and man,
And an evil principle which created chaos, darkness, and woman.

Pythagoras, 6th Century B.C.[4]

Almost twenty years prior ...
Bristol Castle
Home of Robert of Gloucester, Earl of Gloucester
Gloucestershire, England
January 1141 A.D.

Chapter Three

Were Thomas to really think on it (although he never would, for knights never *thought* they only reacted instinctually) he was reborn that day on the Lincoln battlefield. The voice of authority, he soon learned, was none other than Robert, Earl of Gloucester, commander of the enemy army, and *bastard son* of King Henry. King Henry, as in the fourth son of King William I. King William as in William the Conqueror. King William as in *The Bastard of Normandy*. Indeed, Thomas *was* in excellent company.

In the blink of an eye, or rather the snap of King Stephen's sword, the course of Thomas' life was transformed. He walked off the Battlefield of Lincoln a captured prisoner but soon discovered that he was treated better and with more respect than he had ever been as Sir Robert's page.

His world was turned upside down, but he was not entirely sure that it was such a bad thing.

Thomas' country was at war. The worse kind of war for it was a civil war, a war in which brother could fight brother and cousin wished to kill cousin. While he did not understand all the details - so many tangled reasons that caused a hatred great enough to pray for the death of another - Thomas did comprehend the basic facts. At the start of it all had been William I. Supporters had called him William the Conqueror, for he had vanquished the royal house before him so thoroughly that those who battled *then* for the throne *were not* part of this current fight. William's successor, his son William II, had died before leaving any heirs, and that's where the real trouble had begun. As William I's successive children began to fight amongst themselves (he and his wife Matilda of Flanders had had ten children!), Henry, the fourth son, had clawed his way to the top of the pile and claimed the right to the throne. He'd held on to it for a good number of years, too – thirty-five all told.

But King Henry had left behind a tangled web of his own problems at his death. Not that he didn't try to prevent such problems, but the reality of life was that his only surviving *legitimate* heir was a *daughter* - Matilda. Now no one need explain to Thomas of the value of legitimate birth. King Henry's eight bastard children (at last count anyway) may have had all the same hopes and desires as any other royal heir, but had few solid claims to stand on. But, Thomas had also heard the comments and knew that many – male and female alike – would have preferred almost anything to being ruled by a woman. And, if her gender wasn't bad enough, Henry's daughter had married Geoffrey IV, Count of Anjou – *a Frenchman.* (Thomas knew many who spat to get the foul taste out of their mouths after saying that word.) So when King Henry died, the powerful barons had ignored his wishes and gone against the pledges they had made to him regarding Matilda's ascension and instead crowned Stephen King.

King Stephen was Matilda's cousin. He was from the royal line as well, his mother Princess Adela, another of William I's ten children. Who had the true right to the throne? Mere months ago, Thomas would have easily answered that question, having heard all the valid arguments and having watched men willing to lay down their lives in order to help King Stephen maintain his throne and his kingdom. But, as a captive, he was afforded the opportunity to see the opposite side of the horse so to speak, and that view, instead of making the issue more clear, had simply made the picture far more complicated.

The question of rights of succession, wishes of the previous monarch, and broken pledges made by so-called honorable men had muddied the waters to such an extent that Thomas' head swam. As he watched the captive King Stephen at Bristol Castle, he allowed himself the treasonable thoughts of *Are you the rightful King? Have you assumed the throne by right or by treachery?*

To make matters even more complicated, Empress Matilda was not an easy woman to like. Had she been kind, polite and friendly the waters perhaps would not be so clouded. The decision as to who should rule might have been a bit easier, for the people truly wished to *love* their monarch. But she was imperious, demanding, superior, and downright nasty to any but the most senior of her officials. Why even Earl Robert of Gloucester, who had set aside his very viable claim to the throne to support her (he was one of King Henry's illegitimate sons and therefore Matilda's half brother), was not immune to her vicious tongue. Thomas had heard her refer to him as *My Lovely Bastard Brother* on more than one occasion in the presence of an audience of her nobles. No one knew better than Thomas how that label felt.

So Thomas' country suffered under the dark cloud of civil war. In the east were King Stephen's supporters backed by the powerful barons who had chosen to go against their previous pledges to their former King and make their own choices. Their claims that King Stephen was true royalty, the rightful King of England, were powerful but not definitive. To the west and south were the supporters of Empress Matilda and Earl Robert of Gloucester. Cleaved down the middle, with each side alternately attacking, killing, destroying, and capturing all in the name of the cause they believed enough in *to die*, England suffered. Greatly.

And, as if matters were not as bad as they could possibly be, over the western border, hidden in the Marches of England, another threat loomed dark and ugly. The Marches were an area that was *never* truly peaceful: *"March"* for the old Anglo-Saxon word *'mearc'* - which meant simply "boundary". The area suffered the distinct advantage of being next to the wild country of Wales (whose people probably spit every time they said the word *English!*). The Welsh were a proud but vicious people. They would never accept Norman dominance, never acknowledge England's authority, and would always be ready to reclaim what they had lost. As the Civil War raged in England, the Welsh barons quietly dusted off their weapons, targeted their intended conquests, and made ready to avenge past wrongs. Led by a powerful Welsh Prince, Rhys ab Gruffydd, a man of cunning and superior military intelligence, they began to do something amongst the rivaling Welsh clans that had never, *ever* been done, let alone thought of. They began to actually plan and talk amongst themselves. In truth, nothing was a greater force at bringing enemies together than a mutual, all consuming hatred of another.

Ironically, being a prisoner was perhaps the best time of Thomas' life. While King Stephen and his captured nobles were kept well guarded at Bristol Castle with their every action carefully monitored, Thomas enjoyed a freedom he had never known. With the death of Sir Robert, his page responsibilities had ceased. Thomas literally, for the first time since he could remember, had nothing to do.

He was allowed to roam the castle and explored it from top to bottom. Old Martin the stable master welcomed his company, and Thomas found Martin's willingness to talk and tolerate his company stunning. Never had Thomas met someone who seemed so content with life or the company of one annoying boy.

"Make yourself useful, boy, and give the horses fresh hay. Mind you don't eat any of that hay, the horses need it more than you do."

Thomas looked sheepish as he used a pitchfork to toss fresh hay into the horses' stalls. It seemed he could not escape his appetite and he couldn't seem to contain it either. He thought he'd kept it well disguised, however. "I don't eat hay, Martin," he grumbled in embarrassment.

"Aye, you don't, but God's feet it seems that you eat anything else you can get your hands on. I saw you eating scraps off the plates that you were helping clear last night. Is Kitchen Mary not giving you enough food? I'll have a word with her about that …" As Martin joined Thomas in the haying of the horses he said, almost as an afterthought, "Did those cowardly English see fit to starve children under their own care as well as kill innocent men and women?"

Thomas had already listened to days and days of Martin's litany of hate for King Stephen and his followers. He certainly didn't need to add an additional day to the list. "Yes, Martin, they fed me," he said in an effort to placate Martin and his rising temper. Thomas hayed faster, trying to impress Martin with his work and distract him from his temper.

"How often? Once a week?"

Thomas suddenly had a flash of himself searching through the rubbish pile for edible bits and eating dinner remains from the bucket of slops he carried out to the pigs. He shrugged, "No, more than that." He had no idea how telling his answer was.

"Tell me truth, boy, are you not getting enough to eat here? Is that why you're still stealing scraps?"

Thomas kept his back to Martin to hide the embarrassment he knew stained his face. "No, they feed me plenty. It's just …" he struggled for words and his own understanding, "it's just that I worry that there won't be enough … next time, and so I try to get as fulled up as I can *now* when the food is here, just in case."

He kept forking the hay methodically into each stall, but the silence behind him became something Thomas couldn't ignore. When he turned, Old Martin was looking at him with a thunderous expression.

"Don't be mad at me, Martin. I won't do it no more, if you say so."

Martin threw the pitchfork down and said in barely contained fury, "Come with me," and stalked out of the barn.

Thomas followed, for disobedience was not in his understanding, although he dragged his feet and felt the spark of fear ignite in his belly. The spark turned to a full-fledged flame as he realized they were headed to the kitchens. What was Martin about? Would he tell the others on him? Would he be punished? While he knew asking for more was forbidden, eating scraps should be allowed. Shouldn't it? Did the amount of scraps he ate make that much difference? Good God, would they be angry with him for stealing food destined for the pigs? Thomas knew how precious a good sow was. A farmer could live his whole life and never be able to afford just one. By all that's holy, it had never occurred to him that while he filled his belly with table scraps he was depriving the pigs of their much needed food. Oh no, Thomas thought, as the dawning realization of his actions came to him. Now he was in for it. He'd get a beating for sure. He thought back in his mind and realized that the last beating he'd gotten had been just before the battle. He'd not been quick enough securing Sir Richard's gauntlets as he'd dressed.

He sighed as they entered the kitchens. Two weeks. He'd gone two full weeks without a beating. He smiled to himself, for in truth it was the longest he'd ever gone between punishments. Every two weeks wasn't so bad. He hoped they wouldn't use the birch switch …

"This be Kitchen Mary," Martin said gesturing to an enormously fat woman standing by the cook fires. "We call her *Kitchen* Mary because there are at least three other Marys working here in the castle." Kitchen Mary's face was flushed beet red from the heat and perspiration dampened the hair that had escaped her mop cap. She smiled and wiped her brow with the edge of her enormous apron.

"This be Thomas," Martin said to Kitchen Mary. He faced her with his back to Thomas. "He's always hungry, Mary. He's eating scraps off the plates at night when he helps clear the tables. I'm worried he might slaughter and eat one of me horses in the stable. Can't have that, you know, Lord Robert would have me head. What can you do about it?"

"Well now," Kitchen Mary said as she looked at Thomas, "first I'll be knowing if this young man is hungry because he finds my cooking not to his liking."

The concept that *any* kind of food would not be to a person's liking was as foreign to Thomas as the idea that a man could fly like a bird. And the food *here* had been better than he'd ever tasted in his entire life. His incredulity at the very idea showed in his voice, "Not like your food

Mistress Kitchen Mary?" he shook his head vigorously, "Nay, not at all. That's why I eat the scraps, no sense such good food going to waste."

"Why don't you ask for more if you're still hungry, instead of eating the scraps?"

Thomas looked from Kitchen Mary to Martin and then back again to Kitchen Mary. Was this a question meant to trick him? To get him into further trouble? He looked down at his feet and mumbled, "I know better than to ask for seconds, Miss."

"And why is that, young Thomas?"

It was the kindness of her voice that made Thomas look up at her and answer honestly. "I know 'tis forbidden," he said in a whisper.

"Mayhap that be the rule in *Royal English* kitchens, but here to ask for seconds is a high compliment to the cook."

Thomas looked up at both of them, gauging their faces and the truth of Kitchen Mary's words. "You speak the truth?" He still could not believe her.

Kitchen Mary nodded. Martin nodded. The two serving girls at the table who were peeling a mountain of potatoes looked at him, smiled shyly, and nodded. The big man who had just carried in a new load of split logs for the stoves and who had obviously heard just the very end of the conversation looked at Thomas and nodded.

Kitchen Mary walked over to Thomas, put her hand on his shoulder, and smiled. "I'd be most pleased to have you ask for more of my cooking."

Thomas licked his lips at the thought. "At every meal?" He needed to clarify, get it all straight, know where the parameters of this treasure extended.

Kitchen Mary nodded and smiled again. "In fact," she said as she went back to kneading the bread dough rising on the table, "those who are in my *good graces* and see fit to help me out with small chores and such have the free run of the kitchen and can eat *any time they want.* Ain't that right, Jack?"

The man who had brought in the wood had traveled to a corner of the kitchen where a mound of tarts and small pies and biscuits sat on a small table. There were a few crude chairs and a pitcher and mugs as well. The man called Jack took a tart and crammed the entire thing into his mouth in one swift motion. "Absolutely," he mumbled, his mouth stuffed to bursting. He winked at Thomas and left the kitchen.

Thomas' mouth hung open in stunned shock. The idea, *that you could eat until you were full and then some* was unbelievable. He shut his mouth, afraid that he would drool, for his mouth had begun to water at all the possibilities.

"You've finished helping me hay the horses," Martin said to him. "Perhaps Kitchen Mary has a few chores she'd like you to do for her."

"Well, Thomas the Hungry, what say you?" Kitchen Mary's eyes twinkled, and as she brushed a stray lock of damp hair from her forehead she left a slash of flour across her cheek.

Thomas nodded his head still in a daze.

"Well then, young man, grab yourself a tart and then quick follow after Jack. I need at least five more loads of wood just to get us through to the nooning meal." Thomas didn't need to be told twice.

From then on his days fell into a comfortable routine. He helped Kitchen Mary before and after every meal as much as she needed and for as much as he could eat. He helped Martin in the stables before breakfast, mucking out the stalls, hauling and forking hay, currying and brushing the horses. Through Martin he met the blacksmith and armorer, Colin, who oversaw the care, repair, and creating of the weapons an army in the midst of civil war required. When Old Martin and Kitchen Mary ran out of chores for him, then he'd wander over to Colin's forge to sit and listen, and maybe do some chores. Colin didn't seem to mind his endless questions and seemed quite happy to talk as he worked.

As the summer ended and the cool of autumn began to creep into the air, Thomas was forced to make the acquaintance of Sewing Mary for it seemed he was in desperate need of new clothes. Old Martin said it best, "Thomas, you'll catch your death walking around naked as the day you were born, not to mention the stir you'll cause, and if you wait much longer that's how you're going to be. Why you're fair busting out of those rags you're wearing."

And then Earl Robert was taken captive during another of the many battles and things were stirred into a complete uproar. King Stephen, prisoner for nine long months, now became a valuable pawn in the bargaining between the two sides. Talks of prisoner exchange and retaliation were the only topics discussed in the kitchen, in the stables, in the armory, and in the training yard.

At the start of December Thomas found himself standing in his new clothes in the great hall before William FitzRobert, Earl Robert's son. He was as imposing as his father, with just as commanding an air. Beside him sat the Empress Matilda. While the sight of the food on the massive table caused Thomas' mouth to water, he knew for sure that Kitchen Mary would be waiting for him with a tray full of tarts. That confidence allowed him to concentrate more on the people present rather than the food. His eyes took in the haughty stare of Empress Matilda, the tolerant gaze of Sir William, and the questioning gaze of King Stephen who sat off to the side.

"It seems your capture has agreed with you, young Thomas," Sir William began.

Thomas struggled to remain calm, forcing the uncertainty and fear of the unknown down deeply – below his stomach's rumblings and over the rich food aromas. He bowed formally, "Yes, Your Grace." He turned and bowed respectfully to the Empress. "Your Highness." He saw, out of the corner of his eye, Empress Matilda's somewhat surprised expression by his proper formality.

"You have been busy while you have been here." It was a statement, not a question and Thomas struggled with what was required of him.

"Your Grace?" What did Sir William wish of him? Thomas fought his rising panic.

"You have many here in the castle who have spoken in your favor. Do you know who I speak of?"

Thomas was at a loss. He shook his head no.

"Within a fortnight, King Stephen will be allowed to leave this castle." Thomas risked a brief glance at the King and then returned his gaze back to Sir William. "He will be allowed to take with him those who were also captured and have been held here these past months." Still Thomas did not understand the reason why he stood before these nobles. "There are those within these castle walls who have stepped forward in defense of you and wish for you to remain here instead of returning to London."

Sir William paused for a moment to let his words sink in. Thomas had many questions but feared his voice would not cooperate. His eyes darted around the room, past the nobles he stood before. He returned his frightened gaze to Sir William. What was he to say?

"Martin wishes to take you on as a stable hand, Mary of the kitchens wishes to keep you on the household staff, and Colin, a man of few words and fewer friends, wishes for you to apprentice with him as a blacksmith." Sir William's expression was unreadable. "What say you to all of this, young Thomas?"

Thomas swallowed the enormous choking mass of fear in his throat and managed to croak out, "I am at your will, Your Grace." As an afterthought he bowed again.

Sir William continued. "I remember my father congratulating you on the battlefield for the first of what he had hoped to be many wise decisions. So I ask you, if given the choice, do you wish to return with Stephen or remain here? I would know where your loyalties would lie."

Thomas was nothing. He was a bastard, abandoned by his mother, who knew nothing of his father. He was small, weak, and easily frightened. He heard Sir Robert's voice, which still haunted his dreams, saying, *You cause me more grief and coin than you will ever be worth, you puny little bastard.* Through those painful memories came Sir William's words spoken not moments before, *There are those within these castle walls who have stepped forward in defense of you and wish for you to remain here instead of returning to London.* Someone actually *wanted* him? How could that possibly be?

Thomas glanced at Empress Matilda, who appeared bored and impatient. He glanced at King Stephen, who appeared furious at his hesitation. His gaze traveled back to Sir William, who did not smile, but had fair eyes just like his father. Thomas could not begin to claim a full understanding of the war that was being waged within the boundaries of his country, but he *could* understand where he had felt happier than he had ever felt in his life. Heart pounding practically out of his chest, he went down on one knee and bowed as formally as he had seen the knights and nobles in court. "It would be my greatest wish to swear fealty to the Empress Matilda, rightful heir of the throne of England, and remain here in her service."

He did not look up, but stayed kneeling, head down, waiting. He heard Sir William rise and step around the great table to stand before him. He saw Sir William's leather shoes come into his line of vision. Still he did not look up. "You have showed great industry while here at the castle, working diligently and earning the respect and admiration of those servants I value most highly. On the battlefield you showed courage and stamina and impressed both my father and me. However, I will not honor the request of those who spoke in your defense. You will not be allowed to remain with Martin, nor Mary, nor Colin."

Thomas' heart ceased its frantic beating. It just about stopped for the sorrow and disappointment that threatened to break it. Sir William's voice came from a distance, "A person with such commitment to hard work, the ability to command respect in such a short time, and the courage to face what you faced on the battlefield deserves more. I would be honored if you would become my newest squire." Thomas felt Sir William's hand on his shoulder. "Stand, young Thomas, and let us all hear your answer."

Thomas stood before the unsmiling gaze of Sir William. He found his voice, from where he was not sure, but spoke loudly and clearly so that all could hear, "It would be my utmost honor to serve you, Your Grace." And then Sir William smiled.

Current Time
Goodrich Castle
Home of the Earl and Countess of Hereford and Essex
Herefordshire, England
August, 1162 A.D.

Chapter Four

Rosamund should have been able to do this.

She could, of course, with prayer, accomplish anything that was required of her.

She had seen to her duty. She was now a wife. A countess! *The Countess of Hereford and Essex, the Lady of Goodrich Castle.* From that first night of their wedding she had made ever effort to face her new husband with love, understanding, and … *bravery.* But even that first night, all she had had to offer had not been enough. She should have known …

Was it not a beautiful wedding, Milord?

Yes.

What a compliment to both our families that Earl William went out of his way -"

Rosamund, I have no desire to converse with you.

Milord?

There is but one purpose for this marriage and conversation is not it.

But shouldn't a husband and wife have companionship and conversation? Does that not enrich a marriage and make it stronger? I had simply hoped …

I need a legitimate heir, Rosamund, not companionship or conversation. If you require such I will make every effort, once we arrive at Castle Goodrich, to secure a lady's maid or companion to provide you with all the camaraderie you wish.

But I -

Come here, Rosamund. I grow weary of the wait.

She prayed for patience. Lord knew that she needed it. Lord also knew that she was running out of it. She had tried. Lord Almighty, He knew she had tried.

In the face of cool disinterest she had been open and friendly.

In the face of blatant dislike she had been polite and respectful.

In the face of impolite condescension she had been articulately magnanimous.

But the reality of her life was slowly killing her, sapping her will to live and pray and continue to put one foot in front of the other. After more then a full year of marriage, it was time for her to concede that nothing she said or did was going to make one bit of difference here in this place she was expected to call home. *Not one blessed thing.* The very proof was right in front of her, making her face the reality of her life yet again.

Castle Goodrich itself was similar to Castle Clifford, where she had been born and raised. Although larger and more foreboding, it was still surrounded by familiar lands, nestled in the Marches of England and the wild country of Wales. She understood the pace of life, the people's wants and needs and fears, and Rosamund was certain, had she been given the opportunity, she would have done well in the role of lady of the castle.

But that was not meant to be. Standing in the shadows of the walled garden, Rosamund watched her husband passionately embrace Nell, the housekeeper. The very same man who had yet to kiss her, embrace her, or speak words of love to her – simply mated with her quickly and efficiently as was required - was crushing the life out of the woman in his arms and pressing feverish kisses anywhere he seemed to be able to get his lips.   Rosamund lifted her hand up to her mouth to stifle any sound. Words of fury? Screams of injustice? Shouts of shock?

In a detached way she watched for a few moments more, her mind flashing through a kaleidoscope of scenes from the past year.   Slowly, understanding solidified in her mind as real as the stone wall she was leaning against.

The cool disinterest from people from the castle as well as the surrounding village was simply because she was *not needed.* The lord of this castle already had a woman, a woman such as themselves, who was one of them, who obviously loved him and whom he loved in return. Rosamond's openness and friendship had been unwanted. Even more so it was a threat, for to befriend her and make her welcome would have shown a disloyalty to the woman currently locked in her husband's fierce embrace.

The blatant dislike Rosamund had felt, mostly from Nell and her son Baldwin, she now understood, would never be turned around by her polite and respectful manner.   Rosamund started with another flash of perception.   Could Baldwin be Humphrey's illegitimate son?   For if that were true, then there was a double purpose for their hate; not only had she displaced Nell as the lady of the castle, but should she bear any children, their legitimacy would undermine any and all of Baldwin's claims to inheritance.

Rosamund shook her head at her naiveté. When she had begun to make overtures to assume the roles the proper mistress of a castle should, she had met varying degrees of outright disobedience. Now she realized with perfect clarity why: she was *not* the proper mistress of this castle *nor would she ever be.*

She sighed. What she was, was a failure. An utter and complete disappointment to her husband. For all he had wished of her, all he had asked of her, all he had needed from her had been for her to produce an heir. One single, solitary, healthy, male child. And she had not even been able to conceive, let alone carry a child to full term, birth it, and have it be male. The enormity of the task and the realization of her inability to accomplish it welled up inside her so that she thought she would burst with the misery of it all. As Rosamund turned and made her way silently out of the castle garden, leaving the lovers' their privacy, she stumbled, blinded by tears and her own humiliation at her gullibility. Why, she was a failure *and* a fool.

She made her way to her rooms and threw herself across her bed. Rosamund allowed herself a good cry, although she knew it would not help her in the least. Tears had not helped when she had begged to be taught by the tutor, Maxwell, to read and write like her brother, Nathan. Tears had not brought Sister Helen back after her death. Tears had not gained her permission to stay safely secluded her entire life behind the walls of Godstowe Nunnery. Tears had not helped when she had pleaded not to be introduced to society and shopped around like a cow at a fair ready to be purchased. And tears had not helped her escape a marriage to a man she did not know, let alone love. But at the moment, tears were the only thing she could do.

The sun had dipped low onto the horizon and shadows were creeping slowly across the floor of her bedroom when Rosamund finally pulled herself together enough to sit up and wipe her face.

You have not prayed … Rosamund heard the soft, reassuring voice of Sister Helen as if she were sitting right now on the soft stool by the dark fire grate and not dead these three years past.

"You're right, Sister Helen," she said with a sigh, "I have not prayed. Shame on me." She closed her eyes, took a deep breath to calm herself, held it for a brief moment and then slowly let it out. As she breathed, she talked silently to her Lord, thanking Him for the things in her life that were precious: her health, the beauty of the world around her, the care and friendship of her lady's maid, Beatrice, the skills she had that made her capable and strong and able … *Never start a prayer of wants without telling our Lord of your appreciation for all the things He has already gifted you with.*

"Lord, please …" she stopped and felt her throat tighten with held back emotion. Would these tears ever reach their end? Rosamund was loath to ask the same prayer that she had asked for longer than she could remember … *The Lord never gives you hopes and desires He does not intend to fulfill.* Heaven help her if she ever ceased to believe in that assurance from Sister Helen. "I want to be happy," she whispered softly, brushing the worthless tears impatiently from her cheeks, "I want to be loved and treasured and valued for *me* and all that I am. *Please* … Please send me someone who will love me as much as I love him."

She had a flash of Humphrey and Nell embracing passionately in the garden and felt a wave of such jealousy and self-pity that the tears welled up and spilled over once again. Resolutely, Rosamund went to the washstand and poured cool water in the basin, wet a rag, and then pressed it against her hot, flushed face. *Be thankful for all things, Rosamund. Even the bad can be turned around when you understand that all things work together for good to those that love Him …*

She snorted a loud unladylike snort through the towel. "What good would you get out of what I witnessed this afternoon in the garden, Sister?" she asked aloud, her voice muffled. *You tell me, Rosamund. Come now, think …*

Ringing the towel out, Rosamund carefully hung it over the edge of the basin. She peered out the narrow window of her room and took a few moments to enjoy the beauty of the sunset. She rested her head against the cool stone, sighed loudly, straightened her shoulders, and pursed her lips in thought.

The first thing she was thankful for was bitter, but viable nonetheless. Humphrey's desire of Nell certainly kept him out of Rosamund's bed! That was top of her list of things she was appreciative for! *Rosamund,* she could hear Sister's reprimanding tone.

Well, she thought, if Humphrey and Nell could experience the passion she had witnessed then it must surely, truly exist. That was a positive thing to know … She had begun to doubt that true love could be real.

She had to admit that there was a level of relief in understanding where all these unwelcome feelings had originated from since she'd arrived at the castle. Rosamund had never experienced such profound dislike from *anyone,* let alone an entire household and village of people. To realize it wasn't *her* specifically after all, but simply the circumstances, caused her to pause and feel a small relief. It was nothing she had done, after all. Yes, that was a positive.

All this is well and good, Rosamund. But what is the positive for you specifically?

"For me? Specifically? What good could I possibly glean from the fact that my husband is passionately involved with the housekeeper? Now that is a far stretch, Sister Helen. Truly a far stretch!"

Sister Helen. Precious, dear, loving, Sister Helen. A woman who had never married and made a conscious effort to surround herself with things that brought her joy and strength. A woman, Rosamund's father said, no man would have, because she refused to bow to convention and the *right way of things* (to which Sister Helen simply laughed, rolled her eyes and said, "Brothers!", for *Sister* Helen, was also *Aunt* Helen, Rosamund's father's sister). A woman who had taught herself to read and write because no one else would do so. A woman who had dedicated her entire life to God ... and Rosamund. *I felt it was God's wish to make you and your upbringing my greatest responsibility.*

Sister Helen had been a buffer that had protected her from her mother's pretensions, her father's greed, and her brother's superiority. Sister Helen, who believed that a person simply by accident of birth was not a prisoner to the dictates of society's whims. Tiny in stature but mighty in will, Sister Helen had faced down each and every member of Rosamund's family who stood in the way of what Sister Helen thought was best for Rosamund.

"Rosamund, you are a mere woman. Higher education would not only be fruitless but a waste of Maxwell's valuable time." Her father, Walter FitzRichard, current lord of Castle Clifford, though he loved her in his own way, had made it perfectly clear how and where she fit within the scheme of things. While Rosamund was valuable to him as far as the eventual marriage she would secure, and in doing so hopefully solidify his own tenuous claims to Castle Clifford, she was not important enough to waste the time of Maxwell, her brother Nathan's tutor.

Rosamund voiced valid arguments that she shared with anyone and everyone. But what no one could or would explain to her was why, just because she was a woman, was she to be denied things that not only would give her great joy but would also enhance her as a person? Would not her ability to do math sums enable her to better manage household duties? Would not her ability to read and write enable her to stimulate her mind and make her a better companion and hostess to a husband? Would not her understanding of political affairs enable her to provide wise counsel and insight in turbulent times such as these? She asked these questions, over and over, politely and with the utmost respect to any and every adult who tried to tell her "No," she could not make use of Maxwell's services.

"Ros, why bother with the headache of learning to read and write? I wish I was as fortunate as you. I'm stuck learning English, French, and Latin while you are *free*. You don't need to know such things to do what is required of a woman." Her brother Nathan might love her but was certainly unwilling or unable to understand her desires.

Rosamund was to be trained in all the responsibilities a proper young woman was expected to possess: embroidery, wifely obligations, and skills to run an estate. In addition, she was expected to learn how to cope with her subordinates and cater to her peers and betters. At each and every opportunity Rosamund pointed out to anyone who would listen that she still had the time and energy and desire to learn whatever Maxwell would teach her.

"Rosamund, why must you always fight the tide? Why must you always challenge the way things must be? Why can you not simply embrace your role in life and revel in your God given rights as a woman: to be gracious, obedient, submissive, and grateful for the protection and guidance from those in your life who care and know what is best for you? Does this mean nothing to you? Do you realize that you could aspire to a superior station in life?" Her mother, Lady Margaret, was perhaps her greatest opponent. Indeed, her most vocal adversary.

It was only Sister Helen who had championed her. Sister Helen. God rest her soul. A person who seemed to understand at least some of Rosamund's desires. Sister Helen had at last added her voice to Rosamund's arguments, volunteered to monitor and step in should things get out of hand, and finally had pointed out that *she* could read rudimentary Latin and was certainly none the worse for it.

And so, finally at age eight, Rosamund had been packed off to Godstowe Nunnery and allowed instruction in the basics of reading, writing, and sums. What she may have lost by starting late, Rosamund made up for tenfold. Originally only to be trained to read and write Latin (the language of the Holy Scriptures) through tenacity, deception, and careful listening in the schoolroom, Rosamund managed to acquire the rudiments of French and English as well. She suspected Sister Helen was aware of this but it was never acknowledged aloud between them. It seemed their secret.

Most importantly, it was from Sister Helen that she had received the gift of faith. The understanding of a loving God who made no distinction between man or woman and who simply required a person to acknowledge His sovereignty, repent of her sinfulness, and embrace the gift of His Son and all that it entailed. This was to be Rosamund's greatest strength. Sister Helen took this job very seriously: sharing faith's benefits, encouraging faith's practices, and modeling faith's instructions.

Sister Helen had taught Rosamund how to pray and how to believe. She had shown her that despite the harsh realities of life, a person of faith could be blessed, protected, and *loved* merely for believing in the one true God. Above and beyond all that Sister Helen did for her, this was truly her greatest gift.

But as much as Sister Helen loved and cared for her, Rosamund was still, in the end, merely another valuable female pawn in the game of political intrigue. With Sister Helen's sudden death Rosamund lost her protective buffer. Only in her prayers could she achieve even a semblance of what she had experienced while Helen had been alive: encouraging, delighting, teaching, modeling … Would that she could have that kind of companionship again? She knew the answer deep in her heart … *no*.

When Rosamund was at the suitable age to begin the search for a husband – ten and three, it was no surprise that her mother, within what seemed mere months of Sister Helen's death, had secured a suitable match for Rosamund.

"Our job was to attract a suitable husband for you, Rosamund," her mother had said. "He must be wealthy, titled, and in good graces with the King. Earl Humphrey could not be more perfect! His family has held the Earldom of Hereford for many years and he has just recently secured the family estates back from King Henry."

"Mother, can I not remain at Godstowe Nunnery? Why must I marry Earl Humphrey? Can he not find another suitable bride? Why must it be *me*? *Please* …"

Lady Margaret had allowed herself a great, world weary sigh before addressing her ungrateful daughter for what, she hoped, would be the final time. "Why can you not appreciate this opportunity, Rosamund? Why can you not comprehend the hard work and delicate negotiation that went into this arrangement? Earl Humphrey is in desperate need of an heir! Two wives over the last two score and ten years have been unable to succeed. You are young, healthy, vibrant … Earl Humphrey has great hopes."

Rosamund's father had joined the conversation. "Remember," her father had said, hands on hips as he glared down at her, "the fate of this castle rests in your hands. We must appear loyal and faithful to the newly crowned King. Earl Humphrey has the King's ear. He would not have had his familial estates reinstated had he not. And don't go spouting any of the ridiculous notions that Helen seemed fit to pack into your head when you have the opportunity to speak with him! You keep your mouth shut, your head down, and your damnable questions behind closed lips. I'll not have you ruin all I've worked for to secure this castle by one idiotic slip of your tongue."

And finally, her brother had said with a smirk, "Well, Ros, think you can handle this? For the first time, it seems, you will be given the opportunity to prove yourself. Too bad all that book learning you so wanted won't be required. Just that sweet female body of yours. Just like we told you."

By birth she was Norman. Her mother's forbearers were direct descendants from the Earl of Tosney, in the oft disputed lands of Normandy to the north of France. Her mother's history stretched back to and beyond the time of William the Conqueror's victorious routing of Harold Godwinson, the Usurper King at The Battle of Hastings in 1066. Why, give her mother just a moment's pause and you would be bound for hours listening to her rattle off the wondrous line of brave and fearless ancestors who had enabled the present King Henry II's current elevated station in life.

By her father's choice she had been raised English, but here the lines of loyalty blurred. For her father, Walter FitzRichard, was not a man to swear allegiance to a side and die in the defense of it. Nay, her father was more likely to change allegiances as he changed his tunics, whenever the need suited him. He was not the true lord of Castle Clifford. Oh, to be sure, he was married to Margaret Tosney, and the Tosney family were the true owner's of Castle Clifford since it had been passed down through the generations through lines of blood and marriage. But the small inconvenience was that the true Earl of Tosney, Rosamund's Uncle Roger, was still alive and well.

Having served King Stephen well and faithfully during the Civil War, Roger Tosney had returned a defeated warrior. But his defeat had been more far - reaching than even he had first realized, for during his lengthy service to his King, his castle had been stolen from him. Walter FitzRichard, his steward and brother-in-law, had taken possession of the castle, and at Roger's return had refused to relinquish it. Why her father had even gone so far as to change his name from Walter FitzRichard to Walter *Clifford*. And in case that was not enough to ensure his ownership – marriage, current possession and name change – Rosamund's father had cunningly claimed allegiance to Henry Plantagenet, the newly recognized heir to the throne. What recourse had Roger? Go and complain to the newly crowned King Henry II, the very man he had just spent the past ten years fighting to destroy? Mount a siege against his own castle with only the fifteen loyal knights he still had under his command? Nay, he had turned and ridden away, the last look at his castle having been the stoic yet victorious expressions of his sister and her husband watching him from the battlements.

With Helen's death Rosamund's life of loneliness had well and truly begun. With the exception of her lady's maid Beatrice, Rosamund had few opportunities for real conversation. It was a state that she became accustomed to gradually. Even when she was seated with a roomful of women visiting in Castle Clifford's solar, she still often felt alone. It wasn't that she didn't fit in.   Oh no, she was an expert at blending in, accommodating, responding, and doing her best to make herself ... invisible to the casual observer. And that was the irony of it all. In a world full of casual, shallow, uninterested people, she was just the opposite. She craved knowledge and depth and laughter and love ...

It was the lack of similarly minded people that made her feel alone whether she was in a crowd or sitting demurely on her horse all by herself. For she knew, with great certainty, that there was no longer anyone in her entire life who really, truly cared about what was on the inside rather than what showed on the outside. She knew with utmost certainty that it was a waste of time and energy for her even to hope. The fortune of having one special person like Helen in her life for a very brief time had now passed. Rosamund was an *anomaly*. When Maxwell, her brother's tutor, had defined her as such she had initially been upset by his perception. But reality had a way of convincing one of things one could not change.   She *was* an anomaly. She always had been and always would be.

Rosamund decided her life was very much like that of a wagon wheel. She was the center, a spot that was almost invisible, and on first glance totally missed in the study of the wheel's design – but absolutely essential in the reality of it all. The spokes that fanned out from the center were the people and things that made up her life: her mother, her father, her brother, her ... husband, her King, her country. The outside part of the wheel, the sturdy wood and iron that held it together and gave it the strength to withstand the deep ruts and large rocks encountered on the road were her faith. *I can do all things through Christ who strengtheneth me.*

What can you gain from today's discovery, my dear? You continue to avoid the question ...

It was dark now.   Dinner would be served at any time and Rosamund must make her appearance.   She must put on the careful outward shell she wore like armor and greet all those below who did not want her, who did not like her, and who wished her continued failure.

And then, suddenly, Rosamund knew what the benefit of her situation was. She was free. No longer did she need to try to impress or win over anyone, for the situation was completely out of her hands. For the first time in Rosamund's life she would just be herself without any concern for how it would be misinterpreted. For she had already lost. She was already a failure. There was nothing she could possibly do anymore. Her husband did not love her. She was barren. There was no value in her life. At age fourteen, all things were over and done.

Rosamund felt lighter all of a sudden. And even felt a small spark of happiness. She felt the tension that defined her life – to do, say, interpret, and respond correctly – released like a taut rope that suddenly snaps.

She went over and looked in the peering glass at her reflection. Her eyes were still a bit red and puffy. Her wimple was half off her head from her lying on the bed crying. She removed it and went through the motions of straightening her hair before she placed it back on. Sister Helen had always hated wimples. She'd joked one time that she had almost decided not to become a nun because of them – only to realize that she was stuck wearing one anyway in "polite" society! It was a warm night and the coolness she felt without the wimple pinned to her head was glorious. She shook her head, feeling her long hair sway, and the air worked its way to the sweat of her scalp.

There was a knock at her door and her maid Beatrice's muffled voice. "Milady? His lordship begs me to remind you that the dinner hour has arrived and you have not come down to the hall? Are you well?"

Rosamund looked at herself in the peering glass. "Aye, Beatrice, I am well. One moment, please." She took a deep breath, closed her eyes, held it, and then breathed out slowly. She looked at the wimple in her hand, tossed it on the bed and walked to the door.

"I am free," she said quietly to herself, desperately trying to bolster her courage and still the trembling of her hand on the door latch. The new protection with which she would now surround herself would no longer be the hard pressed illusionary demeanor that was required of every well bred young lady. Instead, her new protection would be the person that she confidently knew she was: a woman of God, intelligent, well educated, free, *and* a complete failure.

She smiled. Not such a terrible list when you think about it.

In the next two weeks, Rosamund caused more of a stir with the people and circumstances around her than she had in her entire life by *just being herself.* And wonder of wonders, it felt *marvelous.*

For when a woman grows in virtue despite her inherited instincts
and gladly keeps her honour, reputation, and person intact,
she is only a woman in name, but in spirit she is a man!

Gottfried von Strassburg, 13ᵗʰ Century A.D [6]

Goodrich Castle
Home of the Earl and Countess of Hereford and Essex
Herefordshire, England
November, 1162 A.D.

Chapter Five

ne moment Rosamund was asleep and the next she was aware that a man had just sat on the edge of her bed. *Not so soon!* her waking mind screamed. Her monthly had only just finished, surely she would be spared another day or two before it all began again? She willed her heart and her breathing rate to slow and calm. *It is your duty,* her mind reminded her. *Perhaps, this will be the month …* She sighed to herself and willed her head to take her someplace other than the reality of where she was, here, right now. Humphrey would be quick - he always was - and silent. Always well fortified with ale or port, he arrived in the dark of the night, had his way with her, and then immediately left. They were two complete and utter strangers who were both faithful to the duties they were assigned. Rosamund rolled to look at him, for he seemed disinclined to follow the ritual pattern of their brief marriage … and opened her mouth to scream.

It was not her husband! A hand smelling of wood smoke and horse was clamped firmly over her mouth before she could get a proper scream out. Rosamund fought like a mad thing, kicking and flailing and scratching. She felt the stranger's skin collect beneath her fingernails as she clawed him. He seemed unconcerned with most of her struggles and turned to look over his shoulder twice. When Rosamund reached for his eyes, he looked bored almost, and simply pinched her nose closed with the same hand that covered her mouth. Her lungs screamed for air and instead of fighting the stranger, now her entire body fought to be able to breathe. He watched her, dispassionately, while she began to slowly fade away …

"Done fighting, are you?" he said in a heavy Welsh burr.

Rosamund was just drifting into darkness when he released her nose. She spent moments drawing great breaths of air while he waited for her to regain full consciousness.

"Struggle again, and I'll kill you. It matters not to me, understand?" When she made no move whatsoever he looked at her impatiently. "Nod your head if you understand." She nodded.

Still with his hand over her mouth, he began to question her. "You are the lady of this castle?" She hesitated. Well, technically she was, but only in name. The reality was that Nell … He shook her body with the hand still clamped over her mouth and looked furious. He leaned over closely and spoke slowly and clearly, working hard to enunciate the words with as little Welsh burr as possible. *"Are you the lady of this castle?"*

She decided to nod yes.

"Have you children in this castle?"

What kind of question is that? He shook her again and she shook her head no.

"Are you carrying a babe?"

Her eyes grew wide at his boldness. She shook her head no again.

"Do you care for your husband?"

What?! Why does he ask these questions? Questions that she had never even asked her self … She looked at him. He was dark and fierce and she realized that the reason he smelled so strongly of wood smoke was that every spot of bare skin – and there was much of it – was covered in black soot. It made the whites of his eyes and the flash of his teeth stand out in frightening brilliance when caught by the moonlight.

"That seems like too difficult a question for you. Let's try this one: is there someone in this castle you care for?"

Beatrice, her mind screamed. *Oh God, Beatrice.* He saw the panic and the understanding flame in her eyes. She nodded yes, frantically.

"I will remove my hand from your mouth and you will say one name in a whisper. *One name* and nothing else, do you understand?"

She nodded. He removed his hand. "Beatrice."

His hand hovered so close to her face she still felt its heat and smelled its smell. "A lady's maid?"

She nodded.

"Where is she? Is there a way we will know her?" When she hesitated, he leaned into her face and said fiercely, "*Speak, quickly. We take the castle and kill the inhabitants while you gather your fool thoughts together.*"

"In the maid's quarters upstairs. She is short, with ginger hair like mine. When she gets truly frightened she hiccups."

Rosamund heard a muffled cough in the dark corner of her room and realized that the stranger was not the only terrifying man in her room. As if to confirm her understanding, he turned and said brusquely, "See to the maid if it isn't too late."

He stood then. "You have until I return to dress and gather up whatever belongings you wish to take with you. Listen carefully. *You will not ever return here.* Do you understand what you need to do?"

She nodded again.

He smiled at her then. "A silent, obedient woman. And English, too. What a shock." As an afterthought, as he walked out the door he turned to her once more. "'Tis cold, Milady. I would dress for comfort, not for fashion."

He returned mere moments later while she was buttoning up a sturdy, warm woolen gown. He took in her dress and sturdy boots, nodded with approval, lifted the satchel off her bed, and came to stand beside her.

"I am Rhys ab Gruffydd and this castle has been reclaimed by its rightful owners. It now sits on Welsh land. You and your lady's maid will be the sole surviving witnesses to carry our message and our threat back to the English King, who would go against promises made in the past. You English must learn to fear us and believe our threats. Now come."

Rosamund stumbled in the semidarkness of the night, attempting to swing her heavy traveling cloak over her shoulders while hurrying down the familiar hallway and stairs into the great hall. The whole place was deathly still. Embers glowed in the fireplace, it being too early for the servants to have stirred the fire back to life. She followed the man silently, senses alert, heart pounding. "Are all truly dead?" she had to finally ask him. She needed to know, for the panic and hysteria was rising inside her like a rushing river that had at last encountered a stout dam.

Gruffydd turned then and looked at her. She stopped abruptly, her cloak swirling about her woolen clad legs. He was not overly tall, but fearsome nonetheless, covered in black soot, with sparse bits of armor strapped to his chest. A Welsh longbow was strapped to his back, a sword was at his side, a dagger was hanging from his belt and a most lethal expression of delight was on his face. "Yes," he said to her triumphantly, "every single one of them. Too stupid to properly guard what they'd stolen. Most are dead in their beds, their throats laid wide open, not even knowing who killed them. Need I show you the bodies so that you can bear proper witness?"

She shook her head, feeling the terror rise up in her like a tidal wave. He grabbed her arm and dragged her out into the night as the first rays of dawn were beginning to creep into the sky. There were more black-sooted men than her overloaded mind could count, but she instinctively knew that he wanted her to see and register what was before her.

"*Twll dîn pob Sais!*" Rhys ab Gruffydd shouted to the men silently standing in the yard as he still clutched her arm, instinctively knowing that she was not long for this conscious world.

"*Twll dîn pob Sais!*" screamed the men before her. "*Twll dîn pob Sais!*"

"That is to say," Prince Rhys said quietly in her ear, "An arsehole is every Englishman." And then she fainted.

It was full day before she regained consciousness, riding before the man who had awakened her. *Rhys ab Gruffydd*. She knew not of the man or the name. For long moments she sat quietly before him saying nothing, trying to judge the time and the place in which they were.

"Had a good nap?" the Welsh burr rumbled in his chest behind her.

"Is my maid with us?" She needed to grasp at something that was not horror, but was fearful just the same of the answer to her question.

"Yes, she rides back with one of my men. She's made of tougher stuff than you it seems. She did not faint." Rosamund detected a bit of admiration in his voice. She had nothing to say for a while.

"Where do you take me?"

"You are Rosamund deVerne, Countess of Hereford and Essex, daughter of Walter FitzRichard nee Clifford, current lord of Castle Clifford, are you not?"

How did he know these things about her? she thought frantically to herself. She nodded.

"Make sure your King knows that beside abilities all can see of our strength and stealth and cunning, he should realize that there are things we are aware of that even he is not. We have spies everywhere. Our information is sound and complete. And it will all be used toward our own victorious advantage." Gruffydd's arm around her waist squeezed the breath out of her for emphasis and, she supposed, to assure that she did not faint again. "Tell your father, Walter *Clifford*," the tone implied his disgust, "that he should guard his castle well. Earl Roger Tosney may have *left* his castle without a fight but we will *take it* without a fight. Just as we did your precious husband Earl Humphrey's castle."

They rode again for a time and Gruffydd squeezed and shook her again. "Remember everything you see and hear, Milady, for I would have you give an accurate report. The only reason you have been kept alive is that you do such. Your rank and your blood connections will ensure that you will be believed by those to whom I return you. Do not disappoint me."

"And you return me to …?"

"Why your family, of course. So you can suitably warn them of the Welsh threat. So that the King and his armies can be summoned. King Henry's knights. King Henry's foot soldiers. King Henry's paid mercenaries. Let me see," he paused for a moment as if in thought, "is there anyone else? Tell your King to be thorough with his selection of fighting men. Tell him his knights will not be effective once he reaches the close dense forests of *Cymru*. Tell him he will need foot soldiers and mercenaries not afraid of their own shadows. Tell your King all these things so that all preparations can be made for war. So that *we can reclaim all that is ours by birth and by right* once and for all, and there be no more dispute about it. So that we can send all of you *twll dîn pob Sais home for good.*"

"Is that all there is for you? Murder, revenge, hate …?" Her heart beat rapidly in fright at her words. She had gotten far too outspoken these last few months since she had accepted her lot as a failure. These past weeks at Castle Goodrich had revolved around one startling admission from her mouth after another; questioning the *way* of things, challenging the *right* of things, defying the *order* of things. The discovery that no one – not even her husband – knew what to do with her and her new outspoken self, but stand with mouth agape, was powerful. It made her bold even here, a captive from a massacre. She licked her lips; they were dry with fear. Was she truly challenging a man who had just killed an entire fortress full of innocent people?"

"You know much of my struggles, mistress?" He sounded vaguely amused. She heard her voice from long, long ago it seemed saying to Thomas, the knight in the moonlight on the battlements of Warwick Castle, *You know much of beautiful women, then?*

Rosamund shivered, but not from the cold. Gruffydd drew her cloak around her, mistaking the reason for her chill. At last she admitted, "No, I know almost nothing, I'm afraid."

He snorted. "At least you are not like most English who think they are *born* understanding the right and wrong of life. You say, "I'm afraid." Why do you fear your own ignorance?"

"Ignorance is death. Stupidity is your grave. Overconfidence is your tombstone."

He was quiet for a moment processing her words. "I like that. What scholar said that?"

"I did."

She heard him chuckle behind her. "You are surprising company, Countess of Hereford. Perhaps I'll keep you."

She shook her head 'no'. He leaned down to look at her face with a fierce expression. "You tell me no?"

Rosamund did not look at him, but sighed her frustration. "No, I do not tell you 'no.' I recognize that as an empty threat. I think you are a man who does not deviate from a set plan. You would not jeopardize your people to please yourself."

He was seemingly stunned by her perception of him. "Hmmm," Gruffydd said after a bit, "best I not keep you after all. You seem to understand me better than some of my men." She heard admiration in his voice.

"Even if I do faint on occasion."

Gruffydd chuckled. "Yes, even if you do faint on occasion."

She heard her voice from the past again, speaking out slightly differently in the present. "Give me some much needed information so I know. Don't let me die ignorant, stupid, and overconfident. If we English have it so wrong, then help me see the right of it." But the conversation, it seemed, was over. He was silent for the remainder of the day not even speaking to her when they made camp, ate food, or as she bedded down for the night in a makeshift shelter. Though she slept alone in the small tent, Gruffydd lay across the opening at her feet. Her feet did not feel cold in the least throughout the night.

After they had broken their fast and mounted up on the horses the following morning, he resumed the conversation as if there had been only a moment's pause. "It would be a waste to explain the complexities of war and politics to a mere woman."

"Ahh, and here I thought there was something *different* about Welsh men. How mistaken I was. You are just as pig - headed as English ones."

He threw back his head and laughed out loud to the consternation of his men who looked back at him once, twice, three times like he had absolutely lost his mind.

"You did not love your husband," Gruffydd challenged.

"That is none of your business," she countered back quickly.

"Ah, but you were allowed to choose one person, Lady Rosamund, and you chose your maid. You could have saved him and *you did not.*" His voice sounded smug.

The enormity of his words came crashing down on Rosamund. She was thrown from a horse once when she was six or seven, and she remembered lying on the ground staring up at the bright blue sky unable to catch a breath or speak. She felt just like that now. Her breath came in shallow gasps and Rosamund realized she had begun to make mewling sounds in the back of her throat.

Gruffydd shook her. "Don't faint on me again, Rosamund," and the familiarity of him using her given name caught her attention in the midst of her growing hysteria. "I'm enjoying this battle of words and wits with you … don't be so quick to give in."

She struggled to regain her composure, thought for a bit, and then said finally, "You would not have spared him even had I requested such."

Rosamund felt Gruffydd nod. "You are correct. He was marked to die the moment he assumed the lordship of a castle that belonged to one of mine. To have left him alive would merely have postponed the time when I met and killed him in outright battle. I spared him the trouble."

"Then why did it matter if I loved him or not?"

Rosamund felt him shrug. "It's easier transporting a woman who is just in shock as opposed to a woman hysterical with lover's grief. I was just gauging what I was up against in the coming days of travel. Same with the children."

"Would you have killed my children?"

He paused. "Do you really need me to answer?"

She was silent, mentally and emotionally exhausted. Physically too, truth be told.

Finally he said, quietly in her ear, "Answer for me, Lady Rosamund. Would I have killed your children?"

She thought and then shook her head 'no'. "You would not have killed them, but I would not have seen them again, just like Castle Goodrich."

Rosamund felt him nod again. "Were they young enough I would probably have done that, yes. If they were too old to adapt, but only carry on the torch of hate and revenge, I would have probably ended it then and there."

"Have you done that?" she asked in a whisper, but he heard.

Gruffydd was silent for a long while. "Yes," he finally said, "I have done that on more than one occasion. *As it has been done to me.* My son Hywel is currently a hostage of your King Henry. Tell me, Lady Rosamund, would Hywel be better off fearful, mistreated, hated by all those around him, kept as a prisoner throughout his entire life, or *dead?* What say you? I would know how good a soldier you would be." He shook her again in his barely repressed fury. *"I would know,"* he hissed through his teeth in her ear.

She struggled to comprehend his grief and sorrow, powerlessness and fear. Rosamund felt him start when she placed a comforting hand on his hand that was tense with emotion and griping her around the waist. "I take back what I said about *all* Welshmen, sir. For to live day to day with these emotions and knowledge indeed makes *you* different than the average pig-headed Englishman. It is rare to find a man who understands the grief, sorrow, powerlessness, and fear a woman faces throughout her life – at the mercy of any and every man with whom she comes in contact. You, of all men, *know.*" She patted Gruffydd's hand and then gripped it firmly with her own. "I am sorry for your anguish, sir. I will pray for you and your son, Hywel."

He very shortly removed his hand from beneath hers and rested it on the hilt of his sword. Although he did not speak, she sensed that the tense fury in him had abated. After a time, Rosamund said, "So now, I ask you again, Rhys ab Gruffydd, give me some much needed information so I know. Don't let me die ignorant, stupid, and overconfident. Now is your chance to educate at least one Englishwoman."

Gruffydd sighed. "Let it be explained this way; *Cymru* – Wales to you – and *Lloegr* – England – have been at odds with each other for as long as known history is spoken of. The only time we have been able to put aside our differences for any length of time is when an enemy appears that is a greater threat than we are to each other. Then, for a time, we manage to put aside our dissimilarity for a superior purpose. During those times, hatreds are set aside, wrongs are forgotten, promises are made, pledges are given, and there are some who are foolish enough to believe that once this new foe is vanquished all will be well and good between us.

"But no matter how many times this path is taken, the cursed *Saeson* – English - always go back on their pledges and promises made to the *Cymry*, and all the old angers are joined with the new betrayals, making the hatred and fighting all that more fierce."

"What betrayals do you speak of that have cost the lives of my husband and his people?" Rosamund asked.

Gruffydd caught that. "They were not *your* people?"

She shook her head. "No, not by my choice, but by theirs, I was …" Rosamund shrugged. "I was just a failure, nothing more."

"A *failure?* That is the only way you choose to describe yourself?" He sounded absolutely incredulous.

Rosamund squared her shoulders. "That is what I am. But I am other things as well. It depends on where I am and who I am with."

"I would hear this list."

She felt embarrassed then and risked a glance over her shoulder to see if he was making fun of her. He no longer had the soot smeared all over his face, but he still had a dark complexion, dark eyes, dark hair … She saw no mockery in his expression.

"I am a woman of God, a daughter, a sister, a niece, a good friend, a wif-" She swallowed, and then squared her shoulders, "a widow, a person who craves knowledge and understanding of things yet discovered …"

"Hmm, this list sounds more accurate. I find it most revealing that you list 'woman of God' first. How does the failure fit in?"

Rosamund hesitated. *Why not tell him?* Be the new bold and forthright person she had decided to be. "I was unable to conceive. A woman's primary mission in life. I am an abject failure, and in being such it is the defining feature of who I am for most people who choose to have an opinion of me."

"You seem rather accepting about it."

She shrugged. "I cannot change the path that God has set for me. I know that. I can only work to be the best example possible in whatever situation He places me. Yes, I am disappointed about my lack of children." She was quiet for a moment and was dismayed to feel tears crowd behind her eyes. She took a deep breath, held it, then let it out slowly. "I had always dreamed of having children. But it seems that the Lord has other plans for me. Mayhap my father will let me return to the Godstowe Nunnery now. He refused me once before."

Gruffydd was quiet for a bit and then spoke, "Who says *you're* the failure?"

Rosamund frowned down at her hands folded carefully in her lap. "I do not understand."

He sounded somewhat impatient. "Since you are a failure in the conceiving department, I assume you understand that the act involves two participants. Consequently, why must you be the one that is the failure?"

Rosamund looked off into the trees and finally said quietly, "Not only did you kill Humphrey de Vern, but if you killed all who lived at the castle you also murdered his mistress, Nell, and their son, Baldwin."

"Ahh," Gruffydd said, "now the picture becomes more clear." They rode in silence for a time and then he finally said, "I will speak with you when you are three score years old and childless, and then maybe we will both agree on your failures."

"You were speaking of betrayals to you and your people by me and my people," she finally prompted him yet again.

"Ah, yes. We were summoned by Robert, Earl of Gloucester in his battle to win the crown from Stephen de Blois for Matilda. Robert was a man of his word and my father supported him in the Battle of Lincoln with numerous Welsh warriors. We were promised, should they be victorious, that eventually lands that had been taken from us by force would be returned. I am the last of my father's four sons, all of whom fought and died for this just and righteous cause – that of regaining land that is rightfully ours.

"Now, many years later, Henry FitzEmpress sits on the throne. Robert, though long dead, has his victory at last. This same Henry whom you call kind, who knows of the promises and pledges made to my people, now works to eliminate the border barons that took advantage during the years of unrest in your country and had claimed still more of our land. Your King recognizes these baron's disreputable and treacherous actions – for they secured land, equipped an army, and built strongholds for *their own personal gain* – not for the good of your King. These barons, sought to make a kingdom of their own without the blessing of either the English King or the Welsh people. It is amazing, not only do I understand, but I agree with your King that these barons must be destroyed. But your King does not restore this land back to us, the rightful owners by birth *and* by past royal promises, but rather chooses to reward those from which he wishes to reward and buy loyalty.

"So, my father, my brothers, my cousins, my uncles, our women, and our children have suffered and bled and died *once again* for a *saesneg* lie. And it is my duty to finally avenge all of these wrongs and make right what must be made right." He grabbed her chin in his hand and turned her to face him. Gruffydd's eyes were burning with hate and passion and determination, *"and I will succeed. Tell your father and your King that. Rhys ab Gruffydd will succeed."* He held her face painfully in his hand and stared down at her. She swallowed and nodded, and then he let her go. "Now," he said low in her ear, "you are no longer ignorant, stupid, or overconfident. Now you have all the information you wished." After a pause Rosamund heard Gruffydd speak so quietly, it was almost to himself. "And what good will that knowledge do you, I wonder? *What good at all ...*"

Three nights later they left Rosamund and Beatrice just out of guard distance of Castle Clifford. Gruffydd had said few words to her for the remainder of the time, but had continued to be extremely polite each night as they set up camp. She and Beatrice had not been allowed to speak to each other but had seen each other from a distance on many occasions. Now they stood side by side on the dark but familiar path that led to her family home. At their feet was Rosamund's satchel.

Prince Rhys ab Gruffydd bowed formally to her from the top of his horse. "It has been a surprising pleasure riding with you, Milady, these past three days. I have spent so much of my life on a horse and in the thick of battle, you make me think about what I have missed - and it is much. I make you an offer." He reached up to his neck and removed a leather thong with a hammered silver charm suspended from it. "Though you are English, you do not seem to have their hate or their stupidity. Should you and yours ever wish, you can have a place with us. Keep this; it will assure you safe passage to me anywhere in *Cymru*." Rosamund had nothing to say to him, but took the amulet and hung it around her neck underneath her woolen gown.

One of Prince Rhys's men rode up and handed him something then. He leaned down and handed her a small, carved wooden box covered with intricate Celtic designs. "This *is not* for you. You are *not* to open it. You are to tell your story. I give you leave to repeat anything and everything you have seen and heard during your time with me. Answer their questions, and then give this box to your father. Tell him it is incontrovertible proof that he should summon the King. Give me your word that you will obey this."

Rosamund stared at him for a moment and then said, "Prince Rhys ab Gruffydd, you have the word of Rosamund Clifford de Vern that I will do exactly as you have instructed me. And though it is the word of a mere woman, I assure you it is binding and true." And then, there in the darkness and the cold and the autumn leaves, she curtsied deeply as she had been taught should she ever face the King. As she rose she said to him, "I will remember you and your son in my prayers as well, Prince Rhys ab Gruffydd. I will pray that a solution to this conflict between our two countries can be found very soon without massive bloodshed."

Gruffydd scoffed. "Not even God is powerful enough to do that."

Rosamund flashed him an impatient look. *"That* is the first truly foolish thing I have heard you say, sir. I will prove you wrong, just wait and see." And with that she picked up her satchel, took Beatrice's hand, and set off toward Castle Clifford.

"Some woman," Gruffydd's captain said under his breath.

"Yes," Prince Rhys ab Gruffydd replied softly watching her disappear into the darkness. *"Some woman."* The feeling of regret that filled him briefly was foreign and completely disconcerting.

Choose someone rather who doesn't understand <u>all</u> she reads.
Such matters are men's concerns.

Junius Juvenalis, 1st Century A.D[7]

Castle Clifford
On the River Wye, The Marches
Castle owner Walter Clifford nee FitzRichard and Margaret Isobel Tosney
Herefordshire, England
November, 1162 A.D.

Chapter Six

All she had to tell, all she remembered, still was not enough. Her brother, Nathan, and her father made their frustration with her visible with their words, looks and actions.

"How did they get into the Castle?"

"I know not."

"How many men did Gruffydd have under his command?"

"I know not."

"To where do they travel next?"

"I know not."

It reached a point as they fired their questions at Rosamund that she became mutinously silent standing before them. They had not offered her a chair, food, or even a warm drink to calm her. And her mother had not even bothered to rise from her bed. (And there was not a doubt in her mind that everyone had heard the shouts of the guards the moment she and Beatrice had been discovered standing outside in the dark night.)

Rosamund glimpsed one of the servants peering around the alcove and said, with as much cool authority as she could manage, "Mabel, bring me some bread and cheese and a hot mug of tea. Since no one sees fit to see to my needs then I shall do it myself." As the servant scurried to do Rosamund's bidding her father flew from his seat in agitation and came to stand by her side.

"Do you appreciate the enormity of the news you have brought this night that you expect us to believe?" He hissed in her face. "Do you appreciate that the level of information you give us – should this tale be true – is wholly unsatisfactory?" She studied him, calmly. She had been here before so many times: he furious and she unable to please. Failure, failure, failure ... The words danced around her head like butterflies. And Rosamund had seen him like this before, many times. Anytime *his* castle was threatened. No concern for his wife or his children, just his castle.

Her brother, Nathan, stifled a yawn and scratched his chin. "Mayhap she's just had a bad dream and a *really long* sleepwalk, Da," he said, voice dripping with sarcasm. "She claims to have seen no bodies, no blood, heard nothing but silence." He snorted. "We are expected to believe that the invader escorted her *and her maid* safely here untouched and unharmed. Christ, Rosamund, the way you described your conversation with him you made him sound like a courtly gentleman rather than a murdering Welshman." Nathan said the word *Welshman* like the foulest of curses. He snorted again. "Best we send word to Castle Goodrich of her whereabouts, for no doubt they are combing the grounds looking for her!"

She did not rise to the bait. They did not believe her. What could she do? Instinctively she knew that to show the silver medallion currently lying between her breasts would not help her cause in the least. Likely they would begin to accuse her of being unfaithful to her husband.

With a start she remembered the carved box and frantically searched through the pockets of her cloak to find it. Her father watched with suspicious eyes, and then he expressed stunned surprise at what she finally held out in her palm toward him.

"Prince Rhys ab Gruffydd bid me answer any and all your questions truthfully and with as much detail as I could remember. Then he bid me give this to you as final proof that it was indeed time to summon the King." She handed her father the box and he snatched it from her hand. He looked at her questioningly. "I know not what is in the box, Father. Prince Rhys had me give my word that I would not to open it and I have done as he commanded." She couldn't resist. "I am just a mere woman, but I do always keep my word."

Nathan had risen from his chair and come along side them, his curiosity getting the better of him. He rolled his eyes at her. "Calm yourself, Sister," he said low and impatiently. He glanced at his father. "I know not the crest, do you?"

For the first time since she had arrived, she saw concern, nay fear, in her father's eyes. A light bead of perspiration formed on his upper lip. "Aye, it is the crest of the Gruffydd clan. I have seen it only once, but it is not something you forget when it is coming at you in the thick of battle." The cold silver disk between Rosamund's breasts suddenly seemed a bit larger and harder to ignore. She put her hand to her heart, but her intention was to warm the disk and in doing so cease to be aware of it.

Her father opened the box and Nathan peered in anxiously. Her father hissed in his breath and her brother paled considerably. *Don't look,* her head shouted loudly, *don't look, don't look, don't look!!!* But Rosamund's insatiable curiosity got the better of her, that all consuming desire to learn of things she did not know.

It was her husband Humphrey's signet ring.

Still attached to his ring finger.

Prince Rhys would have been wholly disappointed in Rosamund again, for she fainted once more.

They, of course, summoned the King. *And* they locked Rosamund in her room. Her only communication with those outside was through Beatrice, for the guard standing at her door refused to answer any of her questions – despite the fact that she had known him all her life.

"Beatrice, why am I confined to my rooms?"

Beatrice busied herself with the necessary duties in the room. Setting down fresh towels and the pitcher of water she had just carried up to Rosamund, gathering soiled linens, straightening the bed ...

"*Beatrice.*"

Rosamund's maid stopped and looked at her. Then looked at the guard, braced forebodingly in the door listening to all that was being spoken between them.

Rosamund looked at the both of them for a moment, blew out a frustrated breath and said, "I have naught to hide, Beatrice. Warin has known me since I was a child. He is welcome to listen to *and repeat* any and all things we say to each other. *I care not.*" Still Beatrice was silent. Rosamund stood in the center of the room while Beatrice gathered the ashes from the hearth and lay a fresh fire. She went to her maid, *her only friend* her head said quietly to her, and laid a hand on her shoulder. "Beatrice?"

Eyes brimming with tears, Beatrice looked up at her. "I will not repeat to you, Milady, the things that are being said. *I will not.*"

"By whom?"

Beatrice mutinously pursed her lips and went back to laying the fire.

Rosamund sat. "Ahh, it comes from the top down, does it Beatrice? For were it only in the servants quarters you would fight to the death for me, would you not, my dear companion?"

Beatrice did not answer, but continued to work furiously in the hearth, sniffling loudly.

"So they believe that it is necessary to summon the King, but they are not sure of my involvement. My own family questions my loyalty." She sighed a great sigh that felt almost as if it came from her toes. "So I am a failure to my husband and now, it seems I am suspected of being a failure to my country as well."

"No, my lady," Beatrice said earnestly to her, "that is why I will not repeat the talk. There are some that puzzle over the bizarre circumstances of your arrival here, some that question whether the whole story has been told, some," she glanced accusingly at Warin as he stood stoically in the doorway, "that have no intelligent thoughts of their own and simply believe what they have been told to believe. But no one has said that you have failed King or country. No one." She hesitated and then added, "Not even your father or your brother."

"Would that I could be as certain as you. So I am to remain here until the King arrives?"

"Aye, that is what I have been told. I may see to your wishes and needs but you are not to leave the rooms for any reason. Warin is to keep you in as well as others *out*."

"I see."

But she didn't see really. And as the days stretched into weeks, the confinement bore heavily on her head and her heart and her spirit. The circumstances of her life seemed to delight in making her feel as absolutely powerless as possible. She spent long hours standing, wrapped in her wool gown and travel cape looking out the uncovered window at the changing landscape. Winter was coming fast and furiously, chasing the last of the autumn leaves away and leaving patterns of frost on the stone sill. She felt exactly like a leaf. Once young and new, green and vibrant, now she felt old and withered, blowing in the cold wind, and soon to be crushed to bits. She was just fifteen and yet she was already perceived as a profound failure in the two most important areas of a woman's life: the ability to conceive and her personal loyalty to King and country. *And there was nothing she could do about it.*

Oh, yes there is, my dear. Why must we have these conversations so frequently? She sighed and rested her head against the cold stone of the window's edge. "Why must we have these conversations so frequently, Sister? Have you glimpsed the circumstances of my life lately?"

Only God can see the whole measure of our days, dear. We see only small flashes, infinitesimal glimpses. That is why it is so ridiculous for us to even put one foot forward without seeking the Lord's guidance. So Rosamund began to pray. She spent hours doing it. She recited all the rote prayers she knew and still had hours of daylight left. So she talked to God, actually having long conversations with Him. She began, as taught by Aunt Helen, by listing all the things she was thankful for, making herself remember what she had already listed previously and then making herself add new blessings each and every day. In her desperation to find fresh things for her list, she went so far as to be thankful for her confinement and the opportunity to rediscover her prayer life and the close relationship it brought her with God.

Beatrice noticed the change in her. So did Warin and the other guard who shared the responsibility of her imprisonment, Ysac. By the end of the third week, she was stronger, more opinionated, and more confident of herself and her innocence than she had ever been in her life. *How dare they!* How dare they convict her of things she had no control over! How dare they condemn her for telling them the complete truth! How dare they attempt to break her spirit and her confidence simply because of situations and circumstances that *they* put her in originally. Her righteous indignation reached a fevered pitch, and it was then she began to plan.

She went to her door and slammed her fist against it. Repeatedly. "Milady?" she heard Warin's voice through the door. "You wish something?"

Bam! Bam! Bam! She did not answer; she simply continued to pound on the door.

"Milady, I cannot let you out. You know that. Shall I call for Beatrice?"

Bam! Bam! Bam!

Silence answered her from the other side, filled with indecision. At last Rosamund heard the key turn in the lock and the latch give way. Warin's puzzled faced peered around the door. "Milady?" In three weeks she had not sought him out nor spoken to him.

In the most imperious voice she could manage she said, "Summon my father. I would speak with him. Tell him anything you wish to get him here, but *get him here.*"

Warin's eyes widened. She had never spoken to him, ever, in a tone that implied anything but kindness and childlike trust. The young woman standing before him commanded obedience and respect. He bowed. "At once, Milady."

Her father arrived with the evening meal, causing her to loose what little appetite she had. "You wished to see me, daughter?"

"I will soon have an audience with the King, is that correct?"

He had expected tearful pleading, feminine coaxing. He had not expected to feel as if he were conversing with a superior. After a moment's hesitation, he answered. "Yes, we expect him to arrive in about another three week's time."

"Wish you to make a good impression with the King?"

It was a ridiculous question and they both knew it. Walter FitzRichard had spent his entire life trying to become something better than what he really was. He had worked his way up within the castle through hard work, avarice, and deception until he was at last the man that he was today: Walter *Clifford*, de-facto lord of Castle Clifford. A position that was his through the circumstance of war, the benefit of marriage to his equally covetous wife, and the cunning ability to ingratiate himself with whomever had Kingly power over him. He narrowed his eyes at his daughter and said nothing.

"Look at me, Father. This is how I will greet the King in three week's time." She stood before him, hair limp with dirt, skin a ghostly pallor, and in a plain woolen gown that desperately needed a wash. Nay, he thought, it needed to be burned. She dropped into an exquisitely orchestrated royal curtsy. She remained at his feet. He knew full well she was bowed but not *cowed*. "Get up, Rosamund."

She rose before him, graceful and, despite her circumstances, tremendously beautiful. More beautiful that her mother had ever been, and she had been quite a beauty he mused to himself. The hair, the eyes, the heart - shaped face ... Trim shape, regal bearing, quick mind ... That was a drawback though, he knew. He had heard some of the men call her "Fair Rosamund". To him she had always been just a willful daughter with potential to secure him things he could no longer achieve on his own. He'd gone as far as *he* could go, but with his children's potential he continued to dream.

Rosamund waited. Watched the thought patterns cross his face. She had been here before so many times. She had learned that begging and pleading had never and would never work with her father. She needed to use her wits (carefully concealed, of course) and appeal to those things that mattered to him. And his primary concern was his precious Castle Clifford.

"What point do you wish to make with me, Rosamund? I am a busy man. In case you forget, there is a war brewing."

"Will I have an audience with the King? Think you that he will wish to question me? Or do you think that he will be happy to hear all that you and Nathan have to relay to him?"

FitzRichard's eyes narrowed. "Spit it out, girl. What is in that too educated brain of yours?"

"Father, the King *will* wish to speak with me. He will want to hear from my own mouth the account I gave both you and Nathan. I merely wish the opportunity to prepare for the audience. Send me some fabric to sew a gown, or send me some old gowns of mother's that I can alter. I brought nothing with me from Castle Goodrich but what you see before you. I grow mindless with this detention. Give me something to do or when the King arrives I will be a drooling, raving, madwoman." She turned from him, walked to the window tapestry, and drew it aside. Cold air rushed in and she took a deep breath, held it, then slowly let it out.

Her profile was exquisite. She was the picture of serenity despite the chaos that had surrounded her in the last few weeks. Perhaps it was as she said and she was not in league with Rhys ab Gruffydd. It was Nathan who had planted that doubt in Clifford's mind and the terror that had filled him, the nightmarish possibilities that accompanied his doubts had just about caused his heart to stop. He could not hazard even the barest risk that his daughter would be foolish enough to align herself with such a man and in so doing destroy everything he had worked to accomplish. Nay, she must stay in this room until the King and his entourage arrived. He could not chance her escape. Clifford could not chance Rosamund's duplicity.

"You have a point. I will see that you are brought materials to sew some appropriate gowns for when the King arrives. He will wish to speak with you. *Do not shame us, Rosamund.*"

She looked at him then with great contempt. "I am *not* the Clifford that has caused shame, Father. Nor will I ever be." She turned back to the window view, dismissing him.

The King arrived three and one half weeks later. Although she could not see the front courtyard, the tension that seemed to emanate from the walls bore witness to his arrival. Beatrice informed her of the outriders' arrival, but when she tried to give additional information, Ysac stopped her. Her eyes told Rosamund *soon*.

Rosamund knew that her audience with the King was nearing when a bath was brought up for her - her first bath in over six weeks. She spent a long time enjoying it, soaping her hair three times and her body twice. She cleaned under her nails and between her toes. It was a glorious escape. She allowed Beatrice to arrange her hair. "Make me look *old*, Beatrice," she'd told her.

"Old, Milady?"

"Grown up. Sophisticated. Worldly. Powerful."

"'Tis impossible, Milady. You will always be lovely, sweet, Lady Rosamund."

"Do your best, then …"

Rosamund knew instinctively that half her battle in convincing the King of her sincerity would be in the first impression she made. She would appeal to the pomp and circumstance that she knew was an important part of court life. Appearances were everything at Court. Reality meant nothing. With a start, she realized she had been preparing her whole life for this moment. She was not afraid. Nothing could be more difficult than facing Sister Helen's death, or facing life as the wife of Humphrey de Vern, or withstanding the doubt and suspicions of her own family.

Why, facing the King, truth be told, was going to be the easiest thing she had ever done. She was certain of it. There was *nothing* for her to be afraid of.

Rosamund had no idea the stir she caused at her entrance. Having been confined in her room these past six weeks she knew nothing of the tension and intrigue that swirled around her, no matter how much Beatrice had desired to tell her. The lady's maid had done her best to prepare her, securing the most glorious gowns and fabrics, even pilfering some lovely scents and oils from some of the other chambers. Beatrice had had one of the older kitchen maids who long ago had been a lady's maid show her some intricate hair arrangements. So as she stood hidden in the alcove as Rosamund descended into the great hall, the murmurs and gasps of approval made Beatrice feel almost as if she were receiving them herself. *You look like a queen, Milady!*

Gavin's mouth had dropped open when he saw Rosamund descend the stairs and make her way before the King. Over these past years he, Thomas, and Brian, eternally willing to work and fight in an attempt to earn enough coins to make a life of their own, had become part of the elite circle of knights that now traveled exclusively with King Henry. They had proved their mettle, demonstrated their loyalty, earned their place, and secured the trust of the King of England. Coupled with the fact that most of their battle experience had been in dealing with issues along the Marches, they were now not only knights of status and mild renown, but absolutely critical to the success against this newest threat they had been summoned hastily to face. His gaze scanned the hall searching for Thomas. But Gavin knew his friend well. He would most certainly not be here, eager to avoid the crush of bodies. The knights had ridden hard after having been summoned, and for Thomas, arrival at a castle meant meals first and foremost. Gavin struggled with himself. Should he go look for Thomas and possibly miss what promised to be a fine show or should he stay and watch so that he could report later?

Gavin knew, although Thomas *never* spoke of the young woman, that he had never forgotten the girl. Thomas revealed his deep, hidden secret in subtle ways that only a true friend would know. The lack of desire to go wenching (although Thomas would go along if dragged), the way Thomas turned when they were traveling through a crowd and there was a flash of hair color *just so*, the way Thomas would argue a maid's unsuitableness by pointing out the lack of specific characteristics such as those Gavin was staring at *right now*.

Gavin watched mesmerized as Rosamund paused before King Henry and then sunk in to a deep and graceful curtsy. As he stared at her slim neck brushed with ginger tendrils of hair as she bowed in submission before the King, Gavin totally forgot what he had been struggling to decide. He just stared.

The hall was completely silent. So silent that the crackling of the hall fire could be heard, as well as a crash of a dish dropped in the buttery followed by a shouted curse from the cook.

"Rise, Lady Rosamund," King Henry said.

She rose as gracefully as she had knelt, stood with her hands clasped demurely before her and her eyes downcast. "Your Majesty."

King Henry licked his lips and struggled to reorganize his thoughts. *My God*, his mind screamed, *Who is this woman?!* He turned to look at the man to his right, Walter Clifford, self styled lord of this castle, so his closest advisors told him. And the look on the Clifford's face caused the King to chuckle. The man looked like he was seeing a ghost.

"Tell me, Lord Clifford, you look quite stunned. Know you this woman?" humor dripped in every word.

Walter Clifford made every effort to regain his composure. He had never seen a more beautiful creature in his entire life and *it was his daughter*. What had she done to herself? She raised her gaze slightly to him, making eye contact. The look, unbowed and slightly contemptuous, grounded him. Clifford cleared his throat. "Aye, Your Majesty, may I present to you my daughter, Lady Rosamund de Verne, wife of the late Earl Humphrey de Verne of Castle Goodrich."

The King smiled at Rosamund. "Lady Rosamund, I understand you have a tale to tell us."

She raised her eyes to look at him and he was once again stunned by what he saw. *No fear.* She was completely composed without a hint of concern on her lovely face. "Yes, Your Majesty. I have given my word that I would recount, to the best of my abilities, everything I saw and heard at Castle Goodrich some six weeks ago. While my father and brother were frustrated with my lack of information and disbelieving of my story, I have done my very best to remember as much as possible."

King Henry arched his eyebrow. "Your father was not happy with your accounting? He did not believe what you had to tell?"

She glanced at her father and Henry noticed that she did not fear him either. *Some woman*, he thought. She looked back at the King. "No, to both of your questions, Sire."

"Then why have I been summoned? Why am I here?"

Rosamund looked King Henry directly in the eye. "You were summoned because my father had no choice. You are here because you are obviously much the wiser, Your Majesty." She heard her father's sucked in breath of anger and the small murmur traveling through the crowd.

Henry grinned. There was only one thing he loved more than a good battle; a feisty woman. He was married to one and all of his mistresses were carefully selected to be of the same caliber. He had come to these Marches to settle this difficulty between he and Rhys ab Gruffydd once and for all. The bastard had already had the audacity to take Llandovery Castle, not but a few months ago. Preparations had already begun for a final confrontation before Henry and his knights had left from Normandy. Then Clifford's man had shown up with his breathless account of the *supposed* happenings at Goodrich Castle. Henry had not for one moment doubted the accounting that Clifford's trusted man had brought to him in Normandy. And that was before he'd seen the finger. The fair Rosamund was right that Henry was much wiser.

But she was wrong in that she should not have been afraid of him.

The male is by nature superior, and the female inferior;
and the one rules, and the other is ruled;
this principle, of necessity, extends to all mankind …

Aristotle, 4th Century B.C.[8]

Castle Clifford
On the River Wye, The Marches
Castle owner Walter Clifford nee FitzRichard and Margaret Isobel Tosney
Herefordshire, England
December, 1162 A.D.

Chapter Seven

Rosamund recounted her story and King Henry listened. He did not interrupt her once. In fact, he never took his eyes off her face. She felt his intense gaze and gained assurance. Surely he must believe her?

"Why did you call yourself a 'mere woman' when you gave Gruffydd your word you would deliver his message?"

A lovely blush crept up her cheeks. "I said something earlier that had made him laugh and it was in reference to it."

King Henry did not have a response to that. "How old are you, Rosamund?" he asked her quietly.

"She is fifteen, just, Your Majesty, and she has been a sore trial to me since the moment of her birth," her father spit out between clenched teeth. She folded her hands and dropped her head demurely.

This time, King Henry was not so easily fooled. "Would that I had had such trials …" the King mumbled under his breath staring at the top of her shiny head. "Rosamund, I ask you this in all seriousness. Where do your loyalties lie within this conflict?"

King Henry's words came crashing down on her. Even he did not trust her. *Even he.* She was a failure again in attempting to convince him of her loyalty and sincerity. She raised her face to King Henry and the king was stunned to see her eyes filled with unshed tears. When she answered her voice was husky, as if choking back strong emotions that threatened to explode, but loud and clear nonetheless so that everyone in the hall could hear, "I am a loyal subject of King Henry the Second, Count of Anjou, Duke of Normandy, Duke of Aquitaine, and King of England. Besides the Lord God Almighty, I serve and honor no other sovereign. This woman before you gives you her oath and her pledge," and with that she bowed once again into a deep curtsy at his feet.

The hall fell absolutely silent once again. People stuck in the back of the hall stood on tip toes and craned their necks to see what King Henry would do next. Slowly the King rose from his chair and walked forward to where Rosamund still bowed. He reached down and touched the shining hair on her head as he had wanted to do since first glimpsing her. "Rise, Lady Rosamond, I accept your oath and pledge and give you one in return. Henceforth you shall be under *my* protection, a *personal* ward of *my* court. No harm shall befall you by *any* hand, for to harm you will be to harm *me.*"

Rosamund felt the King touch her head once more and then reach for her hand to help her rise. As she stood, she registered three men staring intently at her; the King with an unfathomable expression, her father with an overjoyed smile, and Sir Thomas the knight from more than a year past looking utterly defeated.

In her innocence, Rosamund had merely meant to project herself as a sophisticated, loyal, trustworthy woman. It was of the utmost importance to her to have the King believe her account of what had happened at Goodrich Castle. It was imperative for her reputation and it was critical for the lives of the innocent people who might still yet suffer in the ongoing conflict. But she rapidly began to fear that she had danced on the edge of a shallow pond not realizing it was a bottomless pit. She sensed something was radically different after her audience with the King, but could not seem to grasp exactly what.

The first sign of trouble was the absolute joy, nay the sheer *ecstasy* that both her parents radiated towards Rosamund later that evening. "Well done, daughter! *Well done!,*" and her father had actually given her a crushing embrace and a kiss on the cheek.

"Oh, my *dear*, I knew you had it in you! I just knew! Never have I been so proud to be your mother! Who would have thought?"

Rosamund frowned in complete puzzlement at them. Should they not be somewhat put out, that having doubted her, having questioned her loyalty and integrity, they had been proven wrong?

No longer confined to her room, she was suddenly sought out by everyone and anyone. As the evening wore on she fell into her proper identity of hostess and proper lady and conversed and exchanged pleasantries with the constantly milling crowd of excited hangers on. She just didn't understand. She puzzled over what exactly she had done to merit all this attention besides being truthful.

Rosamund's parents put on a lavish spread for the evening meal - course after course of sumptuous foods. Fine wines and expensive port filled goblets and delectable pastries made the rounds for dessert. Rosamund sat at the head table with her parents, her brother, the King, and many of his most senior knights, none of whom she recognized. One knight in particular, Sir Gavin, could not seem to stop staring at her. Whenever she smiled politely at him he became flustered and looked away. Rosamund conversed, smiled, inclined her head when necessary, and in general felt that soon she would die from complete and utter boredom. The gossip and innuendos, some of which she did not understand, swirled around her and made her head ache. When a break in the conversation occurred she seized the opportunity and excused herself.

Thomas would have totally bypassed the entire evening had Gavin not literally grabbed him by the hair as he had tried to slip by on his way from the kitchens. Still rubbing his scalp he had turned furious eyes on his friend. *What?* his expression had said in impatience.

Gavin had simply inclined his head toward the hall and given him a look that said, *You won't want to miss this.*

Thomas had reluctantly stepped into the stifling crush of bodies and there she'd stood in the center of it all. Calm. Serene. Breathtakingly beautiful. Looking very much as he had remembered her that night more than a year ago. And looking more lovely than he had seen her so vividly in his dreams more nights than he could remember. But ... different. More mature, perhaps? One year ago she had radiated confidence both times Thomas had seen her, and yet there had been fragility about her as she stood on the parapet with him that first night. He saw no weakness now. She was magnificent. Thomas drank in the sight of her. He could not take his eyes from her.

His brain could not process all he heard at first. And then he was incredulous. *Lady Rosamund was the emissary from Gruffydd?! She was the one who had brought Gruffydd's message of impending war?* Thomas struggled to process what his ears were hearing. She was *supposed* to be married to that old Earl and be fat and happy with much wanted babies. Not standing here before King Henry – as he practically drooled over her – talking about battle plans and messages from Rhys ab Gruffydd! Thomas spared a glance at Gavin, who looked at him briefly, appearing just as stunned as he, and shrugged his shoulders.

He heard her talking to the King. God, he had heard her voice *every single night in his dreams* for the past year. "... I asked him to give me some much needed information to understand ..." she was relaying to Henry. Thomas flew back in time, *Let me give you some much needed information.* Honestly, he had not been the same since he last saw her. What would this encounter do to him?

Mayhap kill him.

And then Thomas watched in stunned silence – for it all suddenly became crystal clear to him - as she bowed in deference to Henry giving him her oath and pledge. He watched Henry pledge to her his protection making her a ward of his court. Thomas felt a fury well up inside him; at her, at his King, but most of all at himself. Oh, *now* he could distinguish the difference in her! *Mature.* Ha! It had taken just one short year but it was patently obvious now what the true change was. Rosamund had become one of the hundreds of women they encountered that dreamed of nothing but bedding the King. It was almost like she had studied for the part he thought in fury. She had just the right feistiness, just the right coyness, and certainly an abundant amount of beauty. King Henry's perfect woman was currently bowing in acquiescence before him, offering herself as if a lamb to the slaughter. And Henry had been more than willing to accommodate.

As Thomas watched with gritted teeth and clenched fists, King Henry touch Rosamund and helped her to rise. It was then that Thomas knew with absolute certainty that this occasion of seeing Rosamund would indeed kill him.

He refused dinner. Gavin and Brian did their best to convince Thomas to go but he could not. He did not trust himself. On the battlefield he was cold, precise, calculated, and controlled. He wasn't sure he could control anything watching Rosamund from a distance. How would he behave sitting next to her listening to Henry slowly seduce her? Watching her flirt back? His fury would know no bounds. He simply did not trust himself. He needed time to think and to accept this new reality. He needed time to make his dreams disappear.

Over the course of the interminable evening Thomas discovered that this was her family's castle. How was it that he had missed all those familial details before? *Because you never thought to see or hear of her again so you sought no further information.* He did not go up to the parapets. If that was still her place for escape he did not want to run the risk of encountering her here where the habit had been born. He went out into the gardens, far enough away so that the muted inside sounds were almost indistinguishable from the rustle of the bare tree limbs and the crunch of the fallen leaves. He leaned against the far wall and warred with his own thoughts.

He must come to terms with the reality that the young woman of his dreams whom he had made such a paragon of virtue was indeed a dream. A myth. An impossibility. Not that he had ever expected any of his imaginings would have come to fruition. But dreams were what kept the nightmares and loneliness at bay. And these dreams he had woven of the lovely Lady Rosamund had become as comfortable a companion to him as his own sword. He struggled with the great fool he felt himself to be and had a measure of relief knowing that he had kept all his thoughts and dreams quietly to himself. No one need ever know how great an idiot he really was. He battled with the rage of jealousy he felt toward King Henry and the concern over his disloyal thoughts. Because of the circumstances of Henry's birth, the King obtained things that he would never truly value, appreciate, or treasure. Unlike Thomas would have. Had he been given the chance.

Thomas had become good friends with his King. He enjoyed Henry's sense of humor, his thirst for knowledge, and his willingness to listen to those he trusted. They were almost the same age, and sometimes Thomas puzzled over the fascinating accidents of birth. Henry, by right of birth, King of all England and he, by right of birth, nameless bastard. Thomas had been around Henry long enough – warring and laughing and drinking - to know how to avoid his furious fits of temper, how to amuse him with clever anecdotes, how to fence with him over novel thoughts and ideas, and how to find a woman to please him. He snorted to himself, bitterly. Rosamund, had he brought her to Henry himself, would probably have secured Thomas an Earldom.

It meant nothing that the King was married. Marriage, especially among the nobles and in particular among monarchs, held purpose only to make a country more powerful to her enemies. Eleanor of Aquitaine, Queen of England, filled all the suitable roles required of a Queen: regal, commanding, fertile, wealthy, and powerful in her own right. When they married, Henry at nineteen and Eleanor at just over thirty, it had been the ultimate joining of powerful families. In marrying her, Henry as King of England more than doubled the territory over which he was sovereign by acquiring her dowry lands. As Henry had said one night over too many cups of ale, *Sometimes a woman's most attractive attributes are the riches she brings along to the marriage bed.* And in that case, Eleanor had been absolutely *gorgeous.*

But Queen Eleanor was not and never would be King Henry's passion. The King had a multitude of women to provide for him in that category. It mattered not to Henry whether they were married or single, young or old, particularly beautiful or not. His only true requirement was that they be *willing* and had a distinctive spark about them. And Rosamond Clifford de Verne had certainly communicated that to the King and to everyone else in attendance who had eyes and ears and half a mind.

What did you expect? Thomas' head asked him impatiently. He had never, ever dreamed that she would be his. He was enough of a realist to know that she was so far above his social position that, had she known the facts of his birth, she never would have initially spoken to him. No, what he had expected was that for once, *just once,* the reality of what he had seen in her a year ago had not only been true, but it had been lasting; pure, fresh, alive, sincere, curious, kind, unselfish … *Christ,* he thought to himself, *you've got quite a list there, man.* Thomas had created an ideal of the perfect woman in his head. Rosamund was the *model,* not the actual woman he hoped or dreamed of someday having. She was the standard by which he judged all other women, and he hoped one day to find a woman who perhaps came a bit close to being like her. He closed his eyes and threw his head back, letting it hit hard against the stonewall. *You've been a fool, Thomas. Now get over it.*

He must get himself under control. He must cease this unreasonable fury that was not the fault of any one involved – not her's, not the King's, not even his. Perhaps this was good, for at last he was free of the unrealistic ideal of woman he had slowly nurtured in his head. Yea, that was it. He was free!

Thomas made his way slowly back to the castle hall, pausing at an outside entrance, out of the wind to collect his thoughts, brace himself, and run a hand through his windblown hair. As he went to step in, Rosamund stepped out. He closed his eyes briefly, willing her to disappear. *Go away.*

But when he opened his eyes she was still standing there looking at him intently. He blurted out, "You are supposed to be up on the parapets. That's why I'm down here." *What a fool,* his head sang out to him.

Rosamund stared at him silently for a moment, then smiled shyly. "Am I supposed to understand?"

He shook his head, frustrated with himself. "No."

"Sir Thomas! I did not think we would ever meet again." She smiled again. "And once again, in the dark and shadows of the night."

Thomas inclined his head, bowing slightly, respectfully. "Are you enjoying this celebration more than the last one?" He winced inwardly. Had he well and truly just reminded her of her wedding to her recently murdered husband …?

Rosamund shrugged. "There is no more fear. I guess that makes it more enjoyable." She looked at him. "An unhappy marriage, my failure to conceive an heir, the murder of my husband and all his people, the abduction of myself and my maid by an enemy of the crown, and the questioning of my loyalty to King and country have made it a difficult year." She looked off into the night. "Tonight's party surely makes up for it all, though." Her voice dripped with mockery.

"Your acceptance by the King, nay – how did he put it? – *under his protection, a personal ward of his court* – should be everything you've ever dreamed of; certainly worth the inconvenience of this past year." It was his turn at sarcasm laced tightly with vaguely suppressed fury. "Why there are more women than I can count who would wish what you were granted this evening."

Rosamund studied Sir Thomas in the moonlight. First, her parents unexplained delight, then a multitude of strangers desiring to be her closest companion, and now this knight's unearned anger and sarcasm. She was a bright woman. *What was she missing?* Something dark and foreboding seemed to be creeping up on her in the shadows, but try as she might she could not distinguish what it was.

"You toy with me and I know not why" Rosamund said in a flash of impatience and frustration. "You give me everything I do not want and nothing that I need. Go back and join the 'celebration' inside. You fit in better than you think." She turned then in a flurry of full skirts and made to leave.

Thomas was quick, reaching out to grab her arm. She gasped and looked down at his hand, disbelieving that he dare touch her. "Now you presume too much. *Let go of me.*" Her tone was fierce.

He lessened the hold but did not take away his hand. Both of them knew that should she try to walk away a second time she would succeed. "What is it you need?" Thomas asked her quietly.

She did not look at him but looked out again at the evening, closed her eyes, took a deep breath, held it and then let it out slowly. He felt the tension leave her arm still held in his grasp. Still she did not pull away. *God, would he ever see her up close in anything but darkness and shadows?*

"You would not understand," she said after a time.

"You judge me before you even know me," he countered.

"Is that not the way of things in court? No one knows the real person. Everyone judges based on what they see: deception, lies, gossip, greed ... You have been a part of King Henry's court far longer then I. Surely you know of what I speak."

Thomas bristled at the assumption that he was like all the rest. "So, now that you will be a part of Henry's court, you too will become ... like 'us'."

"I hope not ..." she said quietly, missing his point, "but I already grow *so weary* with it all. I feel myself losing faith at times." She shook her head and closed her eyes. "I *cannot* do that. I cannot!"

These were not the thoughts of a young woman who had just achieved such an apparent victory. "You are unhappy with Henry's pledge?"

Rosamund looked at him impatiently. "I hoped for a drink of cool water and ended up being drowned in a bottomless lake. I wished only for someone to believe what I was trying to tell so that no more innocent lives would be lost. My parents did not believe me, why should the King? I tried simply to be sincere, honest, and convincing. Now I am a ward of King Henry's court." She looked off into the darkness. "*I hate court.*"

Thomas was stunned. She simply had wanted to be *believed*? It was *not* her desire to become the King's leman? Had she *any* idea what she had gotten herself into? His mind struggled to readjust itself yet again.

Still his hand encircled her arm. He made himself as still as possible, unwilling for her to remember his touch and pull away. "I ask you again, milady. What is it you need?"

She sighed. Sir Thomas had no idea the length of her list, the extent of her prayers. Without looking at him, in a soft voice, Rosamund asked, "Did you remember me?"

"Yes."

She turned to look at him. "Have you thought of me?"

Thomas met her unwavering stare. "Yes."

"Do you know that I remember you in prayers nightly?"

It was he who hesitated this time. "Yes."

Rosamund tilted her head and asked, "Why did you hesitate?"

Now it was Thomas turn to look into the night and struggle with himself privately. She deserved his honesty, he decided. "I struggled with the fierce desire that you did as you promised, and with the confusion as to why it was so important to me." He looked at her and smiled. "I guess as a result of that confusion I thought even more of you."

Rosamund couldn't help herself and suddenly reached up to touch his cheek. He closed his eyes, willing himself to remember every single aspect of this mystical moment. The coolness of her hand, the scent of her perfume – *was it vanilla?*, the silent sounds of the night, the look on her face before he had closed his eyes. The only thing missing was the taste of a kiss. With eyes still closed, he loosed the grip further on her arm so that his hand still encircled her but barely touched her. With the most noble of control Thomas ground out, "The desire to kiss you is great, milady. It would be best if you left now."

He felt her hand slide up along the side of his face, snake through the back of his hair, and then apply a firm pressure toward her. "I think I would brave a kiss," she said as Rosamund drew Thomas down to her.

Never in his life since his training as a knight had he lost consciousness of his surroundings, of his back, of the sounds of danger lurking where eyes could not see. But at that moment, his entire world was in that kiss; sights and sounds, taste and touch, smell … He was aware of nothing but her mouth. He did not take her in his arms. He only allowed his hand to tighten once again on her arm while she gripped the back of his head by his hair. Other than their mouths and their hands they did not touch.

Thomas thought he was being burned alive.

A door opened somewhere and there was a burst of laughter and noise close by, breaking the mood that the kiss had created. They withdrew their hands and their mouths and each took a step back from the other. He glanced at her, and for some unexplained reason was fantastically relieved to see that she, for once, looked just as addled as he felt. They were silent for a few long moments.

Rosamund smiled but did not look at him. "My first kiss. Something wonderful to add to my memories. Thank you."

Her first kiss?! Her thanks annoyed Thomas but he couldn't explain why. "I do not want your thanks," he said somewhat more harshly than he would have preferred.

She looked at him without smiling. "I know, but beside my prayers that is all that I can give." She turned to head back into the noise and the crush.

"Lady Rosamund," Thomas said, and she stopped and turned to look at him. "I am not good with prayers, so that I cannot give. But I would gladly offer you my friendship, and, as much as possible, my protection."

She frowned then and took a step back towards him, her lovely brow knotted in confusion. "Why think you now, of all times, that I need your protection? Am I not the safest I have ever been? The King's own personal ward? *What do you know that I do not?* Whom do I need protection from?"

"Besides yourself, Milady?" He could not help himself.

Rosamund looked impatiently at him but remained silent, waiting for an answer.

"Rather than answer your question, I will, instead, give you some *much needed information that you do not know.* For it seems you are the *only one* not aware of it. As of this moment – he's fast but not that fast – you are presently King Henry's newest intended conquest for a leman."

Rosamund frowned in confusion. "A 'leman'? I am unfamiliar with that term…"

Thomas sighed and said softly, "Mistress, Milady. *Mistress.*"

A woman takes off her claim to respect along with her garments.
Herodotus, 5th Century B.C⁹

Castle Clifford
On the River Wye, The Marches
Castle owner Walter Clifford nee FitzRichard and Margaret Isobel Tosney
Herefordshire, England
December, 1162 A.D.

Chapter Eight

eman. She rolled the word around in her mouth like a piece of gristle that was too hard to chew and too large to swallow. It now all made terrible sense to her. Her parent's uncharacteristic delight in something she had done, her sudden popularity with strangers, … even Sir Thomas' hostility and Beatrice's refusal to look Rosamund directly in the eye.

"Beatrice…"

"Milady, I have much to do. Your mother is in a fine state, for the King has consented to remain with us long enough to enjoy the start of the Twelfth Night Celebrations…"

Oh dear Lord in heaven. "Does he plan to stay for the entire celebration?" Rosamund asked in a strained voice. The days leading up to the celebration and then an entire twelve days of celebrations…

Beatrice looked at her. "Aye, milady. *The entire celebration.*" Then she gathered a tray in one hand and a bundle of dirty linen in the other and walked out without another word.

Oh dear Lord in Heaven. Twelve days. The thought of dealing with the King overwhelmed her as nothing else before or since had done. No one could refuse the King. No one.

Leman. Just because many people do something does not make it right. "Are you saying I should refuse the King, Sister?" she said aloud to herself in the confines of her room. She could not anymore imagine refusing the King than she could imagine bedding him. Her mind refused to wrap itself around the concept that everyone else had clearly seen and understood. *The King of England desired her and wished to claim her as his mistress.*

"I cannot...," she whispered, "*I cannot...* " At what point did one's spiritual convictions truly override royal authority and personal self-preservation? King Henry had the power of life and death over her, her family, and her people. It could be as blatant as sentencing her to death for treasonous disobedience or as subtle as withdrawing help and support to Castle Clifford in times of dire need. In her naiveté, her attempt to secure her truthful reputation and the safety of innocent lives had placed her soul at its greatest peril. Could she compromise all she knew to be right once again for the good of the whole?

Rosamund, despite her father's perception of her, had been obedient to every responsibility she had ever been given. She had never once shirked her duties despite her desires to the contrary. But she had also never had to compromise what she believed to be truly right and wrong. She had not loved Humphrey de Verne but, deep in the hidden recesses of her heart she knew that it had been her destiny to marry him. It was what was right and required of a young noble woman, and she would be exemplary in her completion of her obligations. Rosamund was proud of herself in that in some small way, her behavior had been of the utmost propriety. Humphrey had not loved her, his people had not wanted her, Nell and Baldwin had probably hated her, but it was through no fault of her own. She could not have done a better job, and she knew that there was no one who could find fault with her. It was the disbelief of her own family and the doubt of her own people that had truly shaken her self worth. These past six weeks, knowing that everyone save Beatrice questioned her loyalty and commitment, had been more defeating than anything she had ever encountered.

Well, she had certainly earned her family's favor back, she thought wryly. She did not think she had ever seen her parents so delighted with her and the world in general. Even her brother had given her a pleased wink and a casual salute across the hall during last evening's meal. She had learned to be a proper lady at the expense of her individuality and personal happiness, she had married the man of her father's choosing to secure the favorable graces of the English nobility, and now ... *now* ... Now she was expected to give up her body *and her soul* to a man simply because he had the power to wish it and receive it.

To follow through on *these* obligations would go against everything she knew to be right and wrong. And what no one realized, aside from Sister Helen, was that her obedience, her responsibility, and her pride were most firmly rooted in the fact that, though she was a failure in many things, she was a woman after God's own heart. She had meant it when she had told King Henry that beside the Lord God Almighty there was no other sovereign that she acknowledged. But she was not certain that King Henry heard the order of things. God Almighty was *first*. And of all the failures she knew she could endure, a failure to her God was not something she thought she would survive.

The start of Twelfth Night Celebrations began with the winter solstice, December 21st, the shortest day of the year. The traditional Yule log would be chopped down and dragged into the great hall amid much celebration and laughter. Twelfth Night Celebrations were the highlight of the year, for it was a time of bounty and feasting for everyone: young, old, rich, poor, servant, and noble. For Rosamund, it was usually a time of great delight and happiness, for traditionally it was a time she escaped the close scrutiny of her parents and was allowed, for once, just to have fun. But for this year's celebration, the enormity of her situation was something she could not escape.

In the few days of preparation before the festivities she was almost too busy to have more than a passing flash of panic over her new and dire circumstances. Her mother seemed to be in a constant state of frenzy preparing, ordering, panicking, and shrieking. It was in some ways ironic that, for the first time, Lady Margaret Tosney seemed to recognize and appreciate Rosamond's calm presence and cool organizational skills.

As they delivered the last instructions to the servants for food preparation and supervised the hall decorations, Rosamund caught her mother looking at her with an odd expression. "I don't know if I would have been able to manage all these preparations without you, Rosamund," she finally managed the afternoon before the festivities were to begin. "Thanks to you."

Rosamund regarded her mother for a moment, surprised at the recognition. Finally she shrugged. "You have taught me well, Mother."

Her mother shook her head. "Nay, I think it was in you all along. You have grown into a beautiful and poised woman. I find great pride in calling you 'daughter'."

Was her beauty and poise so much greater now that she had caught the King's eye? Was this why her mother finally saw fit to notice her value? Rosamund shook her head at her bitter thoughts and went to see to the final preparations. There was still much to do.

"Rosamund," her mother said as she began to walk away. Rosamund looked back at her mother with a questioning expression. "The King holds your future and the future of this entire demesne in his hands."

Ahh, there was the point. She should have known. "Think you I do not know that, Mother?"

Lady Margaret showed familiar impatience with her daughter. "Think you I do not know that you were unaware of the ramifications of the King's pledge? Your innocence is what attracts him, Rosamund."

Rosamund turned away unable to look into her mother's eyes any longer. "He'd best enjoy it while he can, for whatever innocence I seem still to have is disappearing as rapidly as ice in a fire." She took a deep breath. "In fact, within the year, I will probably have more experience than anyone I know in things I wish to know nothing about." Rosamund looked back at her mother. "Even you, Mother."

But in the end, Rosamund got caught up in the excitement of the celebrations after all. The smell of the cut boughs of evergreen, the crisp night air as they tromped through the woods alongside the horses dragging the Yule log toward the great hall, the sounds of the voices – servants and nobles – raised in happy accord as they sang holiday ditties; all crept into her soul and ignited her love of the season. The freedom of laughter and camaraderie seeped into her tired spirit and it burst into bright light.

The crowd of revelers burst into the great hall with much fanfare, the men sweating and straining to pull the huge Yule log into the massive main fireplace. The log was large enough to burn continuously for the twelve full days of the holiday with a bit left over to start next year's fire. Laughing, the people rushed forward, decorating the Yule with their evergreens and boughs of holly. Some took the time to carve names or ancient runes on the log that would eventually be consumed by fire; representing unwanted people or traits that they hoped would be taken away from them forever in the conflagration.

Rosamund's father, happier than she had ever seen him, greeted everyone and anyone with a heartfelt, *"Waes hael to you!"* the customary Old English greeting which meant simply 'be well' as each came in from the cold. Encouraged to secure a cup, each was immediately gifted, 'from his most secret recipe,' he'd say with a sly wink, some of the strong, hot drink of ale, honey, and spices that he carried with him in an overflowing bucket. Rosamund caught herself laughing with delight at the smiles on so many of the faces.

The meal was sumptuous: goose and venison, fine cheese, creamy butter, berries, leeks, onions, nuts, baked apples … all spiced and flavorful with the tastes and smells of the season. No one knew hunger; everyone enjoyed. Helping her mother with the myriad of hostess duties, Rosamund felt safe and invisible in the crush and the chaos.

Thomas watched Rosamund … and the King. Rosamund could not possibly be overlooked - her cheeks flushed first from the cold and then from the warm, her eyes dancing in merriment, her laughter floating delicately over the harsh voices of every other person present. Henry laughed and conversed, in fine spirits filled with Clifford's abundant "special" drink. There was never a moment, however, that the King did not know exactly where Rosamund was. His timing was so precise that on two occasions Thomas knew where she was simply by looking where Henry looked, only to witness her entrance back into the great hall moments later.

Following dinner and dessert of freshly baked ginger snaps, they once again all trooped out into the cold armed with still more hot cider and enthusiasm. They walked into the cold, dark forest, some armed with torches, some with just their enthusiasm and the light of the moon and the stars. They assembled in the orchard, beneath the now bare trees and sang songs and laughed and tipped a bit of their hot cider on the roots of the trees in a toast to a future year of good harvests and blessings.

Walking slowly back home, Rosamund felt exhaustion tugging at her as the elation of the evening slowly ebbed. Drawing her cloak and hood tightly against the cold, she looked forward to collapsing into her bed this evening! There was much to do on the morrow, for each day had a special celebration to prepare for. She was pleased with the evening, though, and happy that she had been able to enjoy the festivities.

As she went to enter into the castle gate she was grabbed from the side and pulled into the shadows. "I had at first thought it was the season, then the ale, then the food, but nay, I think that what has made this evening so memorable has been watching you and all your loveliness," a male voice whispered low into her ear.

Rosamund looked up into the face of the King of England. His eyes glittered in the moonlight and a lazy smile sat on his lips. He held her tightly in his arms, wedged between his body and the castle wall. He let go with one arm to reach up to push her hood back so he could finger her hair.

"It is as soft and silky as I remember," he murmured almost to himself. "I'd thought that my imagination had been exaggerating." He lifted a lock to his nose and inhaled. "Vanilla ..." he said again, almost to himself, "who ever would have thought that vanilla would be such an intoxicating scent ..."

He seemed in no rush, leaning against her, smelling and staring. Rosamund was at a loss for words, not knowing what to say or do that would not offend and yet still garner her safety. She had seen a small sparrow trapped once in a net, unable to move, knowing that death was imminent. She understood now its confusion and fear.

"What think you, Fair Rosamund?" The king's grin was lazy and seductive.

"I think of all the people present at tonight's celebration, we are the only two who's absence will be sorely and immediately missed."

King Henry chuckled and reached warm fingers up to touch her face: her cheeks, the bridge of her nose, her lips … "Think you I care? Think you anyone will voice an objection? Need I remind you who holds you in his arms?"

He smelled of ale and spices and the outdoors. Not a tall man, he was nevertheless of muscular build. *He has red hair and blue eyes*, she thought looking at him in the moonlight.

"I need not be reminded, *Your Majesty*."

His hand reached around to the back of her neck and buried itself in her hair. "After so much sumptuous fare this evening, I would end it with the very best: I would taste a kiss. Mayhap more than one, truth be told … The wait, I would wager, has been more than worth it."

Before she could utter a single sound, her mouth was engulfed in a kiss. It was as if he was trying to swallow her whole, she thought. She struggled to get her hands up between them and braced against his chest, however, that movement simply made him shift slightly, drawing her more tightly into his arms. She could not breathe, she could not think, she could not scream … she made soft mewling noises in the back of her throat. *God help me,* she thought in wild panic. *Help, Help!*

"Sire?"

With a curse against her lips, the King raised his head but did not turn. "Thomas," he said through gritted teeth, "*you try my patience.* Be gone with you." Rosamund could see nothing but a tall dark shape outlined against the night sky.

"Your Majesty, Clifford hunts for you with the determination of a feral hound. He has some precious port he wishes to share with you. Said he promised to open it in honor of your presence ..." There was a brief hesitation. Then, softly but firmly spoken, "I though perhaps 'twas better that *I* found you rather than he ..."

Henry reached up, and with great possessiveness it seemed, pulled Rosamund's hood back in place, covering her hair. He was not to be rushed, however, and as Thomas stood silently in the dark behind him, the King pulled her tightly into his embrace and kissed her briefly once again. "T'would seem that you were right, Milady," he said softly after he finished. "But we have much time. We will talk at length, you and I, in these next few days." He released her and turned to Thomas. "Escort her back inside."

"Yes, Sire."

She stood there for the longest time trying to gather her wits. Thomas stood, like a tall oak: dark, forbidding and silent. *I would gladly give my friendship, and, as much as possible, my protection.* His protection. Here it was already. Tonight. Now. Finally she spoke, "Does my father truly look for him? I would hate for you to face the King's wrath ..."

He did not answer right away. Then finally, in a low voice, Thomas said, "Aye, your father looks for him."

"The irony is my father would be just as furious with you for this interruption, truth be told."

"I know. At least I spared you the embarrassment of your father's acquiescence."

Rosamund found the strength to step forward and he moved at last, turning and offering his arm. She took it automatically, but then could not help curling her fingers tightly into the fabric of his shirt. After a moment's hesitation, he covered her cold hand with his warm one and they walked slowly toward the hall.

"You offered me your friendship the other night," she said to him at last.

"I did."

"I have never had a friend."   When he did not respond, she continued. "I have Beatrice, my maid, who listens to my fears and cares for me with great thoroughness, yet for me, friendship is more ..."   She struggled with the right words.

"Friendship is freely given."

"Yes! That's it." She stopped then, just before they entered the hall, and looked at him in the twilight. "Why do you offer me your friendship, Sir Thomas?"

Because it seems I have a wish for a slow, painful death, his head said clearly. "Because it is all I have to give, at the moment." *Because it seems I do not have even the brains or the common sense I was born with.* "Because, it would seem, Milady, that you are in dire need of a true friend." *Because there seems to be no one but me willing to champion your cause.* "Because, I want to."

"I would accept your friendship then, sir. Will you accept mine?"

I'll accept anything you offer me. "Yes."

She sighed as if a major decision had been orchestrated and completed.   "Then tell me my only friend," and Rosamund looked searchingly at Thomas' face as her eyes filled up with tears, *"what am I going to do with this mess that is my life?"*

He had no real answer for her. None at all. At last he said in a low voice, "The King, to the best of my knowledge, has never forced a woman to his will ..."

She looked at him incredulously, tears slipping down her face. *"You tell me to deny the King?!"* He spoke of treason. He spoke of death.

Thomas shrugged, willing his head and his heart to process things logically, and unemotionally. It was fair hard to do with her nails digging crescent moon shapes into his arm through the fabric of his sleeve and the wonderful warmth of hers seeping into his left side. "T'would be far easier to do what many a lass has done ..." Thomas looked at her pointedly then, willing her to realize the truth of his words. "He is a generous lover. He will loose interest in you far quicker with your capitulation than through your evasion. No one loves a challenge – mental or physical – more than the King."

"Oh, dear God," she murmured to herself and he watched her close her eyes and mumble something under her breath. He felt a blush steal across his face; here he was thinking of kissing the very lips the King had just kissed as they moved in obvious fervent prayer. *Get a hold of yourself, man.*

"Will he expect these things to occur here in my own home under the watchful eyes of my family and my people?"

Christ, she had not any idea. How could she be where she was in this life and be unaware of the way of things? Did she truly believe that the world was so just and honorable and ... *right?* He looked at her, "And why not?" Her expression told him what he already knew: she was an innocent. Raised amidst all the intrigue of royal life, with a father and mother such as she had, and still she believed that people behaved morally and truthfully.

In the moonlight, Rosamund's face was pale and drawn from stress and tiredness, and yet her beauty still transfixed him. "Yes, I see," she said so quietly that he was forced to lean forward to hear, "and why not?"

It was a long twelve days. By the end of a sennight – with almost another full sennight to go - she was exhausted physically, emotionally, and spiritually. It was the longest twelve plus days of her life: seeing to her myriad of duties, praying every moment that she could spare, and trying to avoid being alone with the King of England to the best of her abilities.

What could not be avoided, however, were two private dinners with him – at his request - in the castle solar, a small, intimate room where the family usually spent most of their time. Not that she was left alone with him, for servants had come and gone with the constant ebb and flow of the meal, but she alone had been forced to carry the conversation between herself and *the King of England*. Rosamund had called upon her training as a proper lady and hostess to see herself through all the physical nuances of the meal, and she had called upon the power of prayer to keep her from collapsing in a hysterical screaming heap on the floor.

Surprisingly, dining with the King had been relatively enjoyable - w*hen* she had been able to forget that it was not necessarily scintillating dinner conversation that was primary in his mind. King Henry had made every effort to be casual, ingratiating, and open. He had told her entertaining stories from his life as a boy, had seemed delighted with her questions, and had been eager to hear her perceptions about anything she felt brave enough to mention. And he had made no move to touch or kiss her again. At the end of both evenings, they had strolled outside in the frigid night air, wrapped in their respective cloaks, trailed by one or more of his retainers and had enjoyed the solitude of the evening. In retrospect, she found it highly ironic that she enjoyed his company and his conversation far better than she ever had Humphrey's.

And then everything suddenly changed with the arrival of a breathless royal messenger bringing vital news to the King. Prince Rhys ab Gruffydd had publicly made his whereabouts known, choosing his location for battle and publicly issuing his challenge: at his holdings in Cantref Mawr, near Carmarthen in the southwest. Rosamund heard his voice whispering fiercely in her ear, *I will succeed. Tell your father and your King that Rhys ab Gruffydd will succeed.*

The messenger had arrived during the dinner hour in the Great Hall amid the laughter and fun one of the final Twelfth Night Celebrations. Rosamund watched the jovial, relaxed stance of every man change. They were now tense and alert. She witnessed the King who had been convivial, charming, and persuasive change to a furious, vengeful, battle hungry warrior. Perhaps, she thought in a flash of hope, the King would forget her and she would be allowed to go to Godstowe Nunnery as she so desperately wanted and needed? She dared not hope. Nay, she *prayed* it would be so. Please ... *please* ...

By morning messengers had been sent summoning support for King Henry against this 'damnable curse that must be annihilated once and for all from our sacred shores'. All evidence of royal visitors had vanished, and Castle Clifford was no longer a royal residence but once again a quiet country manor.

But morning also found Rosamund and all her possessions being packed in compliance with the King's command. She had been summoned to Woodstocke Manor, the King's royal residence in Herefordshire. It seemed that in all of King Henry's lust for battle, he had not forgotten his lust for her.

Were the world all mine from the sea to the Rhine,
I'd give all away if the English Queen would be mine for a day.

German Poet, 12ᵗʰ Century A.D.[10]

Château de Chinon, Anjou
Home of The Duchess of Aquitaine and Queen of England
Vienne River Valley, Northern France
April, 1163

Chapter Nine

uch a messy business this all is, Eleanor de Poitiers, Duchess of Aquitaine and Queen of England thought to herself as she breathed deeply. She grew impatient with the servants and the ladies in waiting as they hovered about her room, bringing her cool drinks, wiping her damp forehead, offering her tidbits of food. "Be gone with all of you!" she finally roared at the top of her lungs as she swung her left arm up, smacking the serving maid in the face and sending her and the tray of God knows what flying across the room. There was a flurry of skirts and whispered comments as the room emptied somewhat. There were probably still close to twenty attendants in the room. Privacy. What she wouldn't give for a few moments of privacy and solitude … But even a Queen couldn't have everything she wanted … for after all, rather than be Queen, Eleanor would have preferred to be King.

She certainly had all the qualifications. She was highly educated; able to read, write, and speak Latin, Provencal – the language of her people in Aquitaine, and English. Her father, William, had seen to it that not only was she appreciative of scholarly treasures but also that she was hungry for experiential pursuits as well. At her mother's death when she was but eight, her father and she had become inseparable, traveling constantly like the troubadours he so loved from one of their familial possessions to the other. From her father she developed a passionate hunger for all that made life exciting and alive: the pursuit of knowledge, the pleasures of music and poetry, the restlessness of sought adventures, and the satisfaction of accomplishing one's goals. Her life had been rich and full, and there had been a time when she knew, without any doubt, that she could be and do anything she dreamed. Her father had encouraged that confidence in her, had bred into her the knowledge that anything was attainable with the right combination of persistence and treachery. *See what you want and take it; determine what hinders you and remove it. Those who hesitate fail; those who forge ahead seize the victory.* Along with love and laughter and the joy of life, Eleanor's father had trained her to be efficient and ruthless in achieving whatever she desired.

At her beloved father's death when she was just fifteen, she became the richest heiress in France and the ward of the King of France, Louis VI. Too rich, too powerful, and far too dangerous to be left unmarried, she had immediately been wed to the King's son, Louis VII. At her new husband's father's death, not a fortnight after becoming a wife, Eleanor became Queen of France. Looking at her husband, pious, weak, grave, dull Louis VII, Eleanor felt for the first time in her life the travesty of her sex; she who was more fit to rule never would, simply because she was a woman.

It was not her husband's fault, really. Louis had never wanted to be King but at the death of his older brother he had been thrust into fulfilling his inescapable duty. Just seventeen, a year older than she, he had become King Louis VII. Could two more different people ever have been created, Eleanor had pondered on more than one occasion? She who loved, nay *thrived*, on the excitement and glitter and pageantry of court; she who possessed the passion and the courage and the skill to lead her own soldiers to battle; she who had the flamboyance and expertise to govern not only her own duchy of Aquitaine, but the entire country of France as well, had been married to a man who had wanted to shutter himself up in a monastery and quietly pray for his entire life. Eleanor represented vitality, while Louis was a vacuous hole. Louis's only saving grace, as far as Eleanor was concerned, was that he was dazzled by her beauty and sensuousness. He seemed not sure what to make of her, but *she* certainly knew what to make of *him*. For a time he had been easily maneuvered, and gradually she established almost complete control over him. Life had been palatable.

Under Eleanor's guidance, the court of King Louis VII was filled with culture and beauty, love and laughter. Were the world perfect, it would simply have strived to emulate everything Eleanor achieved within the bounds of her royal court. But the world was not perfect and did eventually intrude. When the grave threat against the Holy Land loomed, Eleanor and Louis could do nothing more than their duty demanded; they sought to fix things with all the might and power their kingdom possessed. Eleanor, Louis, his troops and her troops, servants, retainers, companions, and troubadours made it as far as the glorious kingdom of Byzantium and its capital Constantinople.

Unfortunately, once they ventured out of the magical boundaries of their world, Louis had been influenced by others. Those who had become Eleanor's enemies – jealous of her loveliness and power and strength – advised her husband of ill-conceived plans. Weak-willed that he was, Louis listened. Initially, she had decided to allow him to go ahead and make his own mistakes while she would continue on with her much more sound strategy. After all, she did not need Louis and his army, she had her own loyal troops from her familial possessions of Aquitaine. She knew what battle tactics would assure success, for her father had taught her well. Eleanor would lead a successful force herself into the Second Crusade. She was not afraid to venture into battle.

Louis, however, not only allowed his plans to interfere with hers, he blatantly sought to stop hers. When she would hear none of his blithering idiocy, he resorted to force, abducting her in the middle of the night and sending her home to France. A few weeks later Louis rejoined her - *defeated* - as she knew he would, and faced an Eleanor who would not be mollified. His actions had formed a breach between them that was, in her opinion, unforgivable.

It had *not* been a match made in heaven, although the most powerful forces on earth sought to keep it together. Despite fifteen years of marriage, two daughters, and interventions by both Abbot Suger, the regent of France, and Pope Eugenius, the marriage was pronounced null and void on the ridiculous grounds of consanguinity. But the reality was, rather than bear the stigma of divorce, it was much preferable to claim that being third cousins had made them unsuitably matched. By then she was willing to do *anything* to get out of the curse that was her marriage. Even leave her daughters …

For there had loomed on the very near horizon Henry Plantagenet. Eleven years her junior, but so like her in personality, Eleanor for a brief moment in time dreamed that *perhaps* they would be happy and powerful and united. Both had been born to lead, groomed to fight, and encouraged to succeed at all costs. Within eight weeks of her annulment from Louis she married Henry. And within two years she was Queen of a new country, England.

She brought class and culture to Henry's court, if not to him and his country. He turned a disinterested eye to Château de Chinon, the magnificent manor in Anjou that Eleanor commissioned. Henry tolerated her 'hangers on' as he called them, those attendants and poets and troubadours who brought style and *civilization* to his vastly substandard existence. While she could not convince him to dress with more flourish, he enjoyed the philosophical discussions that were a staple with the people with whom she deigned to keep company. Many a vibrant night was spent with Henry, still in his mud spattered hunting boots and clothes, roaring with fury over points and counterpoints that scholarly guests refused to renounce. In reality, Henry might eschew her fashion sense but he passionately loved a good debate.

The reality of life, however, settled in with great finality during her marriage to Henry. Regardless of Eleanor's capabilities, she would always be *just a woman*. For while she and Henry had many shared passions, in numerous ways Henry was more stifling than Louis had ever been. For instance, she could not control him as she had Louis. At all. Henry refused to discuss politics with her, nor did he wish to hear her opinions or suggestions on how he should rule, even in regard to *her* properties that he now, by right, claimed as his. Henry had enough strong opinions of his own, thank you very much, and had no interest whatsoever in hearing anything Eleanor might have desired to say.

However, revenge was ultimately hers. It was not that she gave up all hope, simply that her wishes were now redirected in a far more productive manner. For no matter how powerful or how successful Henry became, he could never do the one thing that would ensure the longevity of his rule: *he* could not produce the heir apparent by himself, only with Eleanor. And that's where she decided to stake her claim to the throne. That's where she knew that inevitably, were she careful with the selection and the nurturing and the training of the *future* King of England, she could wield as much power as she had always dreamed. And by then, Henry would be dead.

So produce children she had. First there had been William, then Matilda, then Richard, then Geoffrey, then Eleanor. Five babies in nine short years. Let *no one* say that once she set her mind to something – *anything* - she could not do it with amazing success! Only William had not survived infancy, so not only had she produced numerous children she had produced sturdy ones as well. Her greatest concern now was which one she should choose, foster, mold, encourage, and design to be what she needed him to be.

But then there was always this one, now ... number six.

"Push, Your Majesty, the baby's head crowns ..." The numerous pregnancies had taken their toll on her body. She felt it in the lack of energy this time, the longer and more difficult labor. Were she not careful, this victory in producing heirs could kill her. *I will insist that I be allowed some time after this birth to regain my strength and vitality,* she thought.

At last the child was born. Too exhausted to inquire, Eleanor drifted off into a dreamless sleep. Baby number six for Henry, baby number eight for her. She hastily pushed that thought aside, as blackness overtook her, unwilling to think of her two girls, Marie and Alice, whom she never saw or spoke to.

It was daylight when she awakened, feeling remarkably rested. How long had she slept? Why had the child not been brought to her? While she took very little interest in the actual care of the babies, she certainly wished to have a moment alone with the child. Her maids hovered by her bed and at her first stirring rushed to her side to assist her upright, adjusting pillows, rearranging coverlets, bringing tea and biscuits to her bedside. She cast a glance at the closest maid and said impatiently, "*Cease*. Bring me the babe. I wish to see it."

Eight times she had been brought a squirming bundle which she had carefully unwrapped and examined, checking for the right number of fingers and toes, examining occasional birthmarks, trying to gauge, even at this early date, which child appeared alert and authoritative. To be quite honest, none had truly impressed her yet. Well, perhaps Richard, but the jury was still out on that one. She occasionally visited the nursery, ever searching for The One. For if she could not be King, one of her sons would be, and she would groom him so that he would be the most glorious King that England and Aquitaine and Normandy and Brittany had *ever* seen. For she would be beside him. She *would* one day rule.

"Your Majesty," the royal physician, Lord Beutlings stood at a respectful distance from her canopied bed.

"Approach, Lord Beutlings. I grow impatient, where is the babe?"

"Your Majesty, you fell into a deep sleep after the birth and we were loath to wake you, thinking it was wise to let you rest and regain your strength." He looked pained for a moment. "I'm sorry, Your Majesty. The child never drew breath."

Eleanor was stunned into speechlessness. The *idea*. She struggled to wrap her mind around the concept that for the very first time in her life something she had attempted to do had failed. It had never happened. Ever. She looked up at the physician and realized that he was anticipating hysterics or, at the very least, tears. Kings did not cry. Certainly neither would Queens. She fixed him with a penetrating stare and held it long enough until his gaze wavered with nervousness, and she watched him swallow convulsively. "We will not speak of this again, Lord Beutlings. *Not ever.* I will dismiss anyone who breathes even a hint about this ... incident. Have I made myself clear?"

He bowed respectfully to her, "Perfectly, Your Majesty."

"Good. Summon my maids, I wish to bathe and change and dress. I have business to attend to, courtiers to see, and functions to plan. I am a most busy Queen, sir."

"Aye, Your Majesty, indeed you are."

Henry was off to that God-forsaken island. Eleanor shuddered just thinking about it. She hated England. She abhorred the weather, the people, the land, the coarse language, the food. She was appalled at the primitive living conditions that even those who considered themselves nobility survived in. She smiled to herself as she sat before her dressing table while her maids prepared her hair. Henry hated England just as much as she did. It was something else she liked so much about him. He traveled there only under extreme duress, preferring the culture and beauty of the royal continental society she had fostered. Never had he stayed in England for more than a few months at a time. She would be productive with this interval, resting and recovering her strength and vitality. And then, when he returned to her, she would endeavor to work on child number nine and the ever important goal of producing the Most Perfect Heir. Eleanor would be victorious.

She always was.

The Marches
Welsh and English Border
April, 1163

At the moment that Eleanor was certain of her inevitable victory, Henry was facing imminent death. On the road to Carmarthen his army was slowly and methodically being decimated, one bloody skirmish at a time by the damnable Welsh. Word had just reached the King that his naval contingent, set to sail to Pembroke and attack Prince Rhys at Camarthen from the rear, had suffered crippling casualties. While the bulk of his main army was marching towards Prince Rhys' stronghold, Cantref Mawr, Henry and his most seasoned knights had cut inland to complete a three-pronged attack. For once he had let his all-consuming fury override his innate common sense. Without consulting those more experienced with the countryside, he'd forged ahead with his own plans. This had gotten him and his men where they currently were: hampered by the terrain of dense forests along numerous hills and valleys - which offered no solid land on which to mount an adequate defense. They were unable to battle an unseen enemy, who fought like the cowards they were, dropping arrows like raindrops of death from the trees and melting in and out of the shadowy foliage. They were cursed additionally by the weather, a miserable mix of snow, rain, hail, and sleet – they'd seen every miserable combination in just two days. Did the sun never shine in Wales? Henry had the first inkling of real fear and failure. His rage and frustration knew no bounds. He sat on his horse as another emotion, indecision, joined the chaos of thoughts in his mind.

"Your Majesty, will you at last listen to me?" a low voice said to him from his left.

Henry stared into the calm, cold eyes of one of his trusted knights sitting astride his own horse. "What do you have to tell me, Sir Thomas?"

"Sire, we ride to our deaths. *I have been here before*, more times than I wish to count, fighting the Welsh shadows. We are in their territory, at their mercy, following their rules. Our superior strength and training are worthless here; even young David was able to kill the giant Goliath under the right circumstances."

"You preach to me?"

Thomas looked at him and braved a grin. "If that's what it takes to save my skin and yours, Your Majesty. I'll even sing a song or two. I've done worse things to continue to draw breath."

Henry snorted. "You will preach to me, but you will not say to me that I have erred with this plan."

"You wish me to say such, Your Majesty? Thought of imminent death makes me careless." Thomas shrugged his shoulders. "Your main battle plan is sound. You are a magnificent leader and the reason that I and my fellow knights follow you; for the assured victories. This foray into the woods was not wise, though. At another time it may have worked, but I have stayed alive as long as I have by trusting my instincts. And my instincts tell me that if I continue forward I will die. We can correct the error, but we need to withdraw *now* before there are none of us alive to do so." They both heard a subtle whistle and Thomas was instantly alert, turning his attention away from the King. He answered with a distinctive whistle of his own; birdlike and fleeting.

Thomas turned his attention back to the King. "Gavin says that the Welsh approach. We must withdraw – *now* – quickly, back to the small meadow beside the stream where we last watered the horses."

Henry looked at the man before him and liked what he saw: loyalty, commitment, fearlessness, and intelligence. "Command, Sir Thomas, I follow you."

Instantly, Thomas swung into action, wheeling his horse around, shouting orders over his shoulder and thundering down the narrow path they had just traveled. As Henry turned his horse to obey, all others followed. They crossed the stream to the meadow and had just enough time to turn, position, and draw swords before the forest before them came alive with screaming warriors. Their retreat had immediately cancelled the threat of the deadly Welsh archers, whose favorite position – high in the trees – made them nigh onto invincible.

"Let no one climb a tree!" Thomas screamed to the men as they hacked and parried and thrust from atop their horses. The meadow was not perfect, but much better suited to the English fighting style than the close confines of the wood. And it was all the advantage that they needed. Though outnumbered greatly, the English knights and their King overwhelmed the Welsh with their skill and their weaponry.

Afterwards, Thomas always wondered how long a battle really took. Time seemed to bend when the bloodlust of fighting took over. Surveying the aftermath, feeling the tiredness tug at his body, seeing the sweat stream down the sides of his blowing horse, he knew time had passed, but could never tell exactly how much. The moans of the wounded cancelled out the clashes of the weapons as he dismounted and strode over to the King still astride his horse. He looked up into King Henry's sweat-streamed face and patted the neck of the King's trembling horse.

King Henry stared at him for a long few moments and Thomas, in his exhaustion, simply stared back. "I owe you my life," the King finally said at last.

Thomas bowed slightly, "And I've pledged you mine, Sire."

"You had the courage to speak up and the wherewithal to save us all. Look around you, man, not one of my men lies dead."

Thomas nodded. "They are my brothers in arms, Your Majesty. It pleases me as well."

"We will talk more of this, Sir Thomas. I fulfill all my debts and I am in yours." Henry mopped his sweat-streaked face with the back of his sleeve. In the cold air, men and horses alike cast tendrils of steam off their heated, damp bodies. "Water yourselves and your horses! We ride immediately back to the coast to join the main contingent!" The King spared Thomas one last look of appreciation before he made his way to the stream.

Fighting and traveling with King Henry II was an adventure in every sense of the word. He was a man who truly knew that he was set apart from every other human being on earth. Given worldly authority over life and death and further blessed by being sanctioned by the powerful spiritual authority presently ruling the church here on earth, King Henry II was a figure almost bigger than life. His massive army arrived at Camarthen, regrouped, and advanced with precision to Pencader and Prince Rhys' lair of Cantref Mawr. Under his command Henry had some 50 seasoned knights, 150 archers, and 2000 spearmen. Despite the initial disaster at Pembroke, the English army, in reality, had exerted more effort in *arriving* at the battle site than the actual execution of the conflict itself. By sheer numbers the English army forced itself into Prince Rhys' castle and in the end the siege took no more then ten days. Prince Rhys surrendered, agreeing only after Henry's promise to spare the lives of the women, children, and the few surviving soldiers he still commanded.

It was Thomas who was put in charge of guarding Prince Rhys and seeing to his safe delivery to Henry's stronghold of Woodstocke and all knew it for the honor it was. Riding with his personally selected contingent of men, Brian and Gavin among them, Thomas studied the man who was his prisoner.

Rhys ab Gruffydd rode like a King, comfortable and easy with himself, unhurried *and* unworried with his circumstances. Not a tall man, he had a commanding presence nonetheless, with a dark, sinister air about him. He was a man never to be underestimated, never to be trusted. Thomas remembered Rosamund's accounting of her kidnapping, care and conversation while she was with him. Having encountered Gruffydd in battle on more than one occasion, the picture she had painted of him had been impossible to believe. But now, riding beside him, watching him proud, alert, and definitely calculating … well it wasn't so far a stretch after all.

"You fight with precision," Prince Rhys said to Thomas as they rode. Thomas looked at him briefly but did not respond. "You and your King stand out in the melee, you with your height and your calculated exactitude and your King with his red hair and fury."

Thomas looked at Gruffydd. "Is it conversation you wish? I guess it will make the ride back to your confinement pass a bit more quickly."

"Conversation is the most powerful weapon I possess," Gruffydd looked at Thomas, "since you've taken my sword, shield, and bow."

"I fight to stay alive. It is all I know, although not all I necessarily want. It is a means to an end."

Gruffydd looked ahead, at Gavin's armor clad back before him leading the way. "I fight to reclaim what is mine and all I deserve. I will achieve this or die."

Thomas couldn't help but goad him. "You are well on your way to death then, since you have obviously failed this fight."

"I am defeated when I am dead and not a moment sooner."

"I'll not forget that."

"I would have been disappointed in you if you had."

The irony of the present circumstances did not escape Thomas. They were traveling to Woodstocke where Thomas knew Rosamund also was.

Thomas, who desired Rosamund but could never have her.

Gruffydd, who had possessed her but had released her.

And Henry, who had claimed her and who would keep her.

Woodstocke Manor
Royal Residence of Henry II, King of England
Oxfordshire, England
May, 1163

Chapter Ten

oodstocke was the place that dreams were made of. From her first glimpses of it riding up the winding path with the landscape covered in newly fallen snow to her detailed explorations after her arrival, Rosamund was continually amazed and awed. Like nothing she had ever dreamed or imagined, it astonished and impressed her at every turn.

The first week of her arrival, once she had unpacked and settled into her massive suite of rooms, she had attempted to acclimate herself to the place and had wandered extensively throughout the manor's numerous floors and wings. There were, she suspected, at least one hundred rooms and suites, but she had long since lost count and no longer trusted the accuracy of her tally. There was opulence in every corner, finery such as she didn't know existed in every glance, and she was certain that even after a full week of exploration she had not seen everything, and seriously doubted if she ever would. It was a veritable city unto itself with numerous outbuildings for such necessities as a blacksmith, a tanner, a miller, and a butcher. There were so many servants and workers necessary to staff the place that a good sized village a small distance away, also called Woodstocke, was populated completely with manor employees and their families. Perhaps what amazed her most was that there was an army of masons and carpenters and laborers working practically night and day to finish the *addition* that King Henry had seen fit to order. What did he plan to do with all of this?

One morning, unable to go outside because of the weather, Rosamund wandered aimlessly through the dimly lit halls of the manor. Accidentally, she stumbled upon a room that soon became her most treasured location at Woodstocke: the library. Memories flooded her mind of the glorious times spent with Sister Helen learning to read and write, devouring the precious few books she had owned, and attempting to satisfy her endless craving to learn of things she did not know. She stood in the center of the Woodstocke library, looking at books, the number of which caused her heart to pound and her breathing to quicken and she felt, for the first time in a long, long time, deliriously happy. *"Thank you, Lord,"* she whispered quietly aloud, for certainly this gift was from Him. For certainly no one knew how much she desired a place such as this but Him.

And then there were the gardens. Even with the raw weather of late winter she was drawn to them, the peacefulness of the outdoors always bringing her joy and solitude. Rosamund wandered the paths for weeks whenever the weather permitted, certain she traveled a different route each time and doubtful that she had seen all there was to see. In the midst of her fourth week of wandering she rounded a corner and stared in amazement at what was before her. Then she began to laugh and laugh and laugh because of the sheer ridiculousness of what she saw. It was an elephant, stoically standing in its pen munching through a mountain of hay and regarding her with the most disconcertingly intelligent eyes.

"Hello, sir," she began and giggled at her own folly as she fought the silly urge to bow. "It would seem that I am the newest addition to King

Henry's captured zoo. How does he treat his captives, might I ask? You seem content enough. Have you any suggestions for me to help me become more acclimated to my circumstances?"

"Well, miss, you can try being cooperative and docile," said a voice that nearly startled the life out of her, "for any animals that turn rogue on us we have to put down." Rosamund spun around to find a wizened old gentleman in laborer's garb. "I be James, Milady, one of the keepers of King Henry's animals."

"I'm in trouble already then, James, because I've *never* been cooperative and docile." She smiled at him. "My name is Rosamund."

He bowed as much as his bent form would allow, "'Tis a pleasure, Lady Rosamund." He smiled shyly, "Might ya like a tour?"

How could she have been here, over a full month, and not known there was an elephant, a lion, a bear, a tiger, numerous types of monkeys, and even a feisty giraffe being kept on the grounds? James seemed unfazed. "'Tis more than ten thousand acres of property that goes with this manor, Milady. Much of it untouched forests for the King's greatest passion is the hunt. I'll wager ye have not even seen all the gardens, am I right?" When she nodded, he shrugged. "I'm right impressed, I am, that you've found His Majesty's zoo on your own in such a short time. Have you found the lake? The swings? No? How about the maze?" As Rosamund shook her head, James chuckled. "Aye, you've got much to find then still. Mind the maze. 'Tis best not to go in it without his Majesty to guide ya."

"*A maze?*" she asked incredulously. "What do you mean, sir, 'best not to go in'?"

James' eyes twinkled. "I am not jesting when I tell ya 'tis a garden puzzle that His Majesty had built the last time he was here. Every time he visits Woodstocke he swears that he will never leave again, he loves this place so, and he adds bits and pieces that strike his fancy. Swears that he wants it to rival anything that he's ever seen on the continent and is determined to accomplish that goal. The maze was something Her Majesty the Queen's Uncle Raymond of Poitiers had written to her about seeing. Henry thought it would be grand fun to have one of his own and even got involved enough to draw up the actual plans. Far's I know, he's the only one who knows the true path. Different gardeners care for only specific parts of it so that no one knows the true route to get to the center. And I hear tell that there is a grand surprise that Henry has at the heart of it, but no one knows what it truly is."

So, Rosamund's weeks at Woodstocke slipped into months. When the weather began to show the first signs of spring a veritable army of people arrived, all with her as the focus. Designers and clothiers, seamstresses and leather merchants all came and measured and sewed and fitted her with every conceivable item a young woman could want; dresses and capes, camisoles and hats, shoes and boots, reticules and handkerchiefs, day gowns, ball gowns, riding habits ... Her head swam with the constant demands to make choices and decisions about fabrics and colors while her body ached from the frustrating hours she was forced to remain still during all the fittings. When they left, after nearly a full month of their attentions she was quite certain that she could go for a full year without ever wearing the same dress or shoes twice. Were it not for her insistence that the days of their constant attention not begin until after the nooning meal, giving her time to walk and prepare herself mentally for the frustrating lack of inactivity, she knew she would have gone insane.

By her third month at Woodstocke Manor, she imagined she felt like the animals in Henry's zoo: captive yet diligently cared for. Unable to leave and yet relatively content, the luxurious accommodations caused one to forget what, where, when, and why one truly needed to go away. She spent her days walking the grounds – she did find the maze and avoided it completely, heeding James' warning - and reading book after book after book into the wee hours of the morning. Her prayers were full of thankfulness for God-given pleasures, entreaties for safety for those for whom she felt concern and earnest requests for His continued guidance and protection for herself and Beatrice. Were it not for the reality of where she was and why she was there she could, almost, be happy.

Her almost happiness lasted another month. The King's outriders arrived mid - May when the gardens were just beginning to be their most glorious and the days were, at last, warm enough to forgo a shawl on her wanderings. She returned to the manor to find it in an uproar with King's retainers shouting orders and servants scurrying in every direction.

A knight approached her as she made her way into the main hallway with her current book tucked under her arm, and bowed respectfully. "Lady Rosamund. I'm Sir Robert, one of King Henry's knights. He bids me send you his most fervent regards and looks forward to the time when he can see and speak with you directly."

Her heart began to pound and her stomach to clench. "And when will that be, Sir Robert?"

"King Henry is expected here at Woodstocke in a fortnight."

"A fortnight …" she said quietly to herself. She had a fortnight. King Henry returned from battle in two weeks and Rosamund would then face her own combat. She sighed and looked around at the activity. "T'would seem there is little for me to do but wait. Tell me, is the King well? Was he successful in his quest?"

"Yes, milady. The King returns victorious with Rhys ab Gruffydd as his prisoner."

Rosamund looked at Sir Robert, stunned. "He has Prince Rhys ab Gruffydd as his *prisoner?*"

Sir Robert displayed the smile of a victorious soldier. "Aye, milady. His Majesty accomplished all he set out to do."

"What does he intend to do with his prisoner?" she asked quietly, remembering the man who had murdered her husband, kidnapped her, and yet displayed wit, charm, and courtly manners. Gruffydd's passion and conviction for his cause had made him appear invincible to her, and her mind struggled to process the news she had just heard.

Sir Robert shrugged. "Gruffydd is at the King's mercy, and King Henry has little patience for his enemies." He chuckled a bit to himself. "Let's hope that it's an easy trip here, Milady. I've been with King Henry when his frustration became so great he simply mutilated and hung his hostages rather then go through the bother of securing and transporting them."

Rosamund looked at him, unable to find her voice at first. She forced herself to swallow and take a breath. "You speak from first hand knowledge?"

Sir Robert seemed to puff up a bit with his own importance, "I have traveled exclusively with the King since I was knighted by him. I have traveled and battled and been his confidant. I speak only what I know to be the truth."

"I see …"

Sir Robert seemed eager to impress her further. "I also am privy to the knowledge that King Henry has summoned Malcolm, King of the Scots, and Owain, Prince of the northern Welsh to pay homage to him. They are summoned to appear here at Woodstocke in two months time. Even the new Archbishop, Thomas Becket, has been called to attend."

She bowed to Sir Robert. "I am most fortunate that the King had seen fit to send me such a well informed knight. Thank you for your information, Sir Robert."

He returned her bow. "I am at your service, Milady, by the King's command."

The King of Scotland? The Archbishop of Canterbury? A Prince of Wales? Prince Rhys ab Gruffydd as prisoner? *And* the King of England who wished to make her his leman? And *all* would be present in this place within two months time? Could it get any more complicated? God help her if it did!

King Henry, his knights, a large number of his trusted nobles, one heavily guarded prisoner, and innumerable retainers arrived ten days later causing complete and utter pandemonium. Martin, Woodstocke Manor's head house steward, although unflappable, appeared near collapse. Rosamund took pity on him.

"Your Majesty," she heard him say in his most imperious tone as he stood in the opened front portal, "Welcome home to Woodstocke Manor."

"Ahh, Martin!" she heard the King shout, "now it's not your ugly old face I was hoping to see. Is she here?"

"You would be referring to the Lady Rosamund, Your Majesty?"

She heard the King's laugh. "Is there anyone fairer than she currently residing in the country, man?"

"To the best of my knowledge, Sire, *no.*"

"Then where -" but he stopped when she came out from behind Martin, appearing in the massive doorway of the manor and dropping to a low curtsy.

"Welcome home, Your Majesty," she said loudly and clearly.

She heard his boots hit the gravel of the pathway as he dismounted and the distinctive crunch of his footsteps as he approached. "Let me see your beautiful face, Lady Rosamund," King Henry said in a low voice.

She rose slowly and he extended his hand to assist her. He kept a tight hold on her once she was standing, and looked at her for moments. "You are well?"

"Aye, Your Majesty."

"You have been well cared for?"

"Aye, Your Majesty. The staff here at Woodstocke is superior to any I have every encountered. I have wanted for nothing."

"Not even me?" Henry asked quietly and grinned a wicked grin. She chose to remain silent, which made him chuckle at her temerity. "All of your needs have been met?"

She grew uncomfortable with the army of knights sitting quietly on their horses before her in the courtyard while Henry took his time talking with her. "Aye, Sire, I have been well fed, beautifully clothed, and blessedly content these months I have been here. Tell me, are not you and your men tired from the journey? Would you all not enjoy an opportunity for some good food, warm ale, and a cozy fire? Martin has everything ready to accommodate each and every one of you. Let us not delay your comfort one more moment."

"Will you join us?"

She inclined her head. "As you wish, Your Majesty."

"Will you always be this complacent?"

She looked at him then. The battle had well and truly begun. "Absolutely not, Your Majesty." The King threw back his head and roared with delighted laughter.

It was, by far, the most awkward meal she had ever attended in her entire life. Aside from the serving girls, she was the only woman present in a great hall of men who alternately gawked at her or completely forgot she was there and shouted ribald comments that made her blush. She was seated at the head table with the King on one side and Prince Rhys ab Gruffydd on the other. Next to Prince Rhys was Sir Thomas.

"We meet again, Milady," Gruffydd said to her moments after she took her seat. "It seems that circumstances have improved dramatically for you."

"I am here as a result of your interference in my life, sir. You bear full responsibility."

"Oh? How is that?" Gruffydd seemed genuinely surprised.

"I delivered your message to the King."

"And?"

Rosamund looked at him with impatience. "And *nothing*."

"Yes, Rhys," King Henry said joining the conversation, "I believe I am indebted to you. You see, had you not directed Lady Rosamund to deliver your message and your challenge to me personally, then I perhaps never would have had the wonderful pleasure of making her acquaintance."

Gruffydd looked to the King. "How great is your indebtedness? Is your pleasure of Lady Rosamund's company significant enough to warrant my release and the recognition of my claims?" Gruffydd's tone dripped with sarcasm.

The King reached up and put his finger underneath Rosamund's chin turning her face to him and forcing her to look into his eyes. He searched her expression, looking for a sign of encouragement of some kind. But he saw only terror and confusion and finally released her. "Perhaps, Rhys. It still remains to be seen ..."

"How long have you been here?" Gruffydd asked more quietly, once the King began talking to the knight to his left, so that only Rosamund could hear.

"I was brought here mid January," she replied just as softly, "after King Henry left to address your challenge." She couldn't resist the opportunity for a dig. "You made so many people happy, sir. My mother, my father, the King … Had I not known better, I would have thought you were in league with the English rather than at war."

"But I have not made you happy?"

Rosamund looked at him and let him see the despair and the fear in her eyes. "No, sir, you have not made me happy in the least."

Thomas watched her rise at Henry's bidding and allow herself to be led from the dining hall. She wore the same closed expression that she had worn on her wedding day and he felt his gut clench and the bile rise in his throat. There was naught he could do! He watched, his body tensed to do battle, as the King drew her close by putting an arm around her waist. He stared after them until they turned from view.

A low chuckle to his left drew Thomas' attention and he came in direct eye contact with Gruffydd. "Seems that there is yet another man at this table that has taste enough to know a splendid woman when he sees one, eh?"

Thomas ignored Gruffydd, disgusted with himself that he had allowed his enemy to see something so private.

"Ahh, we had a wonderful three days *and nights* together not too long ago, Lady Rosamund and I. She has the softest hair and skin, like it's been kissed by the Gods it seems. And her scent, why it is a most unusual aroma … *vanilla.*" Gruffydd sighed deeply. "One of my greatest regrets was returning her to her father's castle, but duty to my country outweighed my own personal pleasures." Gruffydd nudged Thomas, who sat stiffly next to him breathing deeply, trying to ignore the purposeful jibes. "Tell me Thomas, have you had the opportunity to taste," he leaned closer to Thomas, "vanilla?" And then Gruffydd's face exploded with Thomas's fist.

Gavin and Brian, sitting across from Thomas, had observed the entire evening, watching their friend closely and seeing his control slowly erode with each course of food served. When the King had left with Rosamund, they had thought the greatest danger had passed, but then Gruffydd had begun his talk. They'd looked at each other in silent understanding and waited for the inevitable. When Thomas snapped they were across the table, dirty platters and tankards of ale flying, trying to grab hold of the two men battling with all their might to kill each other.

Thomas, almost a head and a half taller than Gruffydd and weighing upwards of four stone more, had the advantage. But Gruffydd fought with cold calculation and precision, unfettered by Thomas' blinding fury. It took Gavin, Brian and two other knights to finally subdue Thomas, and two other knights to restrain Gruffydd.

Gruffydd, bleeding from his nose, his mouth, and a cut over his eye, had lost none of his cocky demeanor. "You fight well, young Thomas. Were you to learn to control those emotions and fight with only your strength and skill you might be able to best me."

Thomas, sporting a bloody lip and a darkening eye, jerked his arm from Gavin's grasp and wiped the edge of his mouth. "I look forward to the opportunity," he said as he left the observant crowd and stalked into the night.

Much to Rosamund's horror, although were she to admit it she was not surprised, the King's suite of rooms were in the same wing, on the same floor, and only separated by a brief walk from her own. As they made their way from the dining hall, she struggled with what she planned to do and say. *The King, to the best of my knowledge, has never forced a woman to his will.* And yet, Rosamund, in her entire life had been obedient and respectful to her elders and superiors. That didn't mean she was a mindless idiot, she was quick to remind herself, but it did mean that she was cooperative, aware of her responsibilities, and in reality, quite proud of her life's service thus far. None of this helped Rosamund in the least now as she proceeded the King into his rooms.

Upon entering the King's suite, Rosamund instinctively moved forward to separate herself from him, wandering purposefully to the large windows. They were in a spacious and richly furnished sitting room. The candles burned brightly and the fire cast a warm glow. "I imagine you have a lovely view of the gardens from here, Your Majesty."

She heard him moving behind her, heard the clink of glasses, and assumed he was pouring himself a drink. The silence was profoundly awkward.

"The Manor is lovely, Sire. I've enjoyed walking the grounds and have discovered the zoo, the maze, and the lake. James, who cares for the animals of your zoo, tells me there are swings somewhere, but I've yet to find them. And I must tell you that my most treasured place in the whole manor is …" she turned to determine where he was, and he was right behind her, holding two glasses of wine.

"Right here?" he finished for her smiling as he handed her a glass of wine.

"I was going to say the library," and she bit her lower lip and looked down, trying to avoid his eyes.

King Henry laughed. "I'm surprised you can read, but then again I think that's one of your greatest appeals. You are continually unpredictable." He leaned forward and whispered in her ear, "I love a challenge." Rosamund fell silent as he took her elbow, steering her to a settee. "The library is one of my favorite places, too, Rosamund, beside being in the forests enjoying the thrill of the hunt. What have you read so far?"

"I'm working my way through your philosophical section," she said, and smiled across at him. "At the convent where I learned to read and write, there were very few books with other than religious themes."

"Who are you reading now?"

"Cicero."

"*Appetitus rationi pareat.*"

"'Let your desire be ruled by reason,' I was just reading that!" She looked stunned. "You know enough of Cicero that you can quote him?"

King Henry shrugged. "Don't be too impressed. You could name others and I'd not be so quick. I happen to like many of his opinions, so they stayed with me. Do you consider yourself a Skeptic?"

He was delighted to see her blush and laugh. "Quite frankly, Your Majesty, up until these past few months I didn't even know the term existed. But, no, on the whole I cannot embrace Skepticism. It seems to me that the primary function of Skeptics is simply to criticize the arguments of others."

He nodded in agreement and chuckled. "Cicero was a lawyer, so he needed to be able to see both sides of every argument." He took a sip of his wine. "Kings need that ability, too." He studied her intently for a minute. "I guess that you would embrace a Stoic philosophy over an Epicurean one."

Rosamund looked off at nothing in particular, deep in concentrated thought. "Well, were I forced to choose, I would indeed lean toward Stoicism, however the Epicurean doctrine is not all bad."

King Henry leaned forward, hopeful and intrigued. "You embrace the belief that pleasure is the only human good and that the only righteous goal is the pursuit of such?" He looked like he was ready to devour her.

She held her hand up. "Just hold right there, Your Majesty!" He laughed aloud at her audacity, grabbed her hand, kissed it, and continued to hold onto it. So lost was she in organizing her thoughts and her valid arguments, she barely noticed. "The Epicureans did not mean that we were to spend a baseless life of food, wine and, er, *other pleasures*. Their philosophy has been twisted by others who seek to bend it to their will. Epicureans desired the highest pleasure achieved in studying and discussing thoughts, beliefs, and theories with others of like mind to the exclusion of all else – even politics and public life. That sounds very much like what the sisters had at Godstowe Nunnery. It *was* a pleasurable life."

Still holding her hand, he placed his wine goblet on the floor and reached over to touch her cheek. "'Pleasure is the beginning and the end of happy living.'"

"You know quotes from Epicurus as well! I am doomed. I fear, Your Majesty, that I will never be able to best you in an argument or a debate," she sighed with genuine regret.

"That would give you enjoyment?" King Henry murmured.

Rosamund's eyes sparkled with mischief. "Rarely am I given the opportunity to voice my views, let alone encounter someone who wishes to listen and respond." She shook her head, "No, I do not need to *best* you in a sparing with words. The sparring is enjoyable enough, Your Majesty."

"There are other things far more enjoyable than verbal sparring, my fair Rosamund," he said quietly to her, and when her eyes flew up to meet his in shocked surprise he seized the opportunity and kissed her.

What a fool I am, she thought to herself in despair. Once again she had forgotten her situation and let her thirst for knowledge interfere with her preservation of self. Here she was giggling and laughing and holding a conversation with the King of England *in his bedroom sitting room.* Dear Lord, help!

Rosamund pulled away and the King allowed her to do so, searching her eyes and trying, she supposed, to read her emotions. Tentatively, she placed her hand on his cheek and his expression flared with delight at the touch. "Your Majesty," he gazed at her intently, "might I ask what is it that you find so appealing in me?"

He had a start of surprise and then seemed to have a dawn of understanding. "You are the most beautiful woman I have ever lain eyes upon," he said fervently.

She removed her hand from his face and smiled most tolerantly at him. "Come now, Sire, I have not traveled extensively but have not led a completely sheltered life. Surely, over the course of your life there have been other women that share ... my level of attractiveness. *I would hear the truth.*"

The King shrugged. "Beauty comes in different packages, and at different times a man's judgment changes. You have an uncommon beauty, Rosamund. If it is not compliments you are after, then what is it you need to hear from me? Help me know so that I can say it, get it over with, and then you can join me in my bed."

She had the audacity to looked annoyed for a moment. "I mean, why me, Your Majesty? Why do you seek me with such tenacity? What have I done? What do I have?"

King Henry picked up his wine glass, drained it, and walked over to the table to pour himself another glass. "At first it was your looks." He shrugged. "You are right, though, looks in a woman are easy to come by and," he grinned at her, "'when the candles are out all women are fair.'" He looked a bit sheepish at her shocked look. "Plutarch said that." He sighed.

"Then it was your voice and your manner of speaking." He leaned against the wall, twirling the goblet in his two hands and looked at her pointedly. "*Then* it was your pledge. From that moment on I have thought of you as *mine.*"

"I meant to pledge you my loyalty," she said in a stricken whisper, "*not myself.*"

He came over and sat by her, reached his hand out to her, hesitated, and then brushed a lock of hair from her forehead. "I know," he murmured, seemingly mesmerized by what he saw before him. "It was your innocence, your purity, your total lack of guile that pushed everything aside and has filled my head with thoughts that I cannot put away."

Rosamund stared at her tightly clasped hands. "This purity you see in me …" she looked up at the King, "it is *my faith.* Without it, I would be such a different person. I know that because I struggle each and every day to be the best I can be, and *it is hard work.*

"I, I cannot deny you should you wish to force this … relationship between us. But I must be honest and tell you that should you do that, you will take away this honorable life I endeavor to live, and I will not be this woman that you see before you."

He was angry. Very angry. "And you feel this way because …? Why? Because you cannot bear the stigma of being a mistress? Because you find me unsatisfactory? Because you love another? Why?" The King's voice rose as he spoke, almost nearing a shout.

Rosamund shook her head vigorously. "No, Your Majesty, for none of those reasons." She braved to look at him. "I feel this way because it is *wrong.*"

He looked completely flummoxed. "Wrong, how? Because I can give you no marriage vows?"

She stood then and began to pace the small space between the settee and the windows. "Am I the only one that bears concern for this? Does no one see the conflict that I see? My mother fair pushes me out the door, bags packed to join you, my father dances the happiest jig he has ever danced in his life, and you, Your Majesty, stand before me shouting, demanding an explanation as to why becoming your mistress is wrong." Rosamund stopped in front of the windows and looked at the King standing furiously on the other side of the room. "You made an oath before God, Your Majesty. You gave your word before God and man and pledged your life to your wife." When he started to speak, she had the temerity to lift her hand, "Please let me finish," and he glowered at her but stayed silent.

"I know what you will say. 'It was a marriage of convenience.' I know, I had one, too. 'There is no love involved.' I know, I have never loved in my life, and yet I am already a widow. 'Husbands and wives do it all the time.' I know, my husband, his mistress, and his illegitimate son all died the night of Gruffydd's attack. 'No one need know.' Even if that were possible – and it is not for *everyone* already assumes it to be fact, God would know and He is all I care about. It is not for the *lack* of vows, but because of them.

"I have been a failure in many things, Your Majesty. I was a failure to my husband in being unable to bear a child. I was a failure to my parents in being unable to be the kind of daughter they wished me to be. I was a failure to you in that until I pledged you my loyalty you could not be sure of it." Tears began to gather and trickle down her face and she closed her eyes to stop them. She was unsuccessful. "I do not wish to be a failure to my God, Your Majesty." Rosamund opened her eyes and wiped her face with her hands. "I'm sorry."

King Henry approached her slowly, his movements still stiff with anger. "I have never forced a woman and I will not begin with you. But, know this, fair Rosamund. Once I take something I *never give it back*. And you I already have claimed as mine."

"I am not some*thing*, but someone. Does that not make a difference?"

He kissed her then, a kiss filled with force and anger, bruising her lips and crushing the breath out of her. "No, it makes no difference at all."

She looked at him through her tears. "So I will become another curious animal to add to your zoo. At least I will have opportunities aplenty to best you in an argument or two."

"Look carefully, Lady Rosamund. It seems, this night you may have already bested me, for we *stand* here rather than lying abed. But, as Epicurus once said, *The greater the difficulty, the more the glory in surmounting it.* Be on your guard. You may have won this battle, but you have most certainly not won the war."

No one should be deprived of love without a valid reason.
Andreas Capellanus, 12th Century A.D [12]

Woodstocke Manor
Royal Residence of Henry II, King of England
Oxfordshire, England
May, 1163

Chapter Eleven

Dinner the next night was not as awkward for Rosamund. Perhaps it was because she'd had her first confrontation with the King and had survived. Perhaps because she'd made it through one dinner already. Perhaps it was because all at the table seemed to make a concerted effort to make her feel at ease.

And finally, perhaps it was the casual attitude that everyone adopted at the King's table. King Henry was a man so elevated in his station of life that he resisted as much as possible the pomp and circumstance that went with it. He refused to dress for dinner, often arriving in mud-spattered clothes directly from a hunt. He abandoned the formality of a lord's table, eating and drinking with a mixed company of knights and nobles. Dignity and decorum were flouted, laughter and camaraderie were encouraged. For Rosamund, the attitude was delightful and infectious.

Prince Rhys ab Gruffydd began the evening by complimenting her appearance and holding her chair as she sat. When she looked up to thank him, she gasped. "Prince Rhys! What has happened to you?" His face was a mass of bruises, with a split lip and a cut over his left eye that bore five stitches.

"I ran into a tree," he said by way of explanation and claimed the seat to Rosamund's right.

She glanced at Sir Gavin as he coughed rather loudly and sat in the seat next to Prince Rhys.

"Good eve to you, Milady," said Sir Brian as he took the seat opposite her.

She smiled at Sir Brian and then stared in shock at Sir Thomas as he approached the table. The entire right side of his face was black and blue around his eye. "Sir Thomas ... your face ... what happened?"

"I fell out of bed," he mumbled and Sir Gavin coughed loudly once again. When Rosamund looked at Sir Gavin this time he gave her a wink and a smile.

"I see ..." she said.

The dinner conversation was lively to say the least. At first, Rosamund made every effort to remain quiet and proper, but the strain began to wear on her. Her head actually began to ache from the stress of not responding and voicing opinions. She found it fascinating to observe the King and Prince Rhys as they played with each other with their words. Prince Rhys seemed to delight in baiting every one, challenging King Henry's policies regarding the Welsh, the French, and even the English. The King was more than willing to accommodate Prince Rhys with his own observations regarding the Welsh and their lack of intelligence, might and skill. King Henry's knights seemed absolutely accustomed to the verbal sparring, even tending to add fuel to the proverbial fire when things began to look even vaguely calm.

"The only reason Stephen lost at the Battle of Lincoln was because the *Cymry* fought against him," Gruffydd was saying with great certainty, "you *Saeson* are only ever guaranteed victory if others fight with you."

King Henry snorted, "The reason Stephen lost was because his army had the ability of mere children at play. Hell, even my mother defeated Stephen in battle on more than one occasion. You want a *real* fight, try taking her on." Some of the knights, including Sir Brian and Sir Gavin, laughed and nodded in agreement. "Hell," the King said, "Thomas was at Lincoln. Ask him."

All eyes turned to Sir Thomas sitting across the table next to Sir Brian. Rosamund couldn't stay quiet any longer. "But that's impossible, Your Majesty," she burst out. "The Battle of Lincoln was fought years before I was born. Sir Thomas couldn't possibly have been old enough to fight in that battle."

The King's eyes danced with amusement and he spoke across the table to Thomas, "Who's right, Thomas?"

Thomas nodded to the King, "As always, you are Sire."

"How old were you, Sir Thomas?" Rosamund asked him.

"Seven."

Everyone, but Sir Thomas and Gruffydd, were smiling and nodding at her. "He was there," Brian said. "*On the wrong side*, mind you, but he was there."

Rosamund turned to Sir Brian. "What do you mean, 'on the wrong side'?"

Sir Thomas answered her. "I was with King Stephen's army fighting against the accursed plague known as the Welsh," he looked pointed at Gruffydd and then turned to King Henry with a smile, "*and* the usurper King's army."

"Usurper King," Henry repeated aloud and then grinned at everyone, "I like that."

Gruffydd had gone unusually quiet. "You were the young squire that tried to kill Earl Robert with your fallen knight's sword?"

Sir Thomas, in the blink of an eye, drew his sword and rested it beneath Gruffydd's chin to Henry's great delight and encouragement. "Aye, you Welsh plague, that was me," and Rosamund was unable to determine if he was teasing or serious. "Care to examine the sword more closely? I'd be much obliged to accommodate."

Gruffydd didn't look bothered in the least. "I heard the story. Guarding your master's horse and sword and shield on the battlefield, covered in your own vomit. What name did you go by then?" He tapped his chin with his finger and pretended to be deep in thought. "Hmmm, let me think ... let me see if I can remember. Ah yes, I remember. It was Thomas, *the Bastard*, was it not?"

The King said in a commanding voice, "I need him alive, Sir Thomas. At least for the moment. Sheath your sword now, man, and revel in the fine circumstances of your life," he looked at Gruffydd, "while Gruffydd shuts his mouth and ponders his own dire position.

"You sit here among my most trusted knights, Sir Thomas, because of the bravery and foresight you showed when you were no more than a child. Even *I* heard the story from my Mother when she returned to Normandy from her much misguided foray into trying to reclaim what was rightfully hers here in Britain.

"She recounted how you stood up to your captors with such bravery and yet had the wherewithal to make an educated decision when given the choice." King Henry snorted, "It takes a hell of a lot to impress Empress Matilda. I'm still not sure I have."

The King's words calmed Thomas, who slowly withdrew his sword and sheathed it. Gruffydd said quietly, "You'll not believe my words to you now for we are at opposite sides of the sword, but you impressed many Welsh that day." He grinned at Sir Thomas' scowl. "You so impressed them that a number thought that you most surely had to be *Cymry* because no *Sais* could possibly exhibit such bravery."

Henry chuckled under his breath. "Do you goad your own people so, Gruffydd? It is a puzzle to me that you have lived this long if such is true."

"What were you doing on a battlefield at the age of seven years?" Rosamund asked incredulously, heedless of whether it was an appropriate inquiry or not. *My sword, dagger, and horse are all I need,* she remembered him telling her once.

Sir Thomas looked at her across the table and shrugged. "I had no place better to be."

"Even squires do not always go to battlefields until they are seasoned, and you were barely young enough to be a page," she persisted.

Sir Thomas shrugged and picked up his mug of ale to take a sip. "There was no one to instruct Sir Richard in the care and etiquette of his squires and pages. Certainly *I* was in no position to do so. And I had no family to champion me." He nodded towards Gruffydd, "He is correct in his reminding me of my stellar lineage."

"What happened to this Sir Richard?"

"What happens to many men who walk onto a battlefield," Gruffydd said to Rosamund. "He never walked off." He looked at Sir Thomas. "'T'was fierce fighting that day, I know for I was there. I remember you. Standing their holding that damn horse watching the chaos all around you."

Sir Thomas looked at him, obviously surprised. "Were you one who goaded me into my embarrassing display?"

"No," Gruffydd said. "I was the one who summoned Earl Robert to your side when I began to fear for your life." Gruffydd grinned. "I had no idea that one of my guards was so indebted to me." He looked at the King. "Things are indeed looking up for me. You are indebted to me for Lady Rosamund, your knight here is indebted to me for his life. I may still return to Wales; perhaps with a crown on my head instead of a noose around my neck."

King Henry, always in a good mood after a day of hunting and a belly full of fine food and ale, laughed aloud at Gruffydd's comment. "Hold your breath, Gruffydd, while I decide, why don't you?"

Gruffydd looked at Rosamund. "What say you of my fate, fair Rosamund? Were you King, what would you do with me?"

She couldn't resist. "Aside from having you gagged to stop your constant baiting?"

Even Thomas laughed at that remark. All eyes turned to her, waiting to hear her response. The King encouraged her when she remained silent for a bit. "Come, we would hear your opinion." He leaned close and his warm breath tickled her ear. "Have you not a thought of your own, you could always give us a good philosophical quote."

She looked very primly at the King. "I have many thoughts of my own, Your Majesty, just no one has ever seen fit to ask me to share them until now."

That made them all laugh again. "We already know your opinion about children in battle. Let's hear what you have to say about the Welsh plague." Rosamund looked up into the smiling eyes of Sir Thomas.

"I would seek to end the bloodshed." She glanced at Earl Gilbert, one of the King's close nobles, as he groaned and rolled his eyes in impatient disgust, "While at the same time achieving my goals."

"And how would you accomplish that, Milady. Pray tell us quickly so that we can all go home," Earl Gilbert said sarcastically.

Rosamund was not offended by his manner toward her, in fact she felt complimented. She was being treated the same as all the others at the table. The men were listening to her rather then dismissing her entirely. Earl Gilbert was goading her on rather then trying to silence her. For the first time in her life she was being given the opportunity to share her thoughts. It felt magnificent. "A plague is not just one sickness, Sir Thomas. It is an illness that affects thousands, and by its very nature is unstoppable until it has run it course. Prince Rhys, should you kill him, will only be replaced by others even angrier and vengeful." She looked at Gruffydd intently as he stared at her with his hooded, dark eyes. "Prince Rhys shows no fear or concern for his own personal safety because he knows the fight will continue with or without him. And I suspect," she said softly, "that he has already lost everything of importance to him, so you have nothing with which to threaten him.

"But everyone of us has a price, do we not?" She looked at the solemn faces of the men sitting around her. "Gold? Land? Power?" She looked back at Gruffydd. "Even Prince Rhys ab Gruffydd has a price, I would dare to say. So rather than kill him, I'd try to buy him.

"*'The name of peace is sweet, and the thing itself is beneficial, but there is a great difference between peace and servitude. Peace is freedom in tranquility, servitude is the worst of all evils, to be resisted not only by war, but even by death.*'" She looked at King Henry, who was staring at her with a small smile on his lips. "Cicero, the great philosopher said that."

She turned to Gruffydd and slowly shook her head. "He will never be your servant, Your Majesty. He and all his people would rather die. As would you, would you not, Sire, were the situation reversed?"

"And what if the price for purchase is too high?" Earl Gilbert said.

Rosamund looked at Earl Gilbert. "If a person truly wishes to make a sale, then the price must be reasonable. Wise merchants know how to bargain with each other to get the best deal." She turned to Gruffydd. "And sometimes, the merchants must even relinquish goods at a loss, in the effort to secure the best deal for the whole. For he knows that a sound business partnership will always have opportunities for future gains."

"And what do you think my price is, Lady Rosamund?" Gruffydd asked softly. "How low do you think I would go with my asking?"

She blushed suddenly, painfully aware that a table full of men, knowledgeable in the ways of politics and war were listening to her ramble on. "Don't fail us now, Milady, we would all hear," Sir Thomas said in an encouraging tone.

She flashed him a brief smile and closed her eyes, took a deep breath, held it, and then let it out slowly. Only Thomas knew that she was praying. "Why it is quite obvious what both of you want, is it not?" she said at last. "Prince Rhys wants his land, wants to control it, and wants the King's word of his good faith." Rosamund turned and looked at the King. "And you, Your Majesty, want recognition of your sovereignty and Prince Rhys' words of fealty to you in exchange.

"Were that to happen, would we not be able to stop all this bloodshed," she looked at Earl Gilbert, "and just go home?"

No one said anything for the space of a few moments. "Only coming from you does it all sound fair and reasonable," Sir Brian finally said. "How can you not wish to revenge the life of your husband and people?"

Rosamund looked down at her hands folded tightly in her lap and then spoke so quietly that all leaned forward so as not to miss a word. "There are some duties we owe even to those who have wronged us. There is, after all, a limit to retribution and punishment. Will *anything* I do bring those dead back, Sir Brian? I suspect that Prince Rhys and his people have similar stories to tell." She looked at Sir Brian then and he turned away from her gaze with a haunted look in his eyes.

She smiled and took a deep breath. "I must thank you, gentlemen, for allowing me the honor of expressing my opinions in company such as this. As you can see, my head is full of views, that up until this evening no one has been foolish enough to encourage me to share." She rested her hand on Gruffydd's arm and Rosamund felt him tense. "And I suspect, now that I have been allowed to do so, that the King will no longer feel that he is in your debt for the part you played in bringing me here," she said with a smile on her lips and a twinkle of mischief in her eyes. "If you will excuse me, I will take my leave."

All stood as she rose and made her way quietly out of the hall. And every single man at the table silently watched her leave.

My Rosamunde, my only Rose, that pleasest best mine eye,
The fairest flower in all the worlde, to feed my fantasye.

Thomas Delone, 17th Century A.D.[13]

Woodstocke Manor
Royal Residence of Henry II, King of England
Oxfordshire, England
June, 1163

Chapter Twelve

Thomas should have gone to his bed. God knew since he'd arrived here at Woodstocke he had barely slept at all, and tonight Gruffydd's watch was his responsibility. He needed to be sharp at all times with that one. *And* Thomas needed to stop letting Gruffydd get under his skin so easily.

Trouble was, he already had someone under his skin, and he didn't need anyone else there thank you very much. Since the night he'd watched Rosamund leave the hall with the King, Thomas had been plagued – awake or asleep - with thoughts of her. He literally could not get her out of his head, and it was wearing him down more then any battle fatigue he had ever had.

Leaving the stables, he'd spied the edge of Rosamund's gown disappearing into the gardens and on impulse had turned and followed.

Despite what his common sense roared in his head, his feet continued to step one foot in front of the other. Common sense be damned! Caution ceased to function. His inner voice that had saved him countless times in battle remained disapprovingly silent.

Thomas could not count the number of times that he'd been to Woodstocke Manor, but in all those times he'd never bothered with the gardens. He knew the forests, the stables, and the kitchens, but he was lost in the gardens. Standing on the edge of them, he saw neatly manicured bushes, blooming flowers, and flourishing trees as far as he could see, and not one single solitary woman. He sighed deeply in defeat. It seemed that circumstances would protect him where his common sense hadn't succeeded.

Thomas wandered slowly, choosing paths at random, forcing himself to breathe deeply and work at the tension that was threaded throughout his whole body. He was a fool. He should be content and honored simply to sit and converse with her at meals or to gain her occasional brief smiles when they passed in the halls. *Just what were you going to say to her, had you found her?* his inner voice taunted him, *Hello, I just wanted to make sure that you're happy and content now that you are the King's mistress?* The ridiculousness of his thoughts made him snort out loud.

"Are you imitating one of the King's wild animals caged in his zoo? If so, I would know which one it is for I have never heard such a sound ..."

Thomas turned to see her sitting on a bench under an arbor in the shade of a flowering vine, a book in her lap, smiling at him. "Only if the King's newest addition will be a display of fools," he said.

She laughed at that. "You are many things, Sir Thomas, but a fool you are not."

He walked slowly to her and leaned against the edge of the arbor. "That still remains to be seen."

"Have you come here to find a quiet place to read as well?" she teased him.

Thomas looked at her for a moment and then shook his head. He had a desperate need to have her behave towards him in a way that would lessen her appeal and release him from the draw that she had on him. He said slowly, "No, not only am I a bastard, but I am illiterate as well."

He studied her intently, watching for some negative reaction to his pronouncement. Rosamund smiled and shrugged. "And I am a mere woman who cannot wield a sword to save my life. It seems, between the two of us, we are barely one complete person."

At that moment, Thomas knew that he loved her. *God help him.*

He slid down to the ground in the shade of the arbor, stretched his long legs in front of him, and leaned his head against the flowers, closing his eyes. "Tell me of what you read," he said after a time, and then opened one eye to peer at her, "please?"

She settled back against the arbor and Thomas noticed her slippers casually cast beneath the bench. When she began to read, he couldn't resist, and reached over to pick one up. It was light blue, made with a soft material and decorated with fine embroidery in silver thread. It fit completely in his open hand. He sighed deeply and closed his eyes, still holding onto her shoe. *He was doomed.*

"You are most fortunate, Sir Thomas, for up until the other day I was reading through the King's philosophical section and, I fear, I would have bored you to tears should I have read that aloud. However, I've just come upon this story and have been much enjoying it. I think you will, too. Unfortunately, I'm close to finishing it. There are just a few more chapters. Here, I will go back to this very exciting part, I've just read." She blushed a beautiful shade of red, glancing at Thomas. "I thought of you when I read a part of it." Rosamund ducked her head, busying herself with turning pages, trying to find the best part to begin. Gracing Thomas with another shy smile she said, "Feel free to stop me if you wish." She began to read, and Thomas immediately got lost in the rhythm and flow of her voice as it relayed the magic of the story.

"This is episode eleven in which Beowulf fights the dragon. Beowulf, in many ways reminded me of King Henry ... *Beowulf was angry, the lord of the Geats, he who stormed in battle. He yelled into the cave. The horde-keeper perceived a man's voice and didn't plan to ask for friendship. Flames shot out from among the stones, hot battle-sweat. The ground dinned.*

"The hero raised his shield against the dreadful stranger. Then the coiled thing sought battle. The war king drew his sword, an ancient heirloom with edges unblunt. Each of them intended horror to the other. Stouthearted stood the war-prince with his shield upraised, waited in his war-gear. The dragon coiled together, went forth burning, gliding toward his fate." Thomas, caught up in the story, transposed battle memories into the story, could feel the grip and the horror, sights and the sounds.

"His shield protected life and body for a shorter time than the prince had hoped. That was the first day he was not granted glory in battle. The lord of the Geats raised his arm, struck the horrible thing with his ancestral sword, but the edge gave way; that bright sword bit less on the bone than the war-king needed.

"After that stroke the cave-guardian was in a savage mood. He threw death-fire widely sprayed battle flashes. The gold-friend of the Geats wasn't boasting of victory. His war-sword had failed, not bitten home as it should have, that iron which had always been trustworthy. This wasn't a pleasant trip; that famous king, Beowulf, would have to leave this earth, would have, against his will, to move elsewhere. (So must every man give up these transitory days.)" Rosamund looked up at Thomas. "I can feel the terror. The hopelessness. Is battle ...?" she hesitated, swallowed, and looked down at her book.

"Is battle ...?" he hesitated, waiting for her to finish but she remained silent. "Is battle ... such as this in the story? ... life and death?" Thomas tried to erase the fear he had briefly seen in her eyes. "... really against fire breathing dragons?"

Still with her head down, she made a soft 'whuff' of air, which he assumed was a laugh of sorts.

"The only thing I can honestly say about battle, Lady Rosamund, is that it is never something you can truly describe with words and never something you ever get used to witnessing in person." Thomas turned his head, trying to see her expression. "Please, continue reading to me ..."

Rosamund drew a cleansing breath and nodded. *"It wasn't long before the terrible ones met again- The hoard-keeper took heart, heaved his fire anew. He who once ruled a nation was encircled by fire; no troop of friends, strong princes, stood around him; they ran to the woods to save their lives.*

"*Yet in one of them welled a sorrowful heart. That true-minded one didn't forget kinship. Wiglaf he was called, the son of Woehstan, a beloved shield-warrior, a lord of the Scylfings, a kinsman of Aelthere. He saw his lord suffering from heat under his helmet. ... Wiglaf could not refrain, but grabbed his shield, drew his ancient sword that among men was known as the heirloom of Eanmund, the son of Othere ... His spirit did not fail, nor his heirloom; that the dragon discovered when they met in battle.*" Rosamund cleared her throat. "Wiglaf ..." she looked up at him, gracing him with a brief smile, "... is the one that reminded me of you, Sir Thomas."

Again she blushed and hurriedly looked down at the book, continuing to read. "*Wiglaf spoke words about duty, said in sorrow to his companions; 'I remember the times we drank mead and how we promised our lord there in the beer-hall, he who gave us gifts, that we would repay all his largess, the helmets and hard swords, if the need should ever befall. He chose his best men for this expedition, gave us honor and these treasures because he considered us best among spear fighters, though he proposed to do the job alone because he had performed the most famous deeds among men. Now has the day come that our lord is in need of fighters, of good warriors. Let us go to him, help the war-chief in the fire-horror. God knows, to me, my lord means more than my skin. With him I will embrace the fire. It isn't proper that we bare shields back to our homes before we can defend our lord and kill the enemy. He doesn't deserve to suffer alone. We two shall share the sword and helmet, the mail and war-garment.'*

"*Then Wiglaf advanced through the death-fumes, wore his helmet to help his lord.*

"*He spoke these words; 'Dear Beowulf, may you accomplish all well, as you did in youth, as I have heard tell. Don't surrender the glory of your life. Defend now, with all your strength, your brave deeds. I will help.'*

"*After these words the dragon angrily came; the terrible spirit another time attacked with surging fire. Fire waves burned Wiglaf's shield down to the handle, his mail could not protect the young spear-warrior. He ducked behind his kinsman's shield.*

"*When the war-king remembered past deeds, struck mightily with his sword so that it stuck in the dragon's head; Naegling, the great sword of Beowulf, ancient and shining, broke, failed in battle. Fate had not granted that the iron sword would help ...*

"The terrible dragon a third time rushed, hot and battle-grim. He bit Beowulf's neck with sharp tusks – Beowulf was wet with life's blood; blood gushed in waves.

"Then I've heard, Wiglaf showed courage, craft and bravery, as was his nature – he went not for the thought-seat, but struck a little lower, helped his kinsman though his hand was burned. The sword, shining and ornamented, drove in so that the fire abated.

"Then the king controlled his senses, drew his battle knife, bitter and battle sharp, which he carried on his mail, and cut the dragon through the middle. The enemy fell – strength had driven out life; the two kinsmen, together, had cut down the enemy. So should a warrior do.

"That was Beowulf's last victory, his last work in this world."[14]

They were both silent for a few moments. "So Beowulf dies in the end …" Thomas said finally.

"Yes," she said, "the final episode is 'The Death of Beowulf.'" She said very quietly to him, "You remind me of Wiglaf. I can see you have a 'sorrowful heart'. And you are a 'true minded one who would not forget kinship.'"

Thomas looked at Rosamund pointedly then. "Or vows of friendship specifically given. Are you well and happy, Milady? Though it is not my place to inquire, I would hear from you …" He stopped, looking away from her, at a loss to find the right words. *Damn.*

He knew she understood by the blush that flooded her cheeks. Carefully she said, "My *friend* told me that King Henry desires only *willing* women, of which I am not. The King has cautioned me that while I may have won the first battle, I have not won the war. So, as to your inquiry, at this moment, I am *tenuously* well and happy. Tell me Sir Thomas," she hesitated and he finally turned to look at her, as was her intent, "what would you do were I to tell you I was not well and happy?"

Thomas smiled. "King Henry cannot be any fiercer then Wiglaf's dragon. I would slay him or die in the trying."

"Sir! Your loyalty is to the King. How can you say such!" Rosamund said to him in a teasing tone.

"An honorable knight must always show courtesy and offer protection to women …" he teased back.

"But an *honorable* knight is first and foremost loyal to king and country," she challenged. "How could you separate these two?"

Thomas shrugged trying to appear casual, however, the topic was rapidly approaching the center of his own world. "Most probably through the sacrifice of my hopes and dreams and life." Thomas tried to maintain the same teasing tone, but it was no longer possible.

Rosamund reached forward and touched his shoulder, her face serious and intent. "Sir Thomas, *nothing* is worth the loss of your hopes and dreams."

"That is not for you to say, Milady," he said somewhat harsher than he had intended.

"You do not know me, Sir. I am neither sister, mother, wife, aunt, nor cousin to you. I am not worth a sacrifice so great. You must hold onto your hopes and dreams at all costs."

"Why?"

"If you have not dreams, you do not live."

"What are your dreams?"

Rosamund gave him an impatient look. "You seek to change the subject, sir."

"Nay, I do not. I would like to hear your dreams. Isn't that something friends share with each other?" he tried to tease.

She removed her hand from his shoulder and eyed him suspiciously, giving him a look that seemed to say, 'I will not be put off.' But she sighed and gazed off into the distance organizing her thoughts. The bright sunlight beyond the arbor made her squint and wrinkle her nose. "I have always had dreams that never fit my life: the desire for freedom to make my own choices, the craving to learn as much as I can, the yearning for love …" In a businesslike tone she said, "Now I know that those dreams are difficult – almost impossible – but there is a very small part of me that ever hopes. That part is what keeps me alive and moving."

Rosamund looked directly at him. "What are your dreams, Sir Thomas? It would seem that you have accomplished much: you are respected by your King and your peers for your bravery and skill in battle, and you have achieved the status of being one of the King's own personal knights. Tell me what do you still dream of?"

Thomas looked down at his hands and was appalled to see dirt under most of his fingernails. *Christ, clean yourself up a bit now and then, man.* He balled both hands into fists. "Honestly?" She nodded. "You will find it quite funny in its simplicity. I'd like a home."

"A home?"

"Aye, I've never had one. At least that I can remember. My earliest memories were under FitzRichard's care – if you could call it that. I have forever been waiting, moving, traveling, preparing, riding, fighting ..." He looked at Rosamund. "I have never, ever had a home, and I would one day like one. Not big. No place in particular. Just enough land to provide for myself and mayhap a wife and children. It sounds so simple and yet it has always been so very impossible to attain."

Thomas stood abruptly. "I must get back. I guard Gruffydd tonight and must get some sleep beforehand. He tries my patience to no end when I am well rested. Tired and irritable, I might just kill him."

"Your eye is still bruised."

It was Thomas' turn to blush. "Yes, but it will fade. He will always bear a scar." He seemed innately pleased with himself. "I look forward to seeing you at dinner tonight and hearing more of your thoughts. You have the gift of being able to say things succinctly and yet with much weight." He bowed and turned to leave.

"Sir Thomas?"

"Yes?"

"Might I ask that you give me back my shoe?"

Thomas' blush of embarrassment and incredulous look at the slipper still held in his hand made Rosamund laugh and that made him grin. "Are you sure you'll be needing it?" he joked as he handed it to her. "Until tonight, Milady."

As she watched him walk away briskly toward the manor she knew instinctively that he had no idea the enormity of the compliment he had just given her. It was, she realized, the very first compliment she had ever received from *anyone* that mattered to her. He had said he looked forward to hearing more of her thoughts and that she had a gift in the way she expressed herself. Never had *anyone* given her such high praise.

Dinner was another enjoyable event that evening. The men were delighted when she offered a riddle just before she made ready to leave. "What's the prize, Milady?" one of the knights shouted.

"I'll tell you another one," she was quick to respond. "But here is the first. Are you ready?" All eagerly nodded their heads. "I am the lone wood in the warp of battle, wounded by iron, broken by blade, weary of war. Often I see battle-rush, rage, fierce fight flaring – I hold no hope for help to come before I fall finally with warriors or feel the flame. The hard hammer-leavings strike me, the bright-edged, battle-sharp handiwork of smiths bites in battle. Always I must await the harder encounter[15]. What am I?" She smiled at them as she rose to leave. "I bid you all goodnight while you ponder the solution."

King Henry rose with the other men, but he took her arm. "It will be my honor to escort you, Lady Rosamund."

As they left the hall, Gruffydd leaned over to Thomas and grinned at him. "Shall I pick a fight again?"

Thomas leaned back, took a long pull from his tankard and sighed, "We've got all night, Gruffydd, take your time."

Gruffydd threw back his head and laughed.

"So," King Henry said to her as they made their way down the dimly lit hallway, "will you give me a hint as to the solution of your riddle?"

Rosamund smiled, "Certainly not, Sire! But I must admit you have the others at a great advantage."

"How is that?"

"I would suspect that you have already heard of the riddle and would therefore know the answer."

King Henry gave her an admiring glance. "Already you know me so well." He sighed. "Yes, I've heard the riddle. I could not remember it at first, but when you said 'hard hammer-leavings strike me' I remembered it to be a shield." He leaned over and whispered in her ear, an excuse to get close to her, she surmised, "Will you at least tell me if I am correct?"

She mimicked Sir Thomas' words from the other night, "As always, you are, Sire."

He steered her out in the twilight of the gardens and she felt herself relax somewhat. Once again, she was approaching a battle Rosamund knew, but she thought the setting of the gardens rather than a bedroom sitting room gave her a distinctive advantage. "You said," the King murmured, "that you have yet to find the swings. The moon is bright this evening and I will show you the way."

They strolled in silence for a time enjoying the summer evening. Finally, King Henry said, "You gave sound advice the other night regarding Gruffydd."

The stunned look on Rosamund's face made him chuckle. "You are so surprised by my words?"

"Your Majesty, my whole life I have been told to be quiet, to be obedient, and that it is a waste of time for me to be educated. And yet here I have the King of England praising my opinion. Were the situation reversed, you would feel the same way."

He nodded. "I suppose so. Tell me, how can you not hate Gruffydd for what he has done to you and yours?"

"How can he not hate us for what we have done to him and his? You hold his son hostage as we speak."

King Henry could not conceal his surprise. "He told you of this?"

She nodded. "Yes, after he had taken me from Goodrich Castle."

"Did he tell you how I came by him? That his own countryman – Prince Owain - offered the child as a hostage as a show of good faith? He's been with me for longer than he was with Prince Rhys, nigh onto six years. He has been a hostage so long he is practically no longer Welsh."

"Has he been well cared for?"

The King looked affronted. "What good is a hostage who dies in captivity or grows to hate his captors so much that he becomes twisted with revenge? Nay, 'tis much more subtle to be kind and merciful, winning him over to your side and gaining an ally. Hywel has been treated just as one of my own sons. He is hale and happy."

She looked at the King. "Prince Rhys does not know that."

He snorted. "Of course he does not know that. That's part of the 'fun' of holding hostages; that element of the fear of the unknown. The torture of indecision and worry.

"'Tis cruel."

"'Tis *life*," King Henry insisted.

"Well, Your Majesty, then you certainly hold the upper hand in this battle of stubbornness between you and Prince Rhys," Rosamund said emphatically.

"How so?" asked the King intrigued.

"Why," she smiled at King Henry in the moonlight, "you have found Prince Rhys' price: his son, Hywel, returned to him 'hale and happy'. *That* is a debt he could never repay."

"I would have more than a feeling of indebtedness from the man, Rosamund. Gruffydd is cunning and willful. Never, ever underestimate him."

"I am sure, Your Majesty, he has similar opinions about you."

"Here are the swings," King Henry said changing the subject abruptly and motioning to a tall hedgerow that extended even above his head.

"This is the start to your maze, is it not?"

"Aye, but at 'dead ends' throughout the paths there are little surprises. For the swings, you must remember: *always turn right*."

Rosamund looked delighted at the game. The King gestured her forward. "After you, Milady."

At each intersection, Rosamund faithfully turned right and before she knew it they were in a lovely glade with two swings and no way out. She smiled as she made her way to the swings. "James, your caretaker at the zoo, says that you designed the maze and had it built after the last time you stayed here at Woodstocke Manor."

He nodded looking around. "This place is good for me. It is my escape, really. It gives me peace and helps me to forget, occasionally, that I am King and that there are many more who hate me rather than love me."

She sat on a swing, but remained motionless. "Why say such a thing, Sire?"

He chuckled. "'Cause it 'tis true. There are whole *countries* that would see me dead if they had a chance." He leaned against the swing support with his arms crossed watching her swing and grinned. "Why, Fair Rosamund, might it be possible that you care for me?"

"You wish for answers that I cannot give, Your Majesty. Yes, of course I care deeply, for you are my Sovereign, my King."

"I want more, Rosamund."

"I know, Your Majesty," she said quietly.

He came and sat at the swing next to her. "You are a shining light. I am drawn to you. Is it foolish for me to say that your presence brings me happiness? Both of us are so alike. Both of us have spent our lives doing what is expected of us for the good of others. Have you known much happiness in your life, Rosamund?" She slowly shook her head 'no'. "Neither have I. And I'm the King, for God's sake."

He stood and paced with frustration. "I have never felt so close to a chance at happiness as I do when I am with you. There is a delight in listening to you talk, hearing your thoughts, anticipating your independent responses, and watching your beauty change with your emotions. You may not believe me, so short a time we have spent together, but 'tis true, *I love you*. Rosamund, I cannot change the past, I cannot forsake my duties, but I can try to make my future brighter. I want you. I want to offer you laughter and love and happiness like you have never known. I'm not forcing you, I'm *asking* you. Please, Rosamund, accept what I offer you: my love and my life. Don't look at what is behind *either of us,* just look forward to what is before us."

The King stood, walked over to her, gently took her hands, and made her stand. Carefully, slowly, reverently, he kissed her eyes, her cheeks, her nose, and briefly her mouth. When she went to speak, he put his finger on her lips. "No, do not say anything to me tonight. Take some time to think on what I ask of you and search your head and your heart. I will leave you here. Make your way out when you wish. Remember, *always go left* to get out from the swings." He then turned and left her in stunned silence in the moonlight.

Rosamund could not sleep. How confusing her life had become. Awake she was plagued with thoughts that she could not put to rest and asleep she was accosted by dreams that caused her heart to pound and her breath to gasp. She rose from bed, donned a simple gown, and left her chamber.

The King of England had professed his love for her. *For her.* Bemoaned his obligations, his commitments, his station in life ... all because they interfered with what he desired more than anything else ... to love and live with *her.* She had watched him as he had spoken to her, making no move, for once, to seduce her, or even touch her. He had opened his heart to her, let her see the truth of it on his face and in his eyes. He loved her. King Henry truly loved her. She had no doubt.

Lying in bed she realized with a start that he was as imprisoned in his life as she was in hers. At the whim of others holding sway over him, powerless to change who he was, and yet exemplary in fulfillment of his responsibilities. Her perception of him had changed, shifted, and gained a depth of understanding that softened her resolve to what was right and what was wrong. Things were not as clear as they had first appeared.

God wants you to be happy and intends to fulfill that goal. Aunt Helen had reassured her of that on more than one occasion and Rosamund believed it. Rosamund continued to believe it right up until this evening when she had sat on a swing in the moonlight watching King Henry and listening to him pour his heart out to her. She knew, *she knew* beyond a shadow of a doubt that he was dreadfully unhappy. And then the traitorous thought had crept into her head, *Do you truly know anyone who is happy?* She could not name one single, solitary person. Rosamund had lain in bed and thought of every person she knew casually or in depth and could not, for the life of her, find one person she could call happy. It seemed such a simple emotion. So why was it so impossible to achieve?

And if no one knew happiness, then what was the point of life? Why *bother?* Why make every effort to be obedient and proper if all it got you was misery and sorrow? *Why?*

She could make the King happy. And in doing so, she might find a small measure of joy in this life as well. To be loved. *My God,* she craved that emotion - to give and to get - so profoundly that it had become the stuff of dreams and legends in her mind. And someone had offered it to her. Nay, someone had already given it to her. It was hers for the accepting, like a glorious gem she just happened upon in the dust of the road. All she needed to do was stoop down and pick it up. *Someone loved her.*

Rosamund was familiar now with Woodstocke Manor. The muted lamps along the hallway were enough for her to orient herself and find her way down to the Great Hall. Since she could not sleep she would sit beside the fire, think calming thoughts, and pray. Surely God was still in control of this mess her life had become. *Surely He was.*

She slowly made her way down the marble stairs of the great hall, feeling the cool smoothness of the carved wood balustrade. This place, Woodstocke Manor, in and of itself was truly the stuff dreams were made of. A fairy tale palace of opulence and beauty. She could spend her whole life just wandering the gardens alone.

A sound drew her attention to the center of the great room, and through the flickering lights of the banked fire she saw a shape hunched over the table, as if in pain. Hurrying down the stairs she drew closer, intent on offering assistance. And then she heard a low chuckle and a woman's soft gasp in return. She froze.

They were unaware of her, the man and woman, fully absorbed with themselves. The low murmur of voices, more quiet male laughter, more breathless gasps. Rosamund worked hard to still the rustle of her clothes, turn, back up, and leave.

And then she saw a flash of hair. Ginger hair. Her color ... and Beatrice's. They were the only two at the manor with that hair. King Henry had remarked on it on more than one occasion, complimenting the color. *Beatrice?* This was *Beatrice?* Here?! On the table of the great hall?! Was she ...? Did she...? Rosamund stood frozen with indecision, her heart pounding, her mind processing, her senses trying to reach out and determine what, if, ...

Beatrice moaned a deep, throaty sound that Rosamund could not determine was pain or pleasure. But Rosamund could not abandon her maid if there was even the barest hint of distress on her part. She was galvanized. She took hesitant, yet forward steps toward the table and managed to say, "Beatrice, have you need of my assistance?"

Both bodies froze for moments and Rosamund held her breath, her thoughts attempting to order themselves should she need to provide help and protection for both herself and Beatrice. The man straightened somewhat, turned and looked at Rosamund with a lazy, seductive smile playing on his lips. "No, she needs not your assistance, Rosamund. But you are more than welcome to join us," King Henry said.

Rosamund fell back two steps, … three, retreating from the scene before her, yet still unwilling to abandon Beatrice should her maid need her. She glanced down at Beatrice, and Henry turned to follow her gaze. He reached down, grabbed Beatrice by the back of the neck, and helped her sit up. Her hair was loose about her shoulders, her gown was open exposing her breasts to the flickering firelight, and her eyes were unfocused … *languid*, Rosamund thought. Henry spoke to Beatrice, "Tell your mistress you are not in need of her protection."

Beatrice, struggled with herself, and tried to order her thoughts and find her voice. She looked across the short distance that separated herself from Rosamund and said in a clear voice, "I am content, Milady."

Henry chuckled, an arrogant sound in the silence of the hall. "Nay, you are *well sated*," he said with a grin. He then turned to Rosamund and arched a red eyebrow. "What say you, my love? Will you finally take me up on my offer and allow me to offer you the same pleasure?" He laughed. "You need not worry, we can find someplace more suited than the great hall table."

Rosamund turned and fled.

King Henry didn't understand why Rosamund was upset. *Hysteria*, he called it. Neither, surprisingly did Beatrice. "Milady, he sought me out! It was an honor, nay, a privilege." She clasped her hands together and sighed. *"The King of England*, Milady!"

Rosamund kept to herself the conversation she had had with the King, for she was certain that Beatrice would not feel so honored should she know *The King of England's* true perception of things.

"Rosamund, yesterday I bared my heart to you. I told you of my love and my desires, as well as my frustrations with the duties of my life. What more could you wish from me? I cannot understand why an inconsequential dalliance with your maid means aught to you or has any impact on what I desire to share with you." He ran his fingers through his hair and stroked his beard, desperately trying to understand her obvious distress. "We have not been intimate, you and I. You have denied me on many occasions and I have not forced you nor threatened you nor commanded you – all which are my right! My love and respect for you bids me be patient." The King looked earnestly at her and Rosamund closed her eyes finally, then turned to look out the window. "This thing we have between us I sense is something more wonderful than I had ever hoped or imagined ... So I wait, my love, for you to ponder on the things I say and do and show you so that you will know how very much you mean to me."

Rosamund stood with her back to the King, hands clenched, staring out at the finely manicured lawns and gardens, trying desperately to breathe slowly and evenly, attempting to order her thoughts and emotions and words into something more coherent than a blood curdling scream. *What are you most upset about,* her mind pushed at her relentlessly, *what you witnessed last evening in the Great Hall or what you almost decided to do to make the King happy?* "How will what I witnessed last night help me understand how very much I mean to you? Help me understand, Your Majesty."

He chuckled with tolerant humor, "Know you not that men have, at times, ... indiscretions, Rosamund? That we have, at times," he shrugged, "how can I say it?" he thought for a moment, "*base* urges. Brought on by drunkenness and excesses. It is out of respect for you, *for the high regard in which I hold you* that I do not seek you out or even consider you at those times. I hold you in such great esteem. You are a woman of noble birth, pure of heart, lovely of spirit ... You should not be upset or angry with any of this. You should feel honored, even cherished."

Rosamund turned and looked at her King then. "So Beatrice was then an indiscretion, no more?" He nodded, delighted at her apparent understanding. "She was a necessary distraction for a *base urge?*" He inclined his head, smiling at her. "Tell me, Your Majesty, if there is a time when the Queen learns of me, will you explain me to her in the same fashion? Or will you tell her of your great love and respect for me?"

"Ahh, my love," King Henry said to her with a sigh. "I may be the King of England, but I am also Eleanor's husband. Were she to learn of you, I would at first *lie,* next *deny,* and finally," he laughed at his own upcoming humor, "I would run like hell."

You have been the first among my joys, and you shall be the last,
so long as there is life in me.

Bernart de Ventadour, 12th Century A.D.[16]

Woodstocke Manor
Royal Residence of Henry II, King of England
Oxfordshire, England
July, 1163

Chapter Thirteen

King Henry exhibited a possessive attitude toward Rosamund after the night at the swings. He claimed her company in the morning when they broke their fast, he was her companion numerous times on strolls through the gardens, he invited her to ride out beside him with the men when they went on their daily hunts, and he faithfully escorted her from the evening meal each night. To any and all observers, they were a couple in love.

What was she to do? How could she respond except in the way she had been taught, with dignity, respect, and the utmost decorum. She smiled when he spoke with her, laughed when he said something witty, blushed sincerely when he made subtle innuendoes, and behaved with demure shyness when he made numerous overtures by touching her. Only she and the King knew the truth of the way things were between them and neither, for their own reasons, were willing to set opinions straight.

For Rosamund it was the most difficult time of her life. Henry was a charmer, a master of words and thought. With little skill in subterfuge, she found his contradictions disconcerting to say the least. How could he profess his love to her only to seek out Beatrice that very same night? How could he thoughtfully present her with a book he thought she might enjoy and then later at dinner discuss the necessary executions of hostages from prior battles? How could he eschew so many of the trappings of royalty that his station afforded him and yet expect the imminent arrival of the most powerful men in the land with plans to make them accept the subservient status of dependent vassals?

Rosamund was rapidly discovering that King Henry was deeply intelligent and enjoyed the challenge of playing games with people whether friend or foe. And she was wise enough to know that at present, she was his primary quest. She seriously doubted she would ever be able to best him. As the days stretched into weeks, she prayed most fervently to remain clear and focused on the path God truly wished her to travel.

Each evening ended identically. King Henry would escort her from the eating hall. If the weather was inclement, he escorted her to his private sitting room, the library or, should she be so fortunate, her own rooms. When the weather was nice they strolled in the gardens and invariably ended up wandering through the maze.

Though she loved the maze, she would never enter it without the King. Just when she thought she had learned a route, she would discover how very lost she was. Time and time again they would enter, and within moments it seemed she would become completely disoriented. To make matters worse, periodically, instead of following the path, the King would choose to use a key he kept around his neck to open a door. When she asked if it was necessary to pass through the doors to get to the center or if it was simply a short cut, he would only wink and grin at her. She could get to the swings – always going right, and she could get to the lovely pond filled with goldfish the size of her forearm – always going left, but that was the extent of her skill. King Henry was delighted with her confusion, for once they ventured in she became absolutely dependant on him.

It was during these times that the ever present battle of wits and words between them was waged. They discussed philosophy, nature, history, church issues, and politics. She discovered, with some surprise, that she had strong opinions on all the topics. Unafraid to admit her lack of knowledge on occasion, King Henry was more than willing to provide her with 'much needed information'. Her quick mind asked hard questions, focused in on faulty logic, and readily pointed out blatant inconsistencies. There were times, she was certain, that he lost the urge to bed her and simply sought to outwit her.

They argued loudly and most frequently over his policy toward Wales, and after one particularly heated discussion he admitted to her that one of the reasons he enjoyed discussions with her was that she helped him finely tune his opinions. He revered his grandfather, King Henry the First, and sought to restore his kingdom to the organized, sophisticated state it had been until the "False King Stephen" had wreaked his havoc. He was determined to reorganize the judicial system, drastically change the relationship the church had toward the crown and its people and gain complete sway over Wales and Scotland. At all costs. Rosamund was wise enough to realize that any *one* of those goals would have been nigh onto impossible, let alone all three. But it was here that the King surprised her most; he had every confidence in himself that he would succeed.

This night, they were seated in the library. Rosamund was incredulous at his audacity regarding the upcoming meeting. "Your Majesty, you think to make Malcolm, King of the Scots, Prince Rhys ab Gruffydd, and Prince Owain ab Gwynedd, who have all admittedly fought, bled and died over their present Client Status swear to you *Dependant Vassalage?* You think that they will bow before you bareheaded and weaponless in an abject show of submission *and then* swear fealty to you?

He shrugged. "They will or they will die."

"But how? How can you force such a thing?"

Henry grinned at her. "With at little bit of honey and a lot of muscle."

"You said to me once that there were whole countries that would see you dead if they had a chance. Is there no other way to gain what you seek than to humiliate and intimidate? Would you not be far more successful *on the whole* were you to *earn* their allegiance rather than *demand* it?"

Impatiently he said, "Rosamund, I do not have the time nor the desire to woo and win this group of obstinate, unpredictable, and untrustworthy foes. I would much rather let them see my teeth, know my strength, and cow them into submission. Once you beat a dog sincerely, it always knows who its master is."

"Or will finally attack."

King Henry shrugged. "Then so be it. A dog that cannot learn its place in the kennel must be put down anyway." He sought to end the argument, as each evening usually ended by wooing her. "Come, let me see your loveliness in the moonlight."

Now began the final part of every evening, with he advancing, she parrying, he growing impatient, she becoming insistent, he storming out in a fit of rage, and she collapsing in an exhausted heap. He always managed a few kisses before his fury took over.

"How long will you make me wait? I am like a starving man staring at a fully laden table through a window. I have professed my love. Can I buy your affection? Jewels? Land? A title?" She tried to look away from his fierce expression as he cupped the side of her face and stared into her eyes. "I want you so much I *ache*, Rosamund. Why must you torture me so?"

She whispered, "If it is so painful for you to be with me like this, Your Majesty, I beg you to let me return to Godstowe Nunnery. The sisters will welcome me with open arms, and I will be happy and content to live out my days there."

"That would be like hiding the most beautiful rose in a dark, windowless room. Who could stand the waste?"

"Please ..."

"Do not beg. It does not become you. I told you Rosamund, I never give back what I have claimed as mine. That is not negotiable."

It was her turn to be angry. "Then build me a cage like all the other animals in your zoo, Your Majesty. For that is all I am."

He gripped her shoulders painfully and shook her. "Do not tempt me, Rosamund. *Why must you be so damnably stubborn?* Why can you not bend on this one issue?"

"*One issue?* Surely you jest with me, Your Majesty! You know as well as I that it is not an *issue* we debate, but a *principle.* The same honor and integrity you laud in your knights and nobles your find inconvenient in me. I am sorry, but I cannot *bend.*"

"Archbishop Thomas Becket arrives tomorrow. You should get on well with him. He has a head full of *principles* that he is forever debating with me. He is not as beautiful as you, but enjoys verbal confrontations as much as you do." He bent and kissed her mouth and trailed his lips down her neck. "He also does not smell as wondrous, although there are times that he makes me just as angry as you do." He bit her earlobe and she shivered. "Becket will like you; because you are intelligent and because you refuse to bend to me. Becket, too, refuses to bend."

"Will you imprison him, too, in your zoo, Your Majesty?"

"No, he is not unique enough for me to desire full possession." King Henry turned to leave, but at the door stopped and looked at her. "You will stay as visible as you have been once those summoned begin to arrive. I expect you to attend all functions and be by my side."

Rosamund was horrified. "All will think …"

He cut her off. "All *already* think. I believe you pointed that out to me months ago. You seem to think that so much of what I do is merely at my whim. I would have you know the truth of things. I will have your beautiful presence, keen mind, and quick tongue handy should I need it."

"In that order, Your Majesty?"

"Yes, Rosamund, in that order."

And then there was Sir Thomas. She was dismayed to discover that her eyes had begun to seek him out almost continually – in the courtyard, in the great hall, on a hunt, even quietly reading in the garden, wondering if he would suddenly appear again. Perhaps more disconcerting were the number of times that when her eyes *did* find him *he* appeared to be watching *her*. A small smile, a brief nod, a casual phrase spoken between them scattered her thoughts and left her mind in a state of confusion. She thought of Thomas' kindness and his caring when he had offered her his friendship. She remembered the texture of his hair and the warmth of his lips when she had kissed him that one time so very long ago. She still smiled every time she recalled the look on his face when she had asked for her slipper back. What was the matter with her?

Over the course of the next week, the arrival of Thomas Becket, Archbishop of Canterbury, was followed rapidly by the arrival of Malcolm, King of Scotland and Prince Owain of Northern Wales. Each man brought his own retinue of knights, servants, supporting nobles, and other necessary retainers. One never knew whom one would encounter at the evening meal. King Henry was in his element at each meal - loud and boisterous, setting the tone for lively debates.

Rosamund felt wholly out of place and begged the King repeatedly to be allowed to eat her meals in her room. He refused. Worse yet, a number of times when the discussions became heated over topics they had previously discussed in private, King Henry looked at her pointedly and arched his eyebrow. She remained stoically silent.

Rosamund immediately liked Thomas Becket. He was a handsome man with dark wavy hair, intelligent eyes, impeccable manners, and a vivacious personality. Sitting at the table with him and listening to him spout learned opinions about any and all topics, Rosamund could easily see why King Henry enjoyed having him around. Why if the King truly enjoyed discussing topics with her and her limited span of knowledge, he most surely enjoy debating issues with Thomas Becket. Add in Prince Rhys ab Gruffydd, to the rowdy collection of boisterous nobles and knights, and evening meal conversations often went on well into the night.

Each evening was similar. Archbishop Becket debated with the King constantly regarding church topics and Gruffydd argued continually on matters regarding state issues, while all around them were sharp eyes and ears spying, eavesdropping, scheming, and calculating. Prince Owain often expressed his opinion but never provocatively. Malcolm, King of the Scots, was as silent as Archbishop and Prince Rhys were challenging, yet Rosamund sensed he was the most discontent of them all.

King Henry was right, however. It seemed that no one at the table, besides Prince Rhys, loved to bait and argue with the King more than the Archbishop. And yet, King Henry seemed to have a genuine friendly affection for the man. Tolerant of his outspoken opinions, Henry enjoyed teasing him to no end. And that, it seems, was where she came in.

"Might I introduce you to the lovely Lady Rosamund, Archbishop," King Henry said on the first night of their acquaintance. King Henry grinned at the archbishop. "Surely, your new position of archbishop has not stifled your appreciation of a beautiful woman?"

The Archbishop focused his attention entirely on Rosamund, lifted her hand to his lips and kissed it. "God is responsible for all things beautiful, and it is most certainly my job to appreciate and admire. It is my utmost pleasure to make your acquaintance. What brings you to such," he paused and looked pointedly at King Henry and then the surrounding room of men, "masculine company?"

She executed a curtsy and rose gracefully. "I am here at the invitation of the King, my Lord Archbishop."

"Can you blame me, Becket?" King Henry reached over and brushed his fingers against her cheek. "Is she not the loveliest thing you have ever seen?"

Rosamund schooled her face to remain calm and serene. The Archbishop murmured low to the King, "Think you that Queen Eleanor would agree, Your Majesty?" He looked at the King with a distinct challenge in his eye.

King Henry scowled. "She has her own diversions, as well you know. Hell, if that one minstrel she keeps in her court continues to write love sonnets about her, I may be forced to hang him." Rosamund looked from King Henry to the Archbishop, gauging the expressions they both wore. Part of the game, she was rapidly learning, was being able to read the *true* emotions that were always carefully hidden. The Archbishop seemed absolutely delighted with the King's apparent bad mood.

Beckett smiled broadly. "I hear she's brought in one of those artists from Greece to paint her portrait. Seems she wishes to be portrayed as warrior – weapons and armor - but has had great difficulty finding someone to bend to her will." The Archbishop laughed. "You've been away from her for only, what? Seven months? Eight? Sire. You know what she's like left to her own devices." He shook his head in apparent disgust. "'Tis shocking that you cannot seem to control this problem you have."

King Henry looked at Thomas Becket and then at Rosamund. Through the entire discussion he had continued to touch her – her cheek, her hair, her neck. She felt herself grow progressively more uncomfortable with the public familiarity he showed. His arm finally settled possessively around her waist. She held her breath waiting for the explosion of the King's temper and was surprised to hear him chuckle. "Ahh, Becket, better to have *my* problems rather than yours. It's always better to have *too many women* rather than *none,* I always say." With that he leaned forward and kissed Rosamund full on the mouth. She responded with a blush, and the King sighed a sound of pure pleasure. "Yes, Becket, I'll take my troubles *any day.*" Laughing, the King drew her to their seats at the table while Becket followed.

This meal was the first time in which all who had been summoned were finally present. The seating arrangements changed nightly, with those in the most senior positions closest to the King. Archbishop Becket sat to the King's left, Rosamund to his right, and directly across the table sat Gruffydd with tonight's guard, Sir Thomas, sitting with him. Seated to Prince Rhys right was King Malcolm, and seated next to Thomas' left was Prince Owain. Fanning out in every direction were the knights and nobles, attended by their own personal staff as well as the Manor's myriad of servants. While there was no true privacy, the noise and the crush provided a subtle curtain for those outside the distinctive 'inner circle'.

King Henry proposed a toast at the start of the meal, causing the only moment of true silence in which everyone was attentive to one specific speaker. He stood and held his goblet high, his commanding presence instilling a tension that could not be ignored. The King inclined his head to each of those summoned, "Becket, Malcolm, Owain, … Rhys," the spoken acknowledgement an honor in it of itself, yet even Rosamund recognized that the purposeful deletion of all titles as a distinctive reminder of who held the true power in the room, "I welcome you to Woodstocke Manor. May this council between us reaffirm previous alliances and forge new ones!" Each and every man present raised his goblet and drank.

The Archbishop wasted no time. "What are your plans for Prince Rhys, Your Majesty?" he asked between bites of venison.

Rosamund thought that the two Welshmen sitting at the table could have been brothers; their dark looks and fierce expressions making them nearly identical, and giving no hint to their thoughts. The King did not pause in his eating, but looked across at Gruffydd in consideration. "He has been almost as provocative a dinner companion as you have been, Becket. I think, mayhap, I may spare him just to continue the battle of wits."

"I prefer the more challenging verbal encounters with Lady Rosamund," Gruffydd said. Rosamund felt all eyes turn to her.

"And *I* prefer the silence and civility of my own private rooms," she retorted before she could stop herself. Even Prince Owain's expressions showed a hint of amusement at her quick response. She sighed. *Keep your mouth closed*, she told herself firmly, *you are in far too deeply*. But she was not going to be given the opportunity.

"Since Prince Rhys so enjoys speaking with you, Lady Rosamund, and since you have specifically been the object of his brutality, what would you suggest the King do with him?" Archbishop Becket asked.

Gruffydd raised his eyebrow in a mocking challenge and she felt with absolute certainty that the conversation was going *precisely* as he wished it. "I have already voiced my opinions in public and in private, on a number of occasions, regarding my view of Prince Rhys' captivity," she said as primly as possible. Though totally lacking in appetite she forced herself to take a mouthful of food and chew slowly. She was finished speaking, she communicated to any and all who looked at her.

"I have not heard your opinion," the Archbishop said in a most friendly tone. "What were your thoughts?"

"She prefers me to be hung," Gruffydd said with harsh finality.

"I do not!" she said in shocked outrage, and to her profound embarrassment both Gruffydd and the King chuckled.

"You were most eloquent the night you spoke, Milady," said a voice from across the table, and she looked up to meet the kind eyes of Sir Thomas. "Voice your opinion, once again to remind us." He smiled at her. And then he winked.

She took a deep breath, held it, closed her eyes, and then slowly exhaled. Rosamund looked around the table at the powerful men looking at her expectantly. What did she truly have to loose besides her pride and self-respect? "I have not seen battle, although I have lived with the effects of it my entire life. The emotions of fear, hate, grief, and mistrust rule a world that is controlled by war. Each of you are men who have the capacity to change things, and yet I wonder at times if you truly understand that or even believe it. You, too, have spent an entire life at war and know nothing else. Why should anyone assume you would desire or crave something different?"

Rosamund looked at the Archbishop. "You ask me for my opinion about what should be done with Prince Rhys ab Gruffydd. Why do you ask, I wonder? You are a man of great power in the church, and yet your appointment is newly achieved. The King must have had great confidence in you to have encouraged your selection. Do *you* have a strong opinion, yet have not the courage to voice it?" She turned at Gruffydd's soft chuckle and saw admiration in his look.

"And you, Prince Rhys. You have murdered my husband and my husband's people, kidnapped and threatened me, and challenged my King to war. Yet you now sit here, a prisoner. It would seem to me that your talk is apparently bolder than your capabilities." She saw, out of the corner of her eye, Prince Owain's face register surprise at her bluntness. "Tell me, Sir, have you changed your stated goals or are you still prepared to die, uncompromisingly, for a cause you appear at this very moment to be losing?" Gruffydd stared at her, expressionless, and did not respond.

She turned then to King Henry. The look he was giving her was one she was familiar with. It was the expression he had when he was most determined to bed her; a look that made her feel as if he wished to devour her. "And you, Your Majesty. You have summoned these powerful leaders to your table. They are here. What will you do with them? Can you make the most of this opportunity and take bold steps towards peace and alliance such as you spoke of in your toast? Or will you be like the many others that have gone before you, and continue to drag this country through many more years of war. A wise man gets more use from his enemies than a fool from his friends, I think, Sire." She looked at all the stunned, silent faces surrounding her. "You are all wise men, are you not? I pray that you are."

Rosamund shrugged her shoulders. "What should be done with Prince Rhys? I have said I see no benefit in arranging his death, and even more so, I see darker ramifications." She looked at him across the table. "I would have him as my ally rather than my enemy." She looked at all of them, one at a time. "I would have you all as my allies rather than my enemies. It is my opinion that should that be accomplished, all of you could work towards a common purpose. You would become the most powerful, the most insurmountable force this world has ever seen."

There was a moment of silence and then King Malcolm spoke. He raised a goblet and looked at Rosamund, "I toast your courage and your wisdom, Milady. Both are profoundly refreshing." He looked at the men around the table. "You dream too highly and too purely, unfortunately. The egos at this table are far too large to entertain the idea of compromise. At any level."

"Do you include yourself in that description, King Malcolm?" she asked.

He hid what she thought was a small smile behind his goblet as he drank. "Most definitely," he responded.

The formal council was held the next day in the reception hall opposite the Great Hall. A raised chair was set for the King and those attending arranged themselves strategically about the hall, higher rank warranting a closer position to the King. Rosamund, following the King's orders, was present, but claimed a spot far in the shadows to the back of the room. This was not her place and well she knew it.

King Henry arrived in full court regalia with flowing robes and jewels that marked his superior station. For a man who eschewed the trappings of court at every opportunity, a distinctive message was being given: Here Is Your King.

Sir Brian was in attendance to Gruffydd this day, and Rosamund caught herself scanning the crowd for Sir Thomas. When she at last found Sir Thomas, in front near the King, he was looking directly at her and she felt an immediate flush of pleasure. He gave her a barely perceptible nod. She gave him a brilliant smile.

Standing to the King's left were two young men, both dressed regally, and Rosamund briefly puzzled over their identity. But then King Henry began to speak and she focused only on the events as they unfolded.

"Prince Rhys," King Henry began, and she watched as Gruffydd walked before the King. "I have been troubled these past weeks with what is to be done with you, and it seems, in reality, that this is a true test of my intentions toward the Welsh people in general. It is because of this realization and my earnest hope to secure better relations between our peoples that I have made the decision to reinstate you to your former status. I would have your word, as you in return have mine, that the blood that has been shed by our people will not be forgotten, but laid to rest, acknowledging all vengeance met."

For a moment the silence in the hall was so great that Rosamund thought she could hear her own heart beating, waiting for Gruffydd's response. At last, Gruffydd knelt before King Henry and said, "You have the word of Rhys ab Gruffydd, that from this day I acknowledge all vengeance met between our peoples."

King Henry gestured to one of the young men behind him who stepped forward and stood by his side. "In a show of good faith for this mutual pledge, I return to you your son, Hywel, who has for these many years been kept as a hostage. You can see that he has been well cared for; in fact he has been a close companion of my son, Henry." Rosamund watched in stunned amazement as the other young man stepped forward and acknowledged Gruffydd with a regal nod. With that one subtle action the similarity in likeness was immediately apparent between Prince Henry and his father, the King.

Gruffydd stood, but inclined his head toward King Henry. "I extend my gratitude to you and it seems, Your Majesty, I am in your debt."

King Henry gave Gruffydd a victorious smile, hesitated for a moment, nodded, and then said, *"Which I shall claim now."* The King looked out into the crowd and then gestured to Earl Gilbert.

Earl Gilbert stood and said in a loud voice, "Hear ye! Hear ye! All of King Henry's knights and nobles, all of his faithful allies old and new. Now is the time to reaffirm your allegiance to our King in a formal Commendation Ceremony. Let all those who rule over others swear their dependant vassalage to King Henry, *now* and *forever* by performing an act of homage and swearing an oath of fealty." Even from the back of the large hall, Rosamund saw Prince Rhys ab Gruffydd stiffen. His head snapped up, meeting King Henry's unblinking stare.

A low murmur rippled through the crowd followed by an oppressive moment of silence and inaction. The moment stretched on, with King Henry and Gruffydd each waiting for the other to make the first move. Neither did. It was Gruffydd's son, Hywel, who finally moved. He stepped down from the platform and looked first at his father, inclining his head respectfully and then turning to King Henry. Gruffydd turned to look at his son but made no motion, spoke no words.

Hywel removed his cap and removed the sword that hung from his side. Both of these he lay formally at King Henry's feet and then knelt before the King. Clasping both of his hands tightly before him, he offered them to King Henry, head bowed, while saying in a loud, clear voice, "I promise on my faith that I will in the future be true to my King; Henry Plantagenet, King of England, Count of Anjou, Duke of Normandy, Duke of Aquitaine, never to cause him harm. I will observe my homage to him completely against all persons in good faith and without deceit. I make this Oath of Fealty of my own volition, by my own choice, with the express desire before God and man to become his vassal now and forever."

Henry seemed to be genuinely moved by Hywel's formal pledge, standing from his seat and grasping both of Hywel's clasped hands within his own. "I accept your act of homage and your pledge of fealty, Hywel ab Gruffydd and formally recognize before these witnesses this relationship we have now forged between us. May God fortify this bond throughout the years to come, strengthening us both with its benefits."

Hywel rose, retrieved his cap and sword, bowed once again to his King and then turned to his father, who had not moved. Hywel bowed then to his father, cap and sword in place. Respect was given, however the message was clear; Gruffydd may be his father, but Henry was his chosen King.

Rosamund felt her hands cramping and realized that she had been fisting her fingers so tightly that both of her palms were bleeding. *Please,* she prayed, *please Prince Rhys, make the right choice.*

Gruffydd stood for lengthy moments staring at his son's bowed head and then finally turned to face King Henry. Rosamund was certain that there was no one breathing in the span of time it took Gruffydd to act. He took one step, two steps toward the King, and Rosamund noted the tension in the knights surrounding the King.

"I wear no cap and by your command carry no weapon," Rosamund heard Gruffydd's voice carrying clearly throughout the hall. "I have acknowledged a debt to you before this assemblage regarding the care and now the return of my eldest son, Hywel." He hesitated, as though carefully weighing each word he was about to say. "You claim the debt now and so I will give you your due." Before the stunned assembly, Gruffydd knelt before a triumphant King Henry, clasped and raised his hands, bowed his head, and said, "I promise on my faith that I will in the future be true to my King; Henry Plantagenet, King of England, Count of Anjou, Duke of Normandy, Duke of Aquitaine, ..."

In the end, all the nobles present who had possessions and power great enough to have authority over others stepped forward one after another to give homage and swear fealty to King Henry. Prince Owain and King Malcolm were last. Tension built once again as King Malcolm stood before King Henry, bowed formally and gave his oath of fealty. But he did not kneel nor did he present his hands.

King Henry was not pleased. "You distinguish yourself from this group, Malcolm," he said in a low tone yet heard by all.

"I *am* distinguished from this group," King Malcolm answered simply.

King Henry stood and walked forward, coming to stand one step up from Malcolm. "So you are, Malcolm," the King said after a time, "so you are." He turned and motioned Sir Thomas forward and then spoke quietly to him. While Sir Thomas walked briskly away, King Henry looked again at Malcolm. "As you choose to discriminate yourself from this assemblage, I will acknowledge you in like fashion."

All eyes turned as Sir Thomas reentered the hall escorting a man Rosamund had seen with Malcolm's party of attending nobles. A murmur rose throughout the crowd as Sir Thomas and the man came to stand directly next to King Malcolm. "I accept your pledge of fealty, Malcolm. However, I have decided that your brother, David, will remain in my company when you return to your home." King Henry gestured toward the man standing next to Sir Thomas. "He will be a guarantee of the preservation of this peace we have between us. I have chosen to single you out among all others present to bestow this *honor* since you desire to be made separate and apart from everyone else. You have my assurance that he will receive the same courtesies and care that I have shown other guests such as he in the past." King Henry looked to Sir Thomas, nodded slightly, turned and left the hall. The King's retinue of knights and nobles followed, Prince David and Prince Henry included. Rosamund stood in the back of the hall for a long while afterward, observing. When she finally made her way back to her rooms, only King Malcolm was still standing in the center of the great hall before the empty chair of the King.

Rosamund awoke with a start, heart pounding, ears straining, and eyes frustratingly blinded from the pitch darkness. She lay for a long time trying to remember the dream that had startled her so fully awake, but could not. Just as she felt her heart begin to slow and her body begin to relax back into sleep she heard the voice say quietly, "I thought waking you once with my hand over your mouth was more than enough for one lifetime." The disembodied Welsh burr came to her left.

She took a deep breath to steady her voice. "Prince Rhys, to what do I owe this honor?"

He chuckled. "You are far less frightened this time, Milady. Do men visit you regularly in the darkest hours of the night?"

She shifted herself to a sitting position, stacking pillows behind her and drawing the covers up to maintain some semblance of propriety. "No, I get few visitors in this style, but as my circumstances have changed somewhat over the past few months, I have grown better accustomed to sudden shocks and surprises."

She saw him then, by the fire, stirring coals to life and then watched as he carried a burning reed to the bedside to light a candle. The bed dipped as he sat down. *Why was she not afraid?* she wondered to herself.

"Is there ever a time when you are not beautiful?" he murmured almost to himself.

She brushed the mess of her hair out of her face and hastily looked down to make sure she was properly covered. "I fear to tell you for you may certainly show up to find out for yourself," she said in a flip manner. Gruffydd grinned at her.

"I leave for my home," he said at last.

"Now? Tonight?"

"Yes."

"Why do you behave like a thief?"

He shrugged and smiled. "Because I am?"

Rosamund shook her head. "And what do you steal?"

"You."

Rosamund had a moment of panic and looked into dark eyes that twinkled with humor. She could not help herself, groaned, and rolled her eyes. "*Not again.* Look what havoc you caused in my life the last time."

He shook his head, laughing quietly. "No, not again, really. I will not take you against your will."

"I thought not."

"But I will offer you the opportunity to leave with me of your own choice." When she went to speak, he reached over and put his finger to her lips. "Hear me out before you say 'yea' or 'nay'. I do not offer you the same situation that King Henry currently offers you. I look forward to returning to my wife and she would not welcome me with open arms were I to bring along a beautiful young mistress."

"I am not the King's mistress," she said with much force.

He looked mildly surprised. "By your choice or by his?"

"By mine," she said unconscious of the way her chin lifted a small notch.

Gruffydd chuckled. "You are so much more than you first appear." He scratched the side of his jaw and looked at her in the candlelight. "I offer you a fresh start. I do not promise an easy life, I do not promise you riches," he snorted. "Hell, I do not even promise you happiness. But, should you wish it, I will escort you back to my home, Cantref Mawr, where you will have an opportunity to begin anew. The choice is yours to make."

Rosamund studied his face. "Why do you do this?" she said after a time.

"I owe you a debt," he said.

"*Me?*"

He nodded. "Yes, you. I know that Henry is very much his own man, and yet I think that you subtly put certain ideas and perceptions into his head that made him agreeable towards my reinstatement and my son's return."

She shook her head adamantly. "You give me far too much credit, sir."

Gruffydd looked just as determined, "You give yourself far too little."

They were both silent for a time, he seemingly content to watch her and she lost in her own thoughts. At last she said quietly to him, "I cannot …"

"I would hear your reasons. And be warned. Should I deem them to be insufficient, I will simply kidnap you. And this time I shall gag you. You talk overmuch."

She looked anguished. "I will not risk any bloodshed or the destruction of this tenuous peace that is between our countries! Were I to disappear on the night of your departure, who knows what retaliation would result?" She reached over and touched his arm. "I thank you, though, it is a wondersome thing to consider."

He covered her hand briefly with his warm one. "You must not trust Henry, not for a moment. You must always remain on your guard."

She shrugged. "I have been fine thus far." She looked at him pointedly. "You have paid your homage and sworn your fealty. You who were so quick to decry the words of an *Englishman* once before in a conversation with me. Do not tell me that the words you spoke just this day meant nothing?" She crossed her arms and looked at him questioningly.

"As for *my words* spoken today, they were true. For a *Saeson* king he has many good qualities. But he was unwise with how he handled things today. He shamed many and alienated even more. He did not need to make us all *grovel* before him, but we did. Only I came away with something of worth that I did not have previously: my freedom and my son. Either one of those were worth almost anything I could have said or done, but *both of them together* were positively priceless."

Gruffydd smiled a bitter smile. "But only I do not feel as if I have been publicly dishonored. Henry knew what he was asking, and still he did it. Were someone to have done the same to him, he would have considered it tantamount to an act of war."

"What are you telling me?" she said in a stunned whisper.

"I am telling you that there will be a war between the Welsh and the English like there has never been before. Owain already makes plans and has sent out messengers gathering men."

"But I thought ..."

"Malcolm was correct when he told you at dinner that the egos in this manor are far too large to ever entertain a compromise at any level. He will sit and watch, hindered as he is by his brother's hostage status, watching the Welsh wreak their havoc, silently wishing us well."

"'Us'. So you are included in that havoc." The disappointment in her voice was evident.

"Yes and no." He sighed. "I will not forbid my men nor inhibit my Welsh brothers in their pursuit of well deserved justice. They hunger

for it in a way that you can never begin to understand. But for myself ..."
He shrugged. "I need to think. I need to speak with my son. I need to ...
wait before I declare and act."

He grabbed Rosamund by both her shoulders and shook her.
"You must not become complacent in regard to Henry. He toys with you
now," Gruffydd said with anger and impatience. "For the moment, he can
afford to be patient and play this game you have begun with him. But he
will tire of its amusement very soon, and then you will find yourself so
ensnared you will not be able to escape his trap." He released her and she
reached over to touch his sleeve again.

"Prince Rhys, *I am already unable to escape.* Know you not?"

"He does *nothing* that is not for the betterment of himself."

"Are we not all like that?" she countered quietly.

He looked at her, still highly annoyed. "Henry is, I am, Malcolm
is, but I find it hard to believe that you are."

"I do not deserve such high regard."

"What do you know of Sir Thomas?"

Rosamund expression showed great surprise. "Why do you speak
of Sir Thomas?"

"I would know your thoughts about him. Think you can trust
him?"

"Yes," she said without hesitation.

"I agree," he said just as quickly. "I have spent many hours with
the man," he absently rubbed a scar above his right eye, "and have had
some rather heated debates on a few choice topics with him." He paused
as if choosing the right words. "There are not many *Saeson* I can say this of,
but he is an honorable man." He nodded. "I am pleased that you have
already noted that fact."

He looked at her pointedly in the candlelight. "Do you care for
him?"

He caught her off guard and she felt herself blush. "I ... I... no!
yes!" She groaned in frustration. "He has been kind and polite and helpful
to me on a number of occasions," as Gruffydd gave her a knowing look she
hurried on, "as *many* people here at the manor have done." She sighed and

looked at her hand clutching his sleeve and quickly released it. "He has been a friend to me when I have had none. Even you must realize that there can never be any more than that between us."

Gruffydd reached over and touched her neck and Rosamund gasped until she realized what he was doing. Slowly he drew out from beneath her nightgown the charm he had given her so many months before. "You still have it," he murmured in a pleased voice. He looked at her directly. "The offer still stands and will never be rescinded. You are not to forget."

"I will not forget." She repeated, and he nodded his head with satisfaction.

He reached over and with his hand snuffed out the candle plunging them once again into total darkness but for the few embers glowing in the fireplace. She felt him stand, but immediately lost the awareness of his presence as he moved in complete silence. "Prince Rhys?" her voice shook with uncertainty.

"Take care of yourself, Lady Rosamund," he said softly against her ear causing her to jump.

"And you, sir." But she already sensed he was gone.

Give me my lute in bed now as I lie, and lock the doors of mine unlucky bower.

Gascoigne, 16th Century A.D.[17]

Woodstocke Manor
Royal Residence of Henry II, King of England
Oxfordshire, England
November, 1163

Chapter Fourteen

ruffydd had been gone for less than a fortnight when the first reports of Welsh resistance began to filter back to King Henry. The King was consumed with the responsibilities of his office: seeing to the safe transport of Prince David to his Normandy holdings (safety and security was assured with distance, Rosamund was told), carefully monitoring the ever fractious March barons (who seemed never to be pleased no matter what the state of political affairs), attempting to quell the ever-growing contrary opinions of Archbishop Becket (who had the powerful support of Pope Alexander III), and beginning the arduous task of amassing an army to once and for all to eradicate the Welsh threat. There were many evenings when the additional problem the King faced, that of trying to convince Rosamund to let him share her bed, ceased to be something for which he could spare his precious time. And so, on occasion, the nightly battle – to her great relief – did not occur.

A council had been called at Westminster by the King, and all the powerful earls and barons had been commanded to attend. It seemed that nothing short of a major Welsh military campaign, prepared with surpassing thoroughness, could be considered. The hows and whos and wherefores were to be discussed, and by November, anxious reports from the March barons pushed the King's problem with Wales to the top of the heap.

The November evening was cold as Rosamund and the King strolled in the gardens. She was grateful for her fur-lined cloak which she pulled tightly against her to ward off the chill. "It is my last night with you for a time, and our first separation," King Henry said to her.

"I know, Your Majesty." Rosamund knew that on the morrow he left for Westminster to address the Council about the situations concerning Wales, Scotland, France, and the Church. King Henry's four greatest challenges.

"I would like to show you the treasure that I keep at the center of the maze. Would you humor me?"

Rosamund smiled at King Henry. "I must admit that I have had a great interest in what is at the center of the maze, Sire. You have so many beautiful sights here at Woodstocke, that for you to continually call the center of the maze a 'treasure' piques my curiosity."

"Only I know the route and hold the key. Even workers who were brought in were blindfolded."

As they walked in the cool of the autumn evening, Rosamund tried her utmost to concentrate on the chosen path, while the King appeared not even to think about where he headed. *One hundred and fifty doors* the King had informed her. *Seven acres,* James the zookeeper had told her. She studied King Henry surreptitiously as they strolled through the winding paths. *Did he truly know the intricately complicated path?* She was truly in awe if he did.

He stopped at a door like all the others with no apparent distinctive markings. The only thing that made her realize there was something special about *this* door was the way he looked at her. He paused, studying her in the moonlight. Slowly he reached up and touched her cheek. "Even though you have refused me, angered me, argued with me, and caused me frustration as I have never known, I still love you, Rosamund."

"Your Majesty, I ..."

His finger touched her lips, silencing her. "I need not hear any more of your reasons or arguments. Please believe me, *I have heard them all.* It is *you* who have not heard *me.*" He turned then, unlocked the door, and pushed it open. He gestured into the opening, "After you."

Rosamund was entranced. Standing proudly in the center of an enormous garden was a cottage. Beautiful in its architecture, its graceful lines, beckoned her. She wandered into the clearing, curiosity making her almost hurry. She noticed absently that the grounds surrounding the cottage contained all the lovely attractions within the maze; a swing, a pond. King Henry chuckled with delight as he followed behind her.

"Do you like it?"

"It's exquisite. Did you design this along with the maze?"

"Yes, I designed it. But not along with the maze. I added it later. Come, I'll give you a tour."

Inside the cottage was a sitting room with comfortable chairs, a large, beautifully decorated bedroom, a library filled with books, a buttery fully supplied for cooking, and a table and chairs surrounded by windows overlooking the beautiful and wild gardens. She wandered from room to room, touching particularly lovely items, fingering shimmering satins and silks, and gazing out the windows at the moonlit grounds. "Why, Your Majesty? Why go to all this trouble for a place that no one uses? You are the only one who knows of this place. Will you stay here?"

He had settled himself into one of the winged chairs in the sitting room. His legs were stretched out before him, crossed at the ankles, and his arms were crossed at his chest. He studied her for a few moments and the fact that he did not respond made her finally turn to look at him. Finally, he said, "No, I will not stay here. At least not for a while anyway."

"Then why?"

He sighed. "You have accused me on more than one occasion of keeping you like one of my zoo animals, Rosamund." She continued to stare at him, a frown wrinkling her forehead. "This is to be *your* home. I would not risk your safety when I am not here to protect you."

Shock and panic came in a stifling wave, followed by fury. "You mean, you would not risk my escape."

King Henry inclined his head and smiled. "That too. I have told you numerous times. What I claim, I keep. Every man at this manor desires you."

"You think that I would refuse you and yet accept another?" Her voice rose with her emotions.

His volume kept pace with hers. "You refuse me because of my personal circumstances, not for a general principle of chastity! How am I to know what rattles around in your frustrating mind! I have no clear understanding of you even after all these months together."

"So you will lock me up."

He waved his arm to silence her. "I will keep you safe! Do you think all men are as patient, understanding, and respectful of your misdirected standards of nobility and honor as I?"

She stared at him in disbelief. *"Keep me safe?"* She shook her head vigorously. "Nay, I do not think all men are such as you. In fact, I cannot conceive of any other man who would have the audacity to imprison me merely because I would not acquiesce to his selfish whims."

"Selfish whims!" he roared, shooting to his feet and crossing the room to grasp her shoulders. He shook her roughly. *"I am the King of England.* You seem to forget that. I can have anything I wish! I hold authority over men and countries and church! *It is my right by birth.* Nothing I do is selfish. All is *my due."*

Rosamund stared at him for a moment and then said quietly, "You may take all that you feel is *your due* from me, but it will always be *against my will."*

"So be it. My patience grows thinner with each passing day. Perhaps absence will make your heart grow fonder towards me. Perhaps when you next see me you will feel differently." With that King Henry turned and left her. Rosamund heard the front door of the cottage slam shut. Her prison. Her cage.

She had a hysterical thought. Would James now be her keeper as well? Then she panicked. Who would care for her? How long was she to remain on her own? A sob caught in her throat. The isolation would drive her insane. She wandered into the bedroom and crawled up onto the luxurious silken coverlet. When the weeping came it was an uncontrollable flood. She screamed, she raged, and she sobbed until she fell into an exhausted sleep filled with nightmares and more tears.

Thomas had been given strict instructions. The King had been very specific. It had taken all of Thomas' self control to school his expressions into a mask of obedience while King Henry went into specific detail about Rosamund's care. Once a week a guard was to travel to the center of the maze where Rosamund now resided. She was to be provided anything she requested: food, clothes, anything except her freedom. There were to be *no* visitors. Not her maid, not any additional servants, *no one*. The only person she was to encounter was to be her guard and he was forbidden to stay any longer than necessary to inquire of her needs and deliver supplies. After giving his list of specific instructions, Henry asked Thomas whom he would suggest for the task of guarding Rosamund.

Thomas' mouth went dry, struggling with all of the emotions that were battling behind his stoic mask. "Who do you have in mind, Sire?"

Henry snorted. "The only one I trust is you, but I am loathe to lose one of my best knights for such a task."

Thomas shrugged, "Your Majesty, you are off to the Council Meeting of Westminster, not war. I will stay. Should you need me to guard your back, send for me and I will come."

Henry clapped him on the back. "Were I a suspicious man, I would think you a tad too willing," he chuckled. "But of all my knights, you are the one who consistently shows little interest in the fairer sex."

"I have always had other goals surpassing those pleasures," Thomas murmured.

"And those are?"

Thomas looked into his King's eyes. "To have a place to claim as my own, Sire. To have somewhere to go home to. I have never had that, and one day I wish to have it."

Henry placed both hands on Thomas' shoulders. "You have been a faithful knight, Thomas. You are reliable, loyal, and always willing. On more than one occasion you have saved my sorry hide in battle. Now, because you know how important this is to me, you choose to carry out a mundane task rather than travel with me and seek further opportunities to excel. I make a pledge to you, Sir Thomas. When I return from the Council at Westminster, I will see that you achieve your goal of having 'a place to call home'. You have my word and my pledge."

Thomas kneeled in deference to his King, his stomach clenching as he felt torn in two. "My Lord King, I am your loyal vassal, who swears fealty to none but you."

"I accept your pledge, Sir Thomas, with pleasure."

Thomas broke his word to the King before the sun had set the first day after Henry had departed for Westminster. He knew that Rosamund had already been alone for almost a full day and night and could not imagine her fear and anguish over her circumstances. Key in hand he traveled into the maze following the path that the King had mapped out for him.

He stood in stunned silence upon opening the final door. The bower that stood in the middle of the clearing was lovely, stuff that dreams were made of. *A gilded cage*, he thought. "Lady Rosamund?" he called out tentatively. There was no answer.

He took cautious steps into the garden, coming almost to the foundation of the cottage. "Lady Rosamund?" he called out again. Still no answer.

He went to the door, opened it and stepped inside. "Lady Rosamund?" The silence began to cause him tremendous anxiety. Why did she not answer? Was she hurt? *"Lady Rosamund!"* he finally shouted.

Fear made him travel hastily through all the rooms in search of her. Sitting room, library, dining area, buttery, bedroom. All were empty, appearing untouched. He wandered out onto the grounds, searching in the rapidly growing twilight. Just as he was going to call her name again, he saw the contrasting light color of her gown against the dark grass. She was sitting with her back against the well staring off into nowhere. When he was but five short steps from her he spoke, "Lady Rosamund?"

At first, he thought she did not hear him, but slowly she turned to look at him. He took a step back from the haunted misery he saw in her face. "Sir Thomas," she said in the softest whisper, "what brings you to my prison?" She shivered violently, and he realized that she was soaked to the skin.

"Milady! You are cold and wet! Please let us go inside where you can take care of your needs."

"I have no wish to enter that place. If I am an animal to be kept in a cage, then I shall do as I like, sit where I like, live as I like."

The irony of his situation – loyal to the king yet disobedient to his direct orders, concerned for Rosamund yet responsible for keeping her imprisoned – welled up in him making him furious with his impossible position. *Prioritize* his mind said clearly. Dead from exposure to the elements fit nowhere in his list of responsibilities or desires. He bent down, picked her up, and carried her into the cottage.

"Sir Thomas! Put me down! You have no right!"

"You are wrong, Lady Rosamund. I have been commanded by the King to oversee your needs." His movements were stiff with controlled fury.

Rosamund looked at him and he noted that her lips were tinged blue. "How far in the King's disfavor you have fallen, Sir, to be reduced to a lowly prison servant?"

He pursed his lips, unwilling to speak the truth of things, knowing instinctively she would never believe him. "On the contrary, milady," he said brusquely, "as the King's most trusted man, I volunteered for the duty."

They entered the cottage and he placed her in one of the stuffed chairs near the fireplace. When she made a motion to move he glared at her. "Stay where you are," he said in a gruff voice. He stomped into the bedroom, ripped the cover off the bed and dragged it into the sitting room where he brusquely tucked it around her. Next, he started a fire in the fireplace. Lastly, he went to the buttery, found a pitcher of ale and brought her a cup. "Drink this." When she hesitated and gave him a mutinous look he said through gritted teeth, "Do it of your own volition or I will force it down myself."

He wandered into the bedroom, opened the wardrobe, and searched for something dry for her to wear. What an incredible array of garments, he thought to himself, as he rejected one gown after another. Finally, he found a plain, soft woolen gown and a pair of slippers that appeared to be of the same color. He carried them in to her and dropped them in her lap. "I am going out to gather more firewood. You have until I return to have changed into this. If you haven't finished when I come back, I will do it for you." And with that, he walked out into the garden in search of the woodpile.

Thomas released his frustration and anger by cutting wood. There was already a pile, but there would never be enough when winter set in, so he felt he was being productive with his time. When he at last carried an armload into the house, she was sitting quietly in front of the fire, the damp gown casually draped over the other chair. "Thank you," he said pointedly as he dumped the wood into the bucket by the fireplace.

He sat down in front of the hearth and looked up at her. "Are you warmer?"

"Why did you volunteer to be my keeper?"

He sighed, a sigh that was tinged with anger and irritation. "I am the King's man," he said evasively. "I go where I am needed."

"You are the King's man who has reached a level of respect whereas you need not be stuck with inconsequential responsibilities such as I."

Thomas could not resist. "Think you the King would call you 'inconsequential'?"

"Nay, the King calls me far less complimentary things," and she turned from him to gaze at the fire.

Her lips were no longer blue and her cheeks had regained their color. Her hair began to curl about her head as it dried. He could look at her all day and all night and never tire, he realized. God help him. And he was to guard her? He was to be the only one to have contact with her for months? Had he been out of his mind to volunteer for this duty? He turned to look at the fire, too. It was far safer, he realized than gazing at Rosamund. In reality, jumping directly in the fire was probably safer if he really thought long and hard about the situation he was in.

"Why were you outside, cold and wet?"

She looked at him, exhaustion and defeat written across her face. "I'm done, Sir Thomas. I'm tired, Sir Thomas. I can't do this anymore."

"You will not be here forever, Milady. One month, perhaps two."

Rosamund smiled at him. "You do not understand, do you? This," she gestured to the cottage surrounding her, "is just another location in which I have been confined, controlled, and intimidated. It is not the *place*, it is the realization that the *situation* of my life will never, *ever* change. I have always been," she hesitated searching for the right word, "ridiculously optimistic that at some time my circumstances would change." She laughed a bitter laugh that grated on his nerves. "I thought I would find love, happiness, and fulfillment if I were patient, if I were cooperative, if I were *good*." She looked at the fire again. "What a fool I was."

"You are many things, but you are no fool."

"Why?"

"Why what?"

"You still have not told me why you are here."

He turned to stir up the fire and add a log. Once again he avoided the question. "You are discouraged with your circumstances and rightly so. Yet you seem to have a belief that everyone but you enjoys a level of freedom that you can only dream of." He looked at her pointedly. "I cannot, for the life of me, think of perhaps more than one or two times in my *entire* life where I have made decisions solely for my own enjoyment. *There are many people like that.* Yes, your situation is dire. But you are strong, intelligent, and opinionated. You must not give up. You must not view your situation as your fate." Thomas smiled to himself in memory. "A wise man once told me, 'A man's character is his fate.'"

"You quote philosophy to me, Sir Thomas?"

He felt himself blush. "Earl Robert told me that one time when I bemoaned my bastard birthright once too often." He grinned and shrugged, "Heraclitus.[18]"

"What have you chosen to do solely for your own enjoyment?"

He stood abruptly. "It is time for me to go, Milady. Despite the King's orders, I will visit here with you more than once a week. I can bring you anything you wish, you need only ask, and if it is within my power I will obtain it. You must not loose heart. More importantly, you must not loose faith. *You must not.*"

Thomas turned to go and Rosamund grasped his arm. "*What did you choose?*" she asked in a voice the barest of whispers.

He looked at her then and he sensed that *she knew* and yet needed to hear him say it. He sighed, looking up at the beamed ceiling rather than in her eyes. "I sought out a beautiful woman's company in the garden some months ago, and wasted valuable time as I listened to her read to me. I have never known such simple contentment." He looked down at her and watched her eyes slowly begin to fill with tears and her lips start to tremble. He reached up and caught a tear with his finger and she closed her eyes at his touch. He could not keep from speaking then. "And I chose to be your guard rather than go with the King to Westminster, preferring your company above anything else I could think of." He could not help himself and put his hand against the back of her neck and drew her gently into his embrace. He wrapped both arms around her and rocked her gently as she began to sob in earnest. He leaned down and rested his cheek on the top of her head, and inhaled deeply of her wonderful scent. *I can die now,* he thought briefly to himself.

"Oh, Sir Thomas," she finally managed to say, "what now?"

He did not know what to tell her at first and remained silent. But finally he said, "Perhaps you and I shall make a few more selfish choices."

Thomas came to the bower cottage tentatively, at first. He feared the draw that she had on him which, only from their brief contacts, had already caused him to make decisions that went against his honor and his king. What would it be like for them should they allow this attraction they felt for each other to grow any stronger than it already was? It would spell only disaster for both of them. His next nightly visit was expressly to tell her such, and to impress upon her what boundaries they had to maintain.

Nothing went as he had planned.

He found her, much to his shock and amazement, in the maze. "Lady Rosamund! How...!? What...!? Where...!?" He sputtered in shock.

She laughed at him in the moonlight, her cheeks and nose red from the cold, wrapped in a long, fur lined cloak. "Good eve, Sir Thomas," she said and she curtsied there in the icy grass.

"How are you out here in the maze?!"

"I thought that if King Henry so loves puzzles and mazes, surely there cannot be just one entrance to my place. So I searched and searched and was rewarded for my efforts. Come, I will show you." She grasped his hand and pulled him along behind her.

He panicked. "Milady, I have this path that the King bade me follow. Should we deviate from it and become lost, I cannot help us find the way back."

"Calm yourself, Sir Thomas," she said to him. "Look down and to your right."

At first, he did not see what she meant and then, with a turn, he caught a glimmer and stopped. She stood patiently beside him as he bent down to examine what was at his feet. When he looked up at her, having touched the pale silver thread that ran along the edge of the path, she had a most satisfied expression on her face. "He will not win, Sir Thomas. You will not be found at fault, for he did not tell even you of the other exit. I have had much time on my hands. I told you just last night that I am done. Well, *I am*. I will find the way out of this maze and *I will leave*."

He stood before her, his face registering his concern. "Where will you go?"

Rosamund sighed, grasped his hand again, and continued through the maze back to her bower. "I know not." She looked back at him. "And I care not," she said with great conviction. She stopped and pushed her way through what appeared to be a solid wall of ivy and evergreens, but it gave way easily. He had significantly more difficulty fitting through because of his size and she laughed, pulling leaves and small branches from his hair and clothes once they were in her clearing.

"The King will not let you go, Lady Rosamund."

"There is someone more powerful than even King Henry, Sir Thomas. He is honorable, faithful, loving, and true. He wants only what is best for me and I trust Him with my life. 'God hath not given me a spirit of fear and timidity, but of power and love, and wisdom.[19]'" She turned to him and put her hands on her hips. Her hood had been pulled back in her travels through the hedgerow, her eyes flashed anger and she lifted her chin up in defiance. She was magnificent. "The King thought to break me putting me in here. And he has. But not in the way he would think or hope." She stomped her foot in the frost covered grass. "*I am free*, Sir Thomas. Free of the King, free of my familial obligations, free of societies mores. I will make my own choices and my own decisions regardless of what any *person* thinks. From now on, I answer only to my own conscience." She frowned and leaned forward at him, "I don't give a *fig* what anyone, *even the King*, has to say about it."

Sir Thomas bit the sides of his mouth to keep from smiling, for she would misunderstand his mirth. He felt the emotion so strongly it just about brought him to his knees. *I love her.* God help him.

"What?" She stepped towards him, concern written across her face. "What? The look on your face, Thomas." And his heart lurched for she had called him by his simple name without a title. "I do not want to cause you grief or trouble. I will not share anymore of these thoughts with you so that you can honestly tell the King you knew nothing of my plans." She searched his eyes, unease still written across her face. "Tell me your thoughts."

"No."

Rosamund reached up to touch his face, but he stopped her hand abruptly before he could feel its warmth. He turned and walked some distance from her to the well, and sat down on the cold stones. "Thomas…," she realized then what she had said, "Sir Thomas."

"You cannot go back now," he interrupted her and when she looked puzzled he continued, "You called me 'Thomas'. Do not go back to calling me by my title."

She took tentative steps towards him. "Then you must call me simply 'Rosamund'," she said with a smile.

I call you Love.

She was close enough now that her cape brushed against his knees. She sighed. "In my excitement of discovering the other exit and the grand decisions and plans I made, I never took into account what ramifications my leaving would cause you. I cannot cause you grief or trouble. I cannot put you on the wrong side of the King. Thomas, I…"

"I am already on the wrong side of the King, Rosamund," he said in a voice filled with defeat.

"What say you?! You are King Henry's most trusted man! I know it to be true from what I see with my eyes and what I hear with my ears." She thought for a moment. "Is it because you have come here again so soon? Then you must not do so. Your visit last night was invaluable, but I am in a better frame of mind now. I am strong. I am …

"Powerful, loving and wise?" he teased.

She smiled and nodded but then became serious. "I will not have you risk all you have worked for, Thomas. 'Tis not worth it."

Thomas snorted in disgust. "Oh, it's worth it all right."

Rosamund waggled her finger at him. "We have discussed this before, Sir. Nothing is worth giving up your dreams."

He caught hold of her finger and looked at her. "Can dreams change?"

He confused her with his question and delighted in the fierce look of concentration on her face. "Yes, of course dreams can change. I would hope that they would become bigger, better, grander."

Thomas nodded, still holding on to her finger. "And more impossible than ever before?"

Her hand was cold and he carefully laid it in the palm of his one hand while covering it with his other. She watched his tender care. "Is it because of me that you are on the wrong side of the King? I would have you tell me true, Thomas."

He studied her hand in his. So small and delicate. Such tiny nails and wrist. Soft and fragile to his hard and calloused hand. Her skin was so smooth. He ran his finger up the inside of her wrist along its fairest, silkiest part, and he felt her shiver. "Tell me, Rosamund, since you seem to be so much better in understanding the ways of right and wrong." He looked up and smiled at her briefly, willing her to see the sincerity of his question before looking back down at her hand in his. "When a man swears fealty to his King, he promises to defend and uphold – even to the cost of his own life – all that the King commands. As a knight, I am charged with defending the helpless, protecting the general welfare, and upholding the enemies of God and church." He lifted her hand and could not help himself: he rubbed it against his cheek. He smelled vanilla. "What does a man such as this do when he feels the King is wrong? When he believes that he is not defending the helpless, not protecting the general welfare, not upholding those things that are pleasing to God in following the orders of the King. Tell me fair Rosamund, what should a man do? For a man who believes such as this can no longer be with the King…"

"Is it just me?" she asked in a small voice.

"*Everything is you.*"

Her other hand touched the side of his face and he closed his eyes to enjoy the wonderment of it. "I think back to that first night we spoke."

"Your wedding night."

"Aye," she sighed, "my wedding night. You knew not that I was the bride, did you?"

Thomas shook his head. "Not until the next morn, when you came down to break your fast."

"I thought not."

"I have kept you close in my thoughts and prayers since that night. Never thinking, never dreaming, never hoping." She reached up and ran her hand through his hair, moving it from his forehead, smoothing it. Her touch was wondrous. "We are taught from a small age about duty and obligations and who deserves what and when. I was told that dreams were foolishness and that love was wasteful. I was taught that what we should value most is success and power and prestige." Her fingertip traced his eyebrows and he sighed when he felt the exquisiteness of her touch on his eyelids and lashes. She traced the pattern of his nose and his cheekbones and finally the shape of his lips. Thomas thought he would die.

"Every part of me has been controlled and trained and ordered and obligated from the moment of my birth, Thomas. Except my heart. I have kept it closely guarded for it is the *only thing* I truly have to give." His eyes were still closed, and yet he heard and felt her kneel down before him, her hands now resting on his knees. When he opened his eyes at last she was looking at him with great tenderness. "Will you take my heart, Thomas? I wish no one else to have it. You are the only one I know who will treasure it truly." She leaned toward him and kissed him.

His arms came up instinctively, drawing her close, while he concentrated on returning her kiss. Had he but one wish it would be that time would stand still and he could stay just so with her in his arms. Moments later, resting her head on his shoulder, and sitting on his lap, he said, "Thank you…" but she put her finger against his lips before he could go on.

"And now it seems," Thomas heard her say softly, "we are both on the wrong side of the King."

Once a week, on Sunday afternoons, Sir Thomas traveled into the maze to Rosamund with a small cart carrying foodstuffs, clean gowns, and other items just as he had been directed to by the King. Those visits were brief and businesslike. He carried verbal messages to and from Lady Rosamund and her maid, Beatrice. Each woman, concerned about the other, sent words of assurance. On three occasions he brought missives from King Henry to Lady Rosamund. Thomas did not know what the letters contained, or even if she read them; she never spoke of them. Thomas knew of the King's continued frustration towards her, for he had also received verbal messages from the King filled with inquiries regarding her health and state of mind. Thomas did his utmost to report back factually how she fared.

Aside from this once a week duty to Rosamund, there was little required of Thomas about the Manor. He exercised his horse daily, saw to its needs, and had regular conversations with the stable master. He meticulously cared for his equipment, repairing and refurbishing it, and visited extensively with the Manor's blacksmith and amorer. His training with the small number of remaining knights most afternoons was hard and fierce and he even took on two young boys from the town in anticipation of making them ready for page duties. He was a constant visitor to the Manor's kitchens, such that there was always a plate ready for him in the buttery whenever he appeared.

He made every effort to be as visible as possible during the day, for once darkness descended he completely disappeared. To Rosamund's bower.

For Rosamund, her prison, her cage, her bower had become a magical place. Isolated from the reality of her circumstances, she allowed herself for once to be truly foolish. She stopped thinking about the future and simply concentrated on *the now*. Each evening when darkness settled in, at a time when most people were ending their busy days and climbing exhausted into their beds, her day was just beginning. Sir Thomas arrived with the moon and the stars and stayed for a better portion of the night. They laughed and talked and told each other of their lives. They discussed politics and the philosophical theories she had studied. She read books aloud to him that she thought he would enjoy – including the entire story of Beowulf. He gave her simple lessons in wielding a sword and shooting a bow and arrow. She taught him the rudiments of how to read and write. He would leave before the first beginnings of dawn when night was still at its darkest, returning to his room in the Manor. No one was the wiser.

By some unspoken understanding, they never spoke of the future, never spoke of what each did during the day. He knew not if she continued to explore the maze. She knew not of the world outside her bower. To what end? Broaching such topics would allow the harsh impossibilities of the outside world to intrude, shattering the magical place they had created. Rosamund did not miss the irony of her situation: her bower - her prison - had allowed her for the first time freedom and happiness such as she had never known. Thomas did not miss the impossibility of their situation, knowing full well the King would be returning eventually.

Woodstocke Manor
Royal Residence of Henry II, King of England
Oxfordshire, England
January, 1164

Chapter Fifteen

Their magical time lasted just over two months before the outside world made claim to them once again. The King's summons for Thomas to join him in preparation for upcoming battle and to secure adequate arrangements for Rosamund, came far too soon. *Or far too late*, Thomas realized bitterly.

Thomas went to her in daylight on a day that was not Sunday, heedless of who saw him or who would see fit to question him. He headed purposefully through the gardens toward the maze, completely at a loss as to what he would say to her or how he could comfort her. *Hell, he needed something reassuring to tell himself.*

Still, after all the times he had traveled to her bower, he did not know the way by heart, always carefully heeding the King's specific instructions. He searched inside the leather vest covering his tunic for the precious piece of silk on which the path was drawn. He kept it with him always, close to his heart, terrified of loosing it.

She was not in her bower garden. He pushed himself through the hidden exit, found the silver thread, and followed it. Thomas walked a fair distance before the horrifying reality – that of getting lost – occurred to him. Good God, what would he do? He'd hack the damn maze down with his sword, that's what he'd do. The silver thread lead him completely out of the maze, without utilizing one door. He found himself staring in amazement at the face of a lion. *A lion?*

"Good afternoon to you, Sir. Aren't you thankful that the King sees fit to cage his more fearsome creatures in pens that have no exit?" Turning, he saw her sitting, smiling, on an arbored bench very similar to the one in which she had first read him Beowulf. She finally began to laugh at his expression.

"Rosamund," he stood frozen on the garden path, "what are you doing?"

She grinned at him, closed her book, and stood. She was bundled up against the cold, and the tip of her nose was bright red. "Reading, as usual. I do it every afternoon in this spot when the weather and the sun cooperate." She inclined her head toward the lion. "He doesn't seem to mind my company, and on occasion he seems quite pleased to hear me read aloud."

"How long have you know the full way out?"

"We agreed not to discuss that."

"I'm asking you now."

She sighed. "It took me nigh onto three weeks. The more I thought about it, the more it made sense to me. The doors they are just part of the puzzle. How could he have gardeners come in and care for the maze if they needed keys to do the doors? I suspect that this is just one of a number of exits – I'd warrant there to be at least four." She looked at him. "And I suspect that the path he gave you to follow has some rhythm or reason to it as well since he seems to know it so well by heart. Have you figured it out?"

He shook his head and walked over and sat down on the bench. As she sat down next to him he handed her the precious piece of silk. "Why have you not left, Rosamund?" He thought of the news he had to tell her. "You should have."

Rosamund looked up from studying the silk and smiled at him teasingly. "And miss the opportunity of your company? Nay, I think not." At his stricken expression, she reached over and took his face in her hands - the silk was cool and smooth against his cheek - and kissed him lightly, on the lips. "Thomas, *I love you.* 'Tis long past when I could just up and walk away from what I have with you. My heart told me to stay and see this through, and so I shall. I will not loose one moment more than I must in being with you. You are my source of happiness. *Why would I go?"*

Thomas could not resist Rosamund's nearness and leaned towards her to kiss her once again, slowly. But he also could not resist speaking the truth, "To be free," he said against her lips. "You must seize the opportunity when you can."

She frowned at him and moved, handing him back the piece of silk that showed the path. Her eyes were sad. "You have news. You would not come like this had you not. When does he return?"

Thomas could not help himself, and pulled her into his arms and kissed her. They had many nights when they never touched, trying desperately to maintain a manageable detachment from each other. It was another area that they sought to avoid because the consequences were so grave.

She returned his kiss, wrapping her arms around him and dipping her cold fingers into the warmth of the back of his neck. When he finally ended the kiss, she said softly, "That soon?"

He leaned his forehead into hers and shook his head. "No, I have been summoned by him. I am to secure a new guard for you and join him for the impending battle that looms in the near future."

She schooled her expression to be calm. "I see. When do you leave?"

"I am to make all haste to Shrewsbury to begin coordinating the assemblage of troops. The sheriffs of London have authorized the spending of large sums for fitting out mercenaries from the Low Countries. The plan is to make Shrewsbury an arms dump and outfit a large number of infantrymen, for the King knows first hand how disadvantageous his mounted knights are in the Welsh hill country. King Henry, it seems, intends to settle the Welsh problem once and for all. He has even hired a fleet of Norsemen from Dublin to join the fight." Thomas looked at Rosamund, embarrassed. "The King has rewarded my faithfulness and loyalty by putting me in command of a large contingent of infantrymen. And it would seem that it is I who will command things until the arrival of the King."

"So you leave today?"

"It will take me at least until tomorrow to make all the necessary arrangements."

"Ahh, yes, my keeper. I forgot." She could not keep the sarcasm from her voice.

The look of pain that crossed his features instantly made Rosamund regret her words. He touched her face and said earnestly, "Tell me what you wish me to do, Rosamund. You know my loyalty is now bound to you. I will do anything you wish. *Name it.*"

"Oh, Thomas, how I love you! At the risk of all you have dreamed of here it is, right before you! Surely after this campaign and your assured success in battle the King will reward you with lands and title." Rosamund turned his face to look at her. "It is an answer to my prayers, love."

He pulled away and snorted in fury. "There is no victory in the sacrifice of *you* for my dreams, Rosamund," he said through clenched teeth. "Think you that I can truly settle down with the King's reward while he rides off into the sunset *with you?* My honor and my word have sunk to shameful depths, but there is a limit, *even for me.*"

She ignored his fury and his sarcasm. "Is it not good that at least one of us achieves some measure of happiness? Is that not what true love really is – the ability to be happy through the joy of the one you love?"

Thomas grabbed her by the shoulders and shook her. "True love should not hurt more than death, Rosamund. *It should not.*"

She leaned up and kissed him, seeming to try to draw some of his fury from him. "Will you come tonight?" she said against his mouth.

"How can I not?"

She left him standing in the arbor and disappeared into the maze.

He arrived at her bower later than usual, overwhelmed with all the responsibilities preparing for his departure entailed. How ironic that at a time he most wanted to be with Rosamund, his obligations would keep him away.

She looked particularly lovely tonight, and he did not know if it was true or if it was just because his heart was breaking. The cottage was warm and inviting and Rosamund had poured two goblets of warmed wine which sat at the hearth near the fire.

Thomas would not let her distract him with conversation, but insisted that she change her gown into something warm, insisting that she dress comfortably, but as practically as she could. When she questioned him he refused an answer, merely encouraging her to hurry and change.

Once she was clad in a serviceable gown, wool stockings, sturdy shoes, heavy fur lined cape, scarf, and hand muff, he fairly pulled her at a run through the maze. When they finally stood out in the cloud scattered moonlight there were two saddled horses and two pack horses tied and waiting patiently.

"Thomas, what is this?"

"I will take you away."

"Where?"

He shrugged impatiently. "'Tis your choice; Godstowe Nunnery, Castle Clifford. I know of an abbess near the Scottish border that would welcome you to her priory."

She approached him and he backed away. "Do not touch me, Rosamund, and do not argue with me. My mind is made up. You are right. If one of us is happy, then the other should be able to gain some small measure of happiness as well. I will see you free and then have some peace. God knows it's time I found some."

"Why do you not offer to go with me? Surely, once you do this deed King Henry will know of your duplicity. Your life will be forfeit. What are *your* plans for yourself? Think you I can just wave you off?"

Thomas ran his fingers impatiently through his hair. "I know not what I will do. I will get you settled and then I will make that determination. My life has become unmanageable of late. Nothing is as it seems, nothing is controllable." He nodded his head in agreement with himself. "I will make right this mess with you and then, mayhap, things will begin to improve."

"I love you."

He sighed and rolled his eyes. "I loved you *first*. You know that. Now give me your foot so I can help you mount."

"I will not leave here, Thomas."

"You will."

"I will not."

He picked her up, intending to force her into the saddle, and she wrapped her arms around his neck and began to kiss him. Against his lips she whispered, "'Tis too late, my love, my dreams are here with you, *come what may*."

Her words took all the fight out of him. Every last bit. They stood in the cold, as snowflakes began to fall around them, her feet not touching the ground as he held her.

"*What will we do, Rosamund?*" He asked in an anguished voice. "I must know that you are safe and cared for. It is killing me."

"I have always been safe, Thomas. A power greater than me or you or the King has faithfully watched over me over the course of this chaos known as my life. Look at my existence, how it has been! Look at where I have been and what has gone on around me. Should I be standing here in the arms of a man who loves me so very much? *Should I?*"

He willed her to see reason. "I love you, but I am not deserving of you. We are from different walks of life, you and I; you noble, me *bastard*, you loving and encouraging, me *killing and destroying*." He set her down gently, taking both her hands in his, desperate for her to understand the reality of things. "There is *no place we can go*. You are wealthy; I am *poor*.

You have lands and titles; I do not even have a *name*." He gestured to the horses. "*Please*, Rosamund. Let me take you someplace where I will know you are safe."

"I am safe here."

"*Hell.*"

"I will not leave you. I gave you my heart and I have taken yours."

"*Damn.*"

She pulled the pink ribbon from her hair and took his left hand in hers. Slowly she began to twine the ribbon around their clasped hands, over, under, around. She worked to carefully tie the ribbon in a knot, binding them together. Rosamund looked into Thomas' face and said, "Before God I pledge myself to you, mind, body, and soul, Thomas." She felt his hand tense as if to pull away, and she gripped his all the more tightly. "From this day forth, forever more, I am your wife and I take you to be my husband." She trailed her finger over the pink ribbon wrapped around their hands. "Pink; the color of honor, partnership." She looked up at him and smiled with tears in her eyes, "And *happiness.*"

"Rosamund, have you heard nothing I have said to you?"

"*Thomas*, have you heard nothing *I* have said to *you*?"

They stood there as it snowed around them, looking at each other, tied together with one pink ribbon. Both knew that it would hold for a lifetime.

Finally, he took a deep breath. "I hesitate not because I do not want this, but more because I cannot truly comprehend having something so wondrous given to me."

"I know."

He placed his free hand on top of their bound ones. "I pledge myself to you, Rosamund, body, soul, and mind. I will protect you with my own life and strive each and every moment to bring you joy and laughter. Henceforth and until I no longer can draw breath I call you my wife, and I shall be proud to call myself your husband. With these words spoken between us, I have no dreams that have not been made true."

Rosamund smiled at him. "We are handfasted now, Thomas. As legal and binding as my first marriage was with a priest and witnesses.

Neither the King nor the Pope can dismiss this. Come with me, *my husband*, back to my magical bower. We have one night more to pretend that things are everything we dreamed. Let us not waste another moment."

Still bound to her, he turned, untied the horses, and smacked each one of them on the rump to send them galloping off back to the stables. Then he turned and pulled her roughly to him. She let out a startled shriek. "*At last I call you mine,*" he said fiercely, and kissed her there in the cold and the snow with a passion he had worked diligently to keep at bay, "you are a treasure I never, *ever*, thought to even dream of."

When she finally caught her breath, she smiled brilliantly. "Yes, Thomas. *At last.*" She kissed him again, laughing at the awkwardness of their bound hands. "But I have thought to dream of this, for I have prayed *all my life* for a happiness such as this. Always remember this, my love: *you are my heart.* You shall carry it with you until I see you again, and I shall do the same with yours."

In the end, unable to trust any of the men remaining at the manor (he was as bad as the King, Thomas thought bitterly), he approached James the keeper of the King's animals. Would he be willing to see to the enormous responsibility of Rosamund's care and protection? James assured him he would do all Thomas instructed and anything else that Rosamund asked him.

"*Anything,* James. Promise me you will not question her, just do her bidding regardless of what it is she asks."

"What if she asks for me to bring her out of the maze or give her the key?"

"I give you my word, she will not."

"All right, Sir Thomas. You have my promise. No questions asked and follow her bidding and yours precisely."

Thomas left the following afternoon. He could not risk going to see her to say goodbye. They had said their goodbyes at the dawn, but still the desire to go to her and kiss her once again... More than once he caught himself standing in the busy courtyard staring in the direction of the maze. *Get hold of yourself, man, or you will not live to see her again.* He needed to work on his focus and his control or he would not survive the first battle skirmish! Riding away from her was more difficult than the first night he watched her leave the great hall with the King, for with this leave taking he did not know if he would ever see her again.

Pray, my love. If my prayers alone have been so powerful, think what the two of us can accomplish!

All right. *All right.* Thomas would learn to pray.

February, 1164
Château de Chinon, Anjou

David Dunkeld, brother of King Malcolm of Scotland and otherwise known as Prince David, was tired to death of the Angevin court. The whole lot of them were so full of themselves with their philosophical debates, cultural discussions and artistic expression that he did not think he would survive one more day with them. How long must this hostage status go on? No one seemed to know or, for that matter care. Everyone seemed so surprised that he did not wish to continue on in this 'center of civilization' for the rest of his life... *God help him.*

Prince David's frustration with his lot and King Henry grew with each and every moment he was forced to endure. When comments were made about the King's surprisingly lengthy absence from the continent and all of the superior opportunities he was being forced to live without, Prince David laughed. Did they think that his people lived in *caves?* He could no longer keep silent and went on to describe the Royal Palace in Scotland at length, as well as Woodstocke Manor where he had been entertained by the King. He spoke of the food, the accommodations, the entertainment, the gardens, *the women.*

When he said the name *Fair Rosamund,* all who sat with him at the table inquired as to who she was. He described her glorious ginger hair, her eyes as blue as the sky, her wit and wisdom, her sense of humor.

"And *where* does this paragon of femininity reside, Prince David?" The imperious tone of Queen Eleanor brought him to an abrupt halt.

Prince David looked at the Queen and hesitated for the briefest of moments before answering. "Her family owns a small castle in the

Marches, between the oft disputed land of Wales and England, Your Majesty."

"That does not seem to be the answer to my question."

"I met her when my brother and I were summoned to Woodstocke Manor to pay homage and swear fealty to His Majesty the King."

Queen Eleanor, gave him an impatient glare and asked the assemblage, "Has my question been answered or not?"

"No, Your Majesty," came the reply from many. All eyes settled on Prince David, watching him squirm.

Prince David swallowed and said, "Lady Rosamund resides at Woodstocke Manor as a ward of the King, Your Majesty."

"I see," Queen Eleanor said thoughtfully, "and she is married?"

"Nay, she is widowed. Her husband was murdered by one of the marauding Welsh, Prince Rhys. Her husband and all those who resided in the castle were massacred."

"And yet she escaped?"

"Aye, Your Majesty. Just she and her maid were delivered back to her family home to deliver Rhys' message and challenge to the King."

"My, my, she seems quite intriguing, does she not?" Many heads nodded. "And you say she is beautiful?"

"Aye, Your Majesty. Some would say exquisite."

"And young?"

"Aye, Your Majesty, not even a score of years."

"And the ward of my husband?"

"Aye, Your Majesty."

Queen Eleanor turned to one of her nobles, seated nearby. "How long has my husband been away?"

"Over a year, Your Majesty. And, according to his missives, he will be well and truly involved in military action there throughout the rest of this year and into the next."

She looked pointedly at Prince David. "Woodstocke is near the Marches, is it not?"

"Aye, Your Majesty."

"Perhaps," Queen Eleanor said to her retainers, "it is time I visited my husband and gave him my support and encouragement." She looked pointedly at Prince David. "I wish to experience this culture and refinement that has apparently swept across the isle of Britain in my absence. And I am most anxious to meet this paradigm of womanhood. Maybe she can instruct me in a thing or two."

As laughter tittered through the court, Prince David thought perhaps, *just perhaps*, he had achieved the ultimate revenge towards King Henry. *And he hadn't even planned it*, he thought delightedly.

At the same time, Queen Eleanor also considered the solution to a most disturbing situation, although she would not take one step without an extensive plan. She had had an inkling that something was not right. King Henry had never stayed away from her side for such a length of time, and surprisingly showed no desire to return any time soon. Oh true, his letters were filled with his frustrations over the Welsh, the English, and even the damnable Scots – one of which sat before her with a most bemused expression on his face. No, the discovery of this *Fair Rosamund* seemed to make all the disconnected pieces fit to form a very clear picture.

Queen Eleanor was pragmatic about her relationship with her husband. It had not been, nor had it grown into, a marriage of love. No one had expected it to be. It was a powerful merger of bloodlines that had created a kingdom the likes of which England and France had never seen. Inconsequential dalliances, for both her and for him, were acceptable. Why they were even expected! But instincts told her that this time, this woman – this Lady Rosamund - was someone she should not dismiss lightly.

Queen Eleanor was a wise woman. She knew her husband. And she knew women. She must not let this dalliance – she refused to call it a relationship – escalate to a level in which her position could be threatened. To allow her and Henry's separation to last such a long time and ignore Henry and this woman's liaison would be dangerous in the extreme. One king had been foolish enough to divorce her. It would not happen twice. She owed it to herself and her yet unfilled goals and she owed it to her children – born and unborn. She must not risk any thing that could endanger her position or her children's positions. Above all, this was her foremost duty.

Yes, a visit to England was long overdue. Eleanor would view her isle holdings and she would interact as necessary with those nobles who would be beneficial for her future plans. It was certainly not too early to begin establishing powerful connections with those who could support her and her children's claims to the throne.

But most importantly, she would one way or another eliminate this distraction that had kept Henry from her for so long.

Permanently.

Happiness depends upon ourselves.

Aristotle, 4th Century B.C. [21]

Battlefields of The Marches
Corwen, Wales
July, 1164

Chapter Sixteen

od Almighty, he was hungry. Thomas could not remember the last time he had had a filling meal, and had begun to have dreams of his childhood and his time under Sir Richard FitzUrse's care. Nay, Thomas thought, not dreams, nightmares. It did not ease his conscience in the least to know that as one of the King's top men, his conditions were markedly better than that of his men.

Everything should have gone well. The timing had been perfectly chosen to accommodate the unpredictable Welsh weather and the army had departed from Shrewsbury fully equipped and ready at the beginning of July. The change in battle strategy from mounted knights to large numbers of well equipped infantrymen was made in anticipation of the close confines of the Welsh forests. King Henry had struggled once in the Welsh forests, and found his mounted knights at a severe disadvantage. He would not have that happen again.

Massive expenditures were made to insure that all involved were well supplied and preparations were made for any unexpected eventuality. But in reality, gathering together a large army and equipping it was only one problem; moving it into Wales, feeding it, and bringing it to the enemy was another far more difficult problem to resolve. The King had made a particular point in seeking out the extensive expertise of his seasoned knights and barons who had dealt at length – some all their lives – with the Welsh threat. With the added fleet of hired Norsemen from Dublin, the outcome of the battle seemed a foregone conclusion.

But they had been wrong.

The weather had been unseasonable in the extreme. Four times in the higher elevations they had had to deal with snow and freezing rain *in July*. When the snow stopped, torrential downpours and biting winds had managed to keep everyone just as cold and miserable. Marching through the forests of Ceirog Valley, traveling to the strategic confluence of valleys and routes of Corwen, they had been harassed repeatedly by skirmishers and delayed by the necessity of cutting back the dense undergrowth that hindered man and beast alike. Quitting themselves from the forests had been no relief at all, for immediately they had had to contend with the boggy moors that separated them from the valley of the Upper Dee River. Men who had cursed the forests now had railed at the bogs that sucked their boots right off their feet, permanently disabled transport carts, and indiscriminately broke legs of man and beast.

After three weeks of travel – more than twice as long as had been anticipated - tempers were short, supplies were low, bellies were empty, wounds were septic, troops were loosing faith, and leaders were completely frustrated. Not once had they been able to draw out the Welsh enemy and face them in a proper battle, and yet each and every moment of every day *and* night they were continually and repeatedly attacked. No terrain offered the English any respite; the Welsh were masters of it all. No Englishman slept or even rested, certain that the next attack was always just moments away. *And it was*, only it was never the same style, never the same numbers, never from the same direction… Arrival at Corwen found the English troops disheartened and discouraged with nowhere to go but down.

King Henry was in a foul temper. Known for his explosive moods, those who had experienced one knew to keep a far distance when another was brewing. He was at a loss. The idea of retreat loomed large and real. It just about killed him. He and his army had come so far, worked so hard, and achieved *nothing*.

"You summoned me, Sire?"

King Henry looked up from the map spread out on the table before him. "What would you do if you were me, Sir Thomas?"

"Sire?"

"I want your advice."

Thomas sighed. "I feel as if we are sitting, simply waiting for another attack, Sire. The men are hungry, cold, and tired. The Welsh are playing at us like this is some annoying children's game. We know not where our enemy truly is or for that matter *who* our enemy truly is. I would send out scouts to determine where the enemy base is - *if there is one* - and then head for that. Be on the offensive! But we must move swiftly. All of us are hungry and I fear that loyalty will last only as long as the supplies. You cannot command a starving army."

King Henry looked at him for long moments and then finally said, "Will you go?"

"Aye, you know I will, Sire."

The King sighed. "Again I ask you for much, again you are willing, and again I remember I have not rewarded your faithful service." He rubbed a hand across his weary eyes. "How many will you take?"

"No more than six, three teams that will go south, west, and north."

"Choose and leave tonight."

"Yes, Sire."

Thomas chose five fellow knights, all with whom he would have gladly partnered, but ended up with his good friend, Gavin. They spent intense hours pouring over the King's maps of the surrounding areas, each choosing intended routes that could possibly lead to an enemy army's encampment. A timeframe was decided on: no more than three days. Supplies were issued to them, and they left under the cover of darkness.

It was still slow going, but traveling for two was faster than two thousand. Gavin and Thomas guided their horses slowly and carefully through the boggy moor, up slowly into the hills and back into the forests. They followed, roughly, the River Dee, knowing instinctively that an army could not exist without water. Were the Welsh army near their team's direction – South – then most assuredly it was camped near the Dee. They traveled silently all night using the cover of the dark, unwilling to risk any sound that would give away their whereabouts.

High noon found them near a rocky outcrop that shielded their backs and their horses. They ate what meager supplies they had allowed themselves, fed and watered the horses, and then curled up to get some much needed sleep.

The rain awakened them, a torrential downpour that made them bloody miserable but at least cloaked their presence even better than the dark. Horses and riders continued on, the reality of moving just as miserable as the reality of sitting still. The rain kept on all night and Thomas battled the cold that seeped all the way through to his bones. He worked to stay alert and sharp, but could not keep his thoughts from drifting to his last night with Rosamund.

His wife.

He'd told no one, not even Gavin. It was a treasure he kept to himself, unwilling to risk a knowing smirk or a ribald comment. He could not believe that *she* was *his*. He lost himself in thoughts of her as he rode through the frigid rain, clenching his teeth to keep them from chattering. *Keep her safe. Please, keep her safe. I will promise You anything, give up everything, ask for nothing but that You keep her safe. Please, keep her safe...* The prayer played over and over in his thoughts with each step of his horse and each drop of rain. On they rode through the night and into the day.

"Do you smell smoke?"

It was the first thing they had said to each other since early morn. Thomas stopped his horse, raised his nose out of his collar, and sniffed. He looked at Gavin and nodded. Cook fires. Cook fires struggling to stay alight in the downpour.

They slipped off their horses, tethered them, and silently followed their noses through the woods. At the top of the crest they dropped to their bellies, crawling slowly and steadily until they could see the Welsh army, just as cold and miserable as they were, but judging by the cooking smells a hell of a lot better fed.

"Christ," Gavin mumbled under his breath, "you think if they captured us they'd feed us?"

"We need to get back and tell The King," Thomas said, unwilling to think about his stomach.

They had made their way back to their horses, mounted, and turned when the first arrow struck Thomas in the left arm. He stifled a cry and whipped his horse into a gallop, hearing Gavin shout a warning directly behind him.

They rode like madmen, heedless of the tree branches that tore at their skin and their clothes, only trying to escape. Thomas heard Gavin's horse scream in pain and go down, and struggled to turn his mount to go back.

"*Keep going!*" Gavin screamed at him. "*Go!*" But Thomas ignored his commands. He dismounted and struggled to pull Gavin out from beneath his horse. "*Damn it, Thomas!*" Gavin gasped, "Get the hell out of here! My leg's broken and pinned. I can't get loose. *Ride and inform the King!*"

"I'll not leave you, Gavin, and well you know it," Thomas hissed. Strength he did not know he had helped him drag the horse off his friend. Blood poured from Gavin's thigh, the bone protruding starkly white against his leather trousers. Thomas swallowed convulsively, fighting back the sickness.

"Thomas, I cannot…"

Thomas pulled his gaze away from Gavin's thigh to see an arrow newly embedded in his friend's throat. He looked into the dark and rainy forest, unable to hear the enemy approach for the rain. An arrow missed his head so closely he felt the breeze of its passing. Another arrow sunk deeply into his right thigh. So this was it…

Run, Thomas…RUN.

It was Rosamund's voice that made him move. The arrow in his thigh slowed him considerably, but he was still able to vault onto the saddle of his horse well enough. He held the reins tightly in his good hand and he urged his horse forward again. *Good-bye my friend.* He rode and rode and rode, knowing that the dark and the downpour were as much a help as a hindrance. If *he* could not see or hear his enemy, then *they* could not see or hear him.

In the rain, the gloom, the fear, and the pain he soon grew concerned that he would loose his bearing if he continued. The shivering from cold and shock caused him greater pain than his actual injuries. God, he was cold. Colder than he was hungry. The only feeling of warmth was where the blood from his leg and his arm seeped out and ran down his body. Thomas finally stopped, fearful to go any further. He dismounted and crawled into a hole made from a felled tree, its roots still thick and strong enough to keep the rain out.

His injuries needed to be tended. He dealt with the arrow in his arm by breaking off the tip which protruded out the back and, after taking a deep breath, drawing the shaft out quickly. When he next became aware, he realized that he must have slept, or blacked out, for the rain had stopped and night had settled in. He tore a strip from his tunic and tied it, as best he could with one hand and his teeth, tightly across his arm wound.

He had not the strength or the courage to deal with the arrow in his right leg. Even slight exploration around the wound caused him pain he could barely manage. *Help*, he thought, and then he slept.

His horse awakened him, annoyed to still be saddled, wet, and hungry, Thomas supposed. He managed to get himself standing and gave the horse the last of the grain while he ate the last of his supplies. Might as well. He needed whatever strength he could gain. The seriousness of his circumstances came crashing down on him when he realized that he no longer had the ability or strength to mount his horse. He feared he could not *ride* back to camp, let alone walk. He was doomed.

Walk Thomas. One step in front of the other. Just ten steps. Please.

He began to walk, aided by the patient horse who snorted at first with confusion at his foolishness, and then finally settled in to the unaccustomed pace. After falling twice and dealing with the terrible battle it took to stand each time, he tied his good right arm to the saddle with the reins. After that, when he fell the horse just dragged him on.

Just to that hill, Thomas. Just to that hill and then you can rest for a bit.

One step after another. Night came and he fell into a feverish sleep, dreaming dreams that made no sense but awakened him, with his struggles causing his shoulder further agony. When at last he became aware, the sun was high and warm. He didn't quite know what to make of it.

Thomas had lost track of the days. Had it been two? Three? Four? Had he only slept one night, or had it been longer? He needed food. He needed water. He needed to get this damn arrow out of his leg. He drank rain water from a puddle along with his horse, and reveled in the coolness that slipped down his hot, dry throat. He splashed the cool water on his burning skin, only to become chilled and overcome with shivering. God, he was a mess.

Walk Thomas. You are doing so well, my love. A few more steps. Come on then.

He thanked his horse profusely for his patience and promised him a grand feast of oats and hay when they got back to camp. He was not surprised when the horse threw its head back and laughed at his foolishness. "Remember, Thomas? The King's camp had no more food for man or horse. Remember?"

"Ahh, yes, now I remember," Thomas nodded obligingly. "Will you still take me on?" His horse nodded and smiled.

He drifted in and out of awareness, never fully cognizant, never fully unconscious. When he was being dragged more than he was walking he untied his arm and fell, exhausted and feverish, and slept where he lay. Once he awakened, he tied himself to his horse and traveled on again.

At a point near sunset, when he had a moment's clarity, he and his best friend, horse, stopped near the crest of a hill. It was Corwen valley ahead – he was sure of it, the very spot where this nightmare had begun. He could not believe his fortune and took some time to assess what was real and what was not. Horse looked eager enough, but for once refused conversation.

Just over the hill....just a few more steps now, Thomas. See! I knew you could do it.

Horse moved forward and, as his hand was tied tightly in the rein, Thomas was forced to follow. The two of them stopped at the crest, both looking down at the amazing sight before them.

Thomas had made it to Corwen Valley all right. And it was empty. Devoid of men and tents and horses and supplies. The King and his army had left. Without him.

Woodstocke Manor
Royal Residence of Henry II, King of England
Oxfordshire, England
July, 1164

She had nothing left to do but pray. She missed Thomas, *her husband,* so profoundly that she physically ached. She missed his voice, his touch, his thoughts, his smile, his reassurance.

He had not communicated with her in the seven months he had been gone. Unable to write nor ask anyone else to write for him without drawing untoward suspicion, she had been dropped into a void of silence, left to her own private hell of worry. With each Sunday visit she questioned James as thoroughly as she could, eager to gain even the slightest bit of information. Were she starving or thirsty asking for sustenance to keep her alive, she would surely be dead by now.

The King had written to her, and unlike the first letters, these she had read in hopes of gleaning indirect news about Thomas. She should not have. King Henry spoke at length of his frustration regarding continual difficulties: the bad weather, the rough terrain, the *damnable Welsh bastards,* and the low morale of the troops.

After reading the King's letter, she added profound worry to her profound yearning. There were new images along with her already haunted thoughts of Thomas hungry: cold, tired, sick, hurt. Her nightmares intensified, and her worry reached a feverish intensity. She sat in her bower cage, for it no longer felt like a magical place to her, and decried her sex, her inabilities, and her *uselessness*. Rosamund had no way to write to Thomas and send him words of reassurance, making her misery all that more profound.

Pray, Rosamund, pray!

She snorted. Her life was such a shambles, so out of control, that she honestly did not know what to pray for.

Come now, that cannot be true. Think, Rosamund. Think.

Yes, she supposed that she did know what she wanted. She wanted Thomas, safe, peaceful, and brought back to her. *In that order.* She wanted this mess between her and Henry settled, peacefully, quickly, and finally. *In that order.* She wanted to live her life without fear, freely, and happily. *In that order.* Yes, that was what she wanted. *Why don't I ask for the ability to fly,* she thought bitterly.

For in all her fears and worries, it had never occurred to her that her plight could be any worse or get any more complicated. But it had, in a way that she had never, *ever* considered. Rosamund was with child. *Greatly* with child. Just one night with Thomas, *their wedding night,* and she had conceived. The irony of it all was a bitter draught to swallow. Her barrenness during her marriage had caused her untoward misery, while her fertility now assured that three lives – hers, Thomas' and the babe's - were most assuredly forfeit once the secret was out.

She had but a few more months until the babe was born. Already the child had shifted, making her daily walks through the maze slower and more ungainly. Were she residing in the Manor, everyone would have been aware of her condition, but in her cage, with only old James visiting once a week, she had managed to keep her secret.

Early prayers had been to bring Thomas home quickly upon her discovery. What had Prince Rhys said to her when she had bemoaned her failure to conceive? *I will speak with you when you are three score years old and childless, and then maybe we will both agree on your failures.* He had known.

But the King's dismal last letter had been more than two months ago. She need not think overly hard to realize the truth: she was well and truly on her own. She could not stay in the bower. She must get to someplace that would offer her safety and help *before* it was too late for her to seek it. Rosamund would speak to James on his next visit. She truly did not know what she would do, but as James was her only contact with the outside world she must make use of him.

Sunday afternoon was clear and warm a surprise most welcome given the dismal summer so far: cold, windy, and rainy. James' arrival through the door signaled the only time each week that she had someone other than herself and the birds to converse with. It was always a welcome respite.

"Lady Rosamund! How do you fair this sunny day?"

"I am well, James, and how are you? I believe that this is only the second or third time that you have not arrived here dripping wet and cold! Are you still desirous of a glass of wine?"

"Ahhh, Milady," James grinned at her, "I would never be so rude as to turn down a bit 'o your fine hospitality!"

While he wheeled the cart in to her garden and began unloading the supplies she went inside to get the tray of food she had prepared for him. It was a ritual between them; if the weather was fair they sat outside and talked, otherwise they visited by the fire.

James anxiously peered onto the tray that she carried out and grinned. "Milady, you spoil me, so you do. Look at that collection of tarts and sweet meats! If you're not careful, I'll be a coming here more than once a week!"

She gave him a smile and set the tray down in the middle of the bench near the side of the cottage. "Tell me of the Manor news." It was her standard inquiry, for she was always curious of news that would help her know when Thomas would return. Should the news be that the fighting had ended or that the King was returning, then surely she could assume that Thomas would be back soon.

"Oh, I'm staying right far away from the Manor, so I am Milady. It's chaos there, so it is, what with the Queen having arrived and all."

Rosamund stared open-mouthed at James. *"The Queen is here at Woodstocke Manor?"*

"Oh aye! Arrived like a blizzard in July, so she did, not five days ago. Turned the whole place upside down with her orders and requirements. Poor Martin is threatening to quit. Any servants that cannot speak Provencal, the Queen's high and mighty language, are not allowed to serve the guests. And every day new guests arrive – friends of the queen. I was there Wednesday past and swore I'd not show my face again until after things go back to normal."

"Has she ever visited Woodstocke Manor before?"

"Nay, never."

"Do you know what her intentions are?"

He shrugged his stooped shoulders and shook his head. "I do know that she inquired of your whereabouts. Your maid, Beatrice told me."

"Queen Eleanor knows of me?"

"Oh aye, all know of you and your bower here, Milady."

She looked at him. "And what do they say of me, James?"

His furious blush told her everything really, but she waited patiently to hear what he would say. He tried to hedge, "Oh, that ye be the King's ward, that you are uncommon lovely, that he keeps ye safe in this bower garden he built just for you." He sat up straighter and puffed out his chest. "'Tis a privilege that I hold the key."

"Does everyone know of me and your care of me?"

James thought for a moment and then nodded. "Aye, anyone who wishes to be *in the know.*"

"I see." They sat in companionable silence while he continued to eat and then she finally said cautiously, "I would ask a favor of you, James."

James nodded, his mouth full of tart, working to swallow so he could respond. "Ask away, Milady. My instructions were very clear, I was to provide you with 'anything you asked' and was not to question you as to the whys or wherefores."

Rosamund looked stunned. "Who's directions were those?"

"Sir Thomas bid me to provide you with anything you asked, no matter what it was. When I asked him what I should do if you asked for me to give you the key so that you could leave he gave me his word that you would never do so. I gave my word that I would do as he instructed me."

Thomas, you watch out for me even from so far away. If what James said was true then perhaps her situation was not as dire as she had assumed. Why, she could simply go to the sisters at Godstowe Nunnery and place herself in their care. "No, James, I would never ask you for the key. But I would ask you for something almost as surprising. Would you saddle a mare and tie it to the lion's cage tonight after dark?"

James frowned, his face a study of concentration. After a time he said hesitantly, "Aye, Milady, I will do so on Sir Thomas' instructions. And though I am most curious, I will not ask any questions."

"Thank you, James." She reached over and touched his hand. "I do not wish to cause you any harm or trouble. You have been a good and faithful friend to me from the moment we met."

He blushed scarlet. "'Tis always been a pleasure, Milady."

After James left, Rosamund could not ignore the sense of acute danger. It was a new emotion, and she agonized over whether it was danger for herself or for Thomas. Her prayers reached a feverish pitch as she readied the few possessions she would take with her to Godstowe. *Keep him safe, Lord; bring him home, Lord; Keep him safe, Lord; bring him home, Lord.* She had altered but four gowns to fit her changing shape, and chose serviceable, comfortable shoes. She wished to communicate to Thomas but could not see how she could accomplish such a thing without risking the messenger. She would see to her and the babe's safety first and then worry about contacting Thomas.

The night was warm, the stars were bright, and the moon was full when she stepped out into the garden with her satchel. She gazed for a moment at the cottage and what the place had meant to her. In this place, her cage, she had found love and happiness such as she never thought to have. She would dwell on the good rather than the bad.

"Tis a lovely cottage, I must say," said a voice heavy with French inflection.

Rosamund spun around to see Queen Eleanor standing regally before her with a trembling James in the background holding a flaming torch. Tears slipped quietly down his face.

"James," Rosamund said soothingly to him, "'tis alright. Do not fret."

He bowed to her, "Thank ye, Milady," but still continued to cry.

As gracefully as she could manage, Rosamund bowed to the Queen. "Your Majesty, welcome to my bower prison." She stood and stared at the woman before her. Rosamund took a deep breath, held it, and then let it out slowly. Surprisingly, she felt no fear.

"Quite a lovely prison this is," the Queen said.

"But it 'tis a prison nonetheless. I have been here against my will since last November, when the King saw fit to leave me here 'for my own protection'."

"Protection from what?"

"He says from others who will not be so 'patient and understanding and respectful of my misdirected standards of nobility and honor'."

Queen Eleanor looked at Rosamund for long moments and then grimaced, "It seems my husband the King was not particularly happy with you when he left."

Rosamund shrugged and put down her satchel at her feet. "He said he knew not what rattled around in my frustrating mind, so yes, I would agree with you that he was not particularly happy with me." She looked the Queen directly in the eye. "But by the same token, *I* am not particularly happy with *him* either."

The Queen gestured to the bag at her feet. "Are you going somewhere?"

Tell the truth, why not? Her head said. "Yes, I leave my prison tonight."

The Queen looked surprised and then glanced back at James standing with the torch still held high. He had stopped crying, but now simply stood trembling. "Have I interrupted some deep, dark plan?"

"Nay," Rosamund said. "James knows naught of my intentions. He has been faithful and kind to me these past months, but has never once betrayed his word nor his King." The Queen looked skeptical. "There is more than one way out of this prison, Your Majesty," Rosamund assured her. "Would you like me to show you?"

Queen Eleanor waved an imperious hand at James. "Make yourself comfortable, Old Man; the Lady Rosamund and I would have a private talk." To Rosamund she commanded, "I would see your bower," and walked past her into the cottage.

Rosamund stood at the door while the Queen inspected her prison and did not move until the Queen sat in one of the wing chairs by the fire and said, "I would have some wine." After having delivered the wine, Rosamund sat in the opposite chair and waited, staring at the fire.

"The descriptions of your beauty do not do you justice," Queen Eleanor said after a time.

Rosamund made a face. "My looks are a curse to me. Men seem to think they are an open invitation to take every advantage they can of me. Would that I could have been plain and dull and boring. Perhaps my life would have been more manageable."

The Queen chuckled. "Such bitterness in one so young."

"I speak from *vast* experience."

The Queen took a sip of her wine. "I would hear your story before I decide if I need to kill you."

Rosamund hesitated for a moment before saying, "What could I possibly say that would make you believe me, Your Majesty? Everyone else always assumes the worst."

"Because," said the Queen, "I know for a fact that the King has been gone from here since November, just as you have said. So the child you carry now *cannot* be his. Either James is much more than he appears or there is a significant amount of information I still need to know. I hate making rash decisions; it shows such poor taste."

So Rosamund told the Queen her story from start to finish. The only information she withheld was Thomas' identity and any facts that would cause the Queen to suspect him. "I am a woman of God, who all her life has sought to honor what is right and good. I wish to be the best woman God would have me be, yet it seems that here I am, a prisoner of the King simply because of this. I believe that my life cannot become any more complicated and yet it continues to do so. Now you sit here challenging me to tell me my story, and should you not be satisfied with what you hear you threaten to kill me."

"You have uncommon courage."

Rosamund snorted loudly. "I have uncommon *faith*. I know that to remain on this path in my life that God has set, I am assured His guidance and protection. To deviate means death."

"Where do you go tonight?"

"Godstowe Nunnery. I spent some time there as a child. The sisters will care for me until the child is born."

"What of the father?"

"My *husband*," Rosamund said with great force and conviction. "I will not speak of him for I fear for his safety and would protect him with my life as he would do for me."

For the first time, the Queen showed true shock. "The King would take and imprison the wife of another man? Is that what you tell me?"

"The King is unaware of my marriage, Your Majesty," Rosamund assured her. "He believes me to be a widow and nothing more."

"What will you do once the child is born?"

Rosamund sighed. "*Nothing* in my life has gone as planned, Your Majesty. *Not one single, blessed thing.* You ask me what the Lord has in store for me. Only He knows, for I surely do not. I will do as I have been doing: pray and pray and pray."

"Do you love the King?"

Now it was Rosamund's turn to be shocked. "As I told him most plainly, I am a loyal subject, and beside the Lord God Almighty, serve and honor no other sovereign but him. I gave him my oath and pledge on this."

She looked at the Queen. "But I *do not* love him as he would wish me to. I love my husband and only him."

The Queen took from her pocket a glass vial, filled with a dark liquid. "This I would have had you drink were I to think that you were truly a threat to me and mine. But circumstances are not what I was led to believe. I believe you Rosamund Clifford de Verne. You need no longer have concern of me." She stood, uncorked the vial and poured the contents into the fire. She placed the empty vial on the hearth and walked to the door. "Light the torch, Old Man! We leave here now."

She turned to Rosamund, "Go to Godstowe Nunnery. Let the nuns care for you and the child, for that is the best solution for now. But you must see this through to the end, Rosamund. Do not run away in fear, for then you will never truly be free. Finish what must be done before you travel on to find your love and your future. *Keep your faith*; it is your best weapon."

"It is my *only* weapon. I have been accused of being a dreamer but take great pains to not be called a fool. I will continue to follow this path the Lord has set out for me. I have come too far to change now. I have had my brief time of love and happiness. In all honesty, I did not believe that I would have been so blessed to have even that."

Queen Eleanor stared at Rosamund. "We are much alike, you and I. Strong. Opinionated. Pragmatic. The distinction between us seems to be faith and love, for these two qualities are almost tangible about you and completely lacking in me. I would encourage you not to loose your faith nor give up on that love, for perhaps it will gain you this happiness you so desire. Sophocles said, 'One word frees us of all the weight and pain of life: That word is love.'[22] I have always scoffed at that opinion, finding little substance in such an erratic emotion, but perhaps, *perhaps* Lady Rosamund, *you* may yet prove me wrong."

Queen Eleanor smiled for the first time since she had arrived in Rosamund's bower. "My thanks to you and your honorable standards, Lady Rosamund. It would so have spoiled my evening to have had to kill you as I had planned." And with that she left, with James leading the way out of the maze.

Godstowe Nunnery
Oxfordshire, England
October, 1164

Chapter Seventeen

The babe was a miracle she never thought to experience. A son, perfectly formed, with the biggest blue eyes she had ever seen and a shock of black hair that stood up all over his head like someone had just given him a most terrible fright. He was ever quiet, ever content, happy to be fed and cuddled and loved and talked to. It seemed that he had want to study her as intently as Rosamund had want to study him, and they sat for hours just looking at each other. She named him, William for it seemed to sound to her a strong name and to the best of her knowledge there was *no one* in her family who bore the name. With the child's birth, Rosamund was determined to start anew and sought to monitor every avenue to ensure this – even something so elemental as a name.

The sisters were delighted to have Rosamund back with them with her son. In the weeks that led up to William's birth and the subsequent time after, it was an opportunity for Rosamund to restore, revive, and rediscover the person she knew she could be: strong, faithful, and confident. At Godstowe Nunnery she was able to reflect on the circumstances of her life that had brought her here. In retrospect, things that had seemed most desperate were in reality the avenues to her greatest joy. The murder of Humphrey had brought her to the King, the King imprisoning her in the bower with Thomas as her guard had brought her love, her pregnancy had convinced the Queen where certainly her words never could have. Surely it was as the scriptures promised: *The Lord, He it is that doth go before thee; He will be with thee, He will not fail thee, neither forsake thee; fear not, neither be dismayed.*[24] In every dark instance, the Lord had been there before her preparing the way, and had she deviated but once from His path she would have been lost forever. And how close those times had come! She gazed down at William's face, his expression one of studious concentration, and her heart fair exploded from the love and gratitude she felt to God for His faithfulness.

Rosamund closed her eyes, took a deep breath, and let it out slowly. *Keep him safe, Lord, bring him home, Lord; Keep him safe, Lord; bring him home, Lord.* Might she ask for this? Aye, she would with every waking thought and breath.

When the babe was but four weeks old a royal summons arrived which required Rosamund's presence at Woodstocke Manor. She was to return forthwith. All her best intentions of confidence and strength teetered on a precipice that overlooked a bottomless pit of despair. No longer was she just herself, she was William's mother, and the enormity of what she had to lose almost crushed her. She would not hear of leaving the babe behind with the sisters. He was Rosamund's child, her responsibility, and she seriously doubted whether she could maintain her sanity should she be separated from him. William would go with her and she would allow God to direct their fates.

The royal messenger allowed her time to pack, and had arrived with two extra horses, one for Rosamund and one for her belongings. They left within the hour. Having said good-bye once again to the sisters, she could not turn to look at them as she rode away. She did not trust herself not to collapse into an hysterical, weeping mass.

The level of activity at Woodstocke told her immediately that King Henry had returned. Everywhere there were men, horses, supply wagons, children, women, and barking dogs. The possibility that Thomas was within shouting distance caused a scream in her throat that made her head ache with its suppression. *Keep him safe, Lord; bring him home, Lord; Keep him safe, Lord; bring him home, Lord.*

But she was not shown into the great hall. In fact, Rosamund did not even enter through the main portal, but instead followed the messenger in through a back entrance and up a dark set of servant stairs. She was shown to a suite of rooms and left alone without explanation or direction. Rosamund did not hear the door lock, but knew she was confined.

She fed William, laid him down to sleep in the center of the enormous bed, and went to stand by the window and wait. And pray.

Rosamund was summoned in late evening to the Queen's sitting room. She went alone, a servant having been sent to remain with the babe. The Queen wasted no time. "The child lives, I understand."

"Aye, Your Majesty, I have a son. His name is William."

Queen Eleanor eyed closely. "The King and his troops have returned from a disastrous time in Wales. They have been back for nigh unto two weeks. Has your *husband* contacted you?"

Rosamund's heart began to hammer. "No, Your Majesty. Aside from your summons, I have heard from no one." She swallowed her panic. "My husband was unaware of my whereabouts."

"Was he aware of his progeny?"

"No, Your Majesty."

"You will go to the King now. He already has unreasonable fury towards you and your disappearance although he strives well to hide it from me. You will tell him of your deception. You will reveal the identity of your husband and you will tell him of the child so that the King understands the extent of your duplicity. He must know what you are truly capable of so that he can rid you from his head and, his heart once and for all. Finally, you will tell him nothing of my involvement with this."

Panic began in her stomach and extended throughout her body in a paralyzing wave. "Your Majesty, I cannot, I, I…fear for my babe, I…," she stuttered, the panic making it for her to breathe.

"You *can*, Lady Rosamund, for the very reason you give me now. Your child. Should you refuse to do my bidding *now*, and in the style in which I have commanded, you will *never see the child again*. Already he has been taken from this Manor, and without my help you will never see him again. You will tell the King, should he ask, that the child has been hidden for you fear for its life." The Queen shrugged. "All of this is true, so you need not concern yourself that you are lying."

Her legs ceased to hold her up and she crumpled to the floor at the Queen's feet. "Please, Your Majesty, do not take my child, *please*."

"Then pull yourself together, Lady Rosamund. Dry your eyes, wipe your nose, exhibit decorum, and do as I have bid you do."

"How do I know that you…"

"I will stop you there for I have concern that you were about to question my integrity. I am many things, young woman, not all of them good. But above all, I am a *woman of my word*."

"I fear for my husband's life, Your Majesty," Rosamund pleaded. "You ask me to choose between my child and him."

Queen Eleanor shrugged. "That is not my concern. That was *yours* before you began this mess that has become your life. I am only interested in readjusting the King's thoughts so that they will be in a direction that is in *my own* best interests." The Queen assumed a look of complete boredom. "I know for a fact that King Henry is in the library as we speak. If you hurry, you will be able to catch him." Rosamund had been dismissed.

It took her long moments to compose herself enough to begin to think about what she needed to do. She needed to cease crying, wipe her face, and get up off of the Queen's sitting room floor. It took her more time to accomplish that.

At the door, Rosamund turned to the Queen. "How will you get my child back to me?" and the grief that welled up in her over Thomas' welfare was so profound for a moment she thought she would be sick on the fine carpet. She took a deep breath, held it, and then let it out slowly.

"You worry what *you* must do. I will concern myself with what *I* must do."

Rosamund unconsciously straightened her back and lifted her chin. The Queen watched her. "I would have him raised by the sisters at Godstowe rather than my family should something happen," *to me*, she thought but did not say. Could not say.

The Queen stared at her but did not answer.

"I will not leave until I have your word on that," Rosamund told her.

"You *order me?*"

Rosamund shrugged. "What do I have to lose? And you have much to gain."

Queen Eleanor smiled. "Ahhh, we are so alike, you and I." She nodded. "If necessary, the child will be sent to Godstowe. You have my word."

Rosamund left without another word. She took no time to order her thoughts or to fix her appearance, but made purposeful steps to the library. She entered without knocking and found the King sitting in a wing chair before the fire with a bottle of port in his hand. He did not look up when she entered.

"Your Majesty."

He looked up at her voice, and the fury she saw in his eyes caused her to take one step back, then two. He placed the bottle of port down, stood, and began to walk toward her. She retreated further, absolutely terrified by the rage she saw on his face. The wall kept her from retreating further, and still he came toward her. When he was but one step away, he stopped and stared at her for a long time, taking in her tears and distraught countenance. When he had seen all he wished, he raised his hand and slapped her so hard across the face that she was knocked to her knees. Her ear rang and she tasted blood. Wisely, she did not stand up.

"Leave me before I kill you." He said softly and went back to his chair and his bottle.

"I would tell you some information that you need to know about me, Your Majesty."

"I need to know the time and date of your death."

Rosamund stood slowly, and used the sleeve of her gown to blot the blood she felt trickling from her lip. *My babe, my babe, please keep him safe, please keep him safe.* "I have fallen in love with someone here at the manor, Sire, and while you were away he and I…"

He looked at her as if she were absolutely mad. *"Have you a death wish,* Fair Rosamund?" he said to her as spittle flew from his mouth at the force of his words.

You will tell him of your deception. You will reveal the identity of your husband and tell him of the child so that the King will understand the extent of your duplicity.

She swallowed. "And while you were away, he and I became handfasted, and I have born him a child just this past month and…"

"ENOUGH!" the King roared, and he heaved the bottle across the room where it exploded against the wall. He advanced again towards Rosamund, yet she did not retreat this time. She did, however, cringe, draw into herself, and begin to sob. *My babe, my babe, please keep him safe, please keep him safe.*

"Who?"

She knew what the King asked. Now was the time that she would betray Thomas, and in doing so, most probably lose everything: him and the babe. She looked up at the King with tears streaming down her face and said, *"Thomas."*

"Thomas?! Thomas? THOMAS?" The King's eyes took on a fanatical look for moments and then he threw back his head and laughed. He laughed for a good long time. Just as he would begin to calm, he would say Thomas' name again and start the hysterical laughter again. Enough time passed that Rosamund calmed herself somewhat and regrouped as best she could.

King Henry wandered over to a tray that held food and drink and poured himself another glass of port. Finally, appearing somewhat composed, he approached her and leaned forward so that he was just inches from her face. "Sir Thomas is *dead*, sweet Rosamund. The Welsh killed him. Seems like you're a widow again, Milady. I suppose you'll be staying here again with me after all, correct?" and he took a sip of his port, winked at her, and began to laugh again. Rosamund did the only thing that was left for her to do. She fainted.

It was Beatrice she first saw when she came back to consciousness. For a time Rosamund was puzzled as to where she was, why she was there, and what she was doing. The ache in her breasts made her think of William, and then it came flooding back to her. She sat up with a sob. "Milady, I brought you some wine."

Rosamund was back in her rooms, all signs of William gone. She grabbed Beatrice's hand in a death grip, "Beatrice, know you where they have taken the babe?"

Beatrice turned and looked frantically around the room. "Babe?! What babe, Milady? I did not know you were released from the maze until just moments ago when I was summoned to your side."

Rosamund began to sob in earnest, hysterically trying to gather her thoughts. Beatrice sought to calm her. "Milady, you must rest. I know not what has happened here this night, but you seem most upset and must try to compose yourself. You'll make yourself sick."

Rosamund gripped Beatrice's shoulders. "I must see the Queen. Beatrice, go and tell her that I request an audience with her. *Now. Please.*"

Beatrice looked at her with regret shaking her head vigorously. "I cannot, Milady. The Queen forbids anyone to attend her or even address her who cannot speak Provencal. I have been working in the kitchens and the scullery since her arrival, forbidden to even be on this floor until this moment."

Rosamund swung her legs off the bed and stood on wobbly legs. "Then I shall go myself."

"Milady, you cannot!"

'Watch me," Rosamund said through gritted teeth and was gone out the door.

The Queen refused to see her, and after wandering the Manor for a time listening for the cry of a child with no success Rosamund returned to her rooms and collapsed into an exhausted sleep. Beatrice watched her mistress while she twitched with nightmares.

For a day and a night Rosamund remained in her rooms, refusing food and drinking little. Her heart ached, her head ached, her breasts ached, and her jaw ached. She did not wash or change or respond even to Beatrice's numerous attempts to draw her out. As the second day came to an end, a servant arrived with a note. It took all of Beatrice's persuasion to get Rosamund to finally open it and read it.

You will be summoned tonight. Prepare to do battle once again. This will be the final skirmish. —E.

"What does it mean, Milady?" Beatrice asked her.

Rosamund looked at her lady's maid. "It means I need a bath."

How the Queen knew that King Henry would summon her that evening she did not know, but he did. Rosamund appeared before him in the solar, a room that was not as public as the Great Hall. He was attended only by the guard that had brought her to him. She stood before him and said absolutely nothing.

For the longest time King Henry ignored her, sipping his port, looking at papers on the table near him, and gazing off into the fire. She stood there as silently as the guard who stood at the door behind her.

"I've decided I no longer wish to keep you," he said at last. "In fact, I've decided that I want you nowhere near me. You are to leave my presence, tonight. Sir Brian will escort you."

"You release me? I am free to go?" Rosamund was incredulous at the possibility. And rightly so.

The King shook his head. "Nay, I *banish you.* Sir Brian takes you *out of my sight.* You are to leave my Kingdom, *forever,* as you are no longer welcome or privileged to be here. Rather than kill you, as I am so wont to do, I will spare your life." King Henry looked at her, sarcasm dripping in every word, "I do so because I believe, in the end, you will be more miserable alive than dead. Your *husband* is dead, I have been assured that your child is *gone,* and you are *all alone*. This will be done *now*, in the dark of night, so that no one knows your treachery and my discomfiture. *Fair Rosamund* will disappear. No one will ever truly know the story of what became of her. You will simply be remembered as a woman who caught the eye of the King for the briefest of intervals and then vanished like so many others before you. " He looked at the guard at the door. "Take her."

She felt a firm grip on her elbow as she was guided out of the solar. Beatrice stood in the hall with a satchel and her cloak. "They will not let me go with you, Milady. They say you are to go alone," and Rosamund's maid began to cry.

Rosamund was having grave difficulty processing everything happening to her. "'Tis all right, Beatrice. You will be better cared for here than with me. I know not even where I go." She looked into the inscrutable expression of the guard. He simply stared back at her, still gripping her arm. She looked back to Beatrice. "Thank you for everything my friend," she felt the tears begin to choke her, "I will remember you in my prayers."

The guard dragged her forward, took the cloak from Beatrice, and put it around Rosamund's shoulders. As he bent to pick up her bag, she embraced her maid. "Farewell to you."

The night was cool. Two horses were saddled in the dark courtyard, one an obvious warhorse and one a smaller mare. The guard helped her mount, mounted his own horse, and led them out of the courtyard and into the dark forest. Rosamund never looked back.

They rode in silence for quite a time until she finally asked, "Do you have a destination that you take me to or do you just plan to take me to a point and leave me?"

"There is a destination, Milady. 'Tis not that much farther and then we will stop for the night." He turned to look at her then. "Rest easy, Lady Rosamund. I was a good friend of Sir Thomas'. I know that he thought highly of you and I would honor his memory by doing right for you. I will follow the orders of my King, but I will also see to your safety."

Thomas. At his name, a pain so intense doubled her over in the saddle and she leaned forward to lessen the agony. The horse's mane tickled her cheek as she lay against it letting the hot tears flow. *My love, so little time we had.* She sniffled and wiped her streaming face on the edge of the cloak. This sorrow she felt must surely kill her.

They came at last to a small hamlet, no more than a place set up between two crossroads. There was a small inn with candles still lit in the windows. Sir Brian helped her dismount and gestured for her to go inside while he cared for the horses. Numbly, one foot in front of the other, she walked forward.

It was a small common room, quiet and uncrowded, with but one of the eight or so tables occupied as Rosamund stepped inside. She sat on the nearest chair at the first table, staring at the fire. She heard Sir Brian order a hot meal and ale for the both of them. Shedding his cloak, he came and took hers and finally sat down across from her.

"Where do we go from here, Sir Brian?"

"Where do you want to go?"

"Were you not given instructions?" she said with surprise.

Sir Brian shrugged. "I was told to get you the hell out of the King's life, as far as I could possibly take you. That leaves quite a choice as far as I'm concerned."

"Thomas spoke one time of an abbess near the Scottish border that he thought would welcome me."

He nodded, slowly. "I know of where he spoke." He looked at her curiously. "The two of you talked of your ... leaving?"

Rosamund could not speak of Thomas. *She could not.* She swallowed and looked across the room without answering. If she opened her mouth she would scream.

A woman at the only other occupied table was staring at her, and after an uncomfortable few moments Rosamund turned away. God only knew what she must look like, plus the fact that she was traveling alone with a royal guard. When their food was served, Rosamund could not help herself and stole a glance at the woman again. She was still looking at Rosamund. Just as Rosamund felt she should mention the woman's attention to Sir Brian, the woman stood and began to walk toward them. "Sir Brian." He looked up from his meal to her and she nodded toward the woman who approached. He stood, turned and put his hand on his sword.

The woman stopped some steps from their table. "You are Lady Rosamund Clifford de Verne?"

Rosamund looked questioningly at Sir Brian. "Who has an interest?" he finally responded.

"Queen Eleanor."

"*Queen Eleanor?*" Sir Brian said incredulously.

Rosamund stood slowly. "Yes, I am Lady Rosamund."

The woman turned and nodded to the man sitting at the opposite table. He rose, picked up a basket and began to walk slowly toward them. Rosamund began to walk and then almost ran, pushing aside the chairs, moving faster and faster. She heard Sir Brian behind her say, "Lady Rosamund!" obviously concerned for her safety. *Please, my babe, my babe, please keep him safe, please keep him safe.*

The man let her snatch the basket from him and she tore back the covers to see the precious sleeping face nestled within the blankets. "Lady Rosamund, what is it?" she heard Sir Brian's anxious voice directly behind her.

Rosamund could not resist, and lifted the sleeping babe from the basket to kiss, and smell, and touch him. With tears streaming down her face, Rosamund looked up into Sir Brian's shocked one. "Let me introduce you to William," she said with a brilliant smile. As the babe opened his sleepy blue eyes and peered into Sir Brian's incredulous green ones, Rosamund said, "'Tis my and Sir Thomas' son."

"Milady," the woman said, "the Queen wished me to remind you that she has kept her word as promised and bids me tell you thus, '*Truly your faith has saved both you and your son, but you have far to go until you are safe. Travel only west, it is your best hope.*' Then the woman curtsied, the man bowed, and they both left.

Sir Brian looked at her incredulously. "The Queen sends you *west?* To the *Welsh?*" I would caution you, Milady, that she may not have your best interests at heart! She may desire to let the Welsh finish something she wishes King Henry had done for her."

"I suspect you are right, Sir Brian. And yet the Queen knows not the full story." From under her gown she pulled out the small medallion that Prince Rhys had given her a lifetime ago. "I have a guarantee of safety should I step foot on Welsh soil. Given my present circumstances, I suppose it seems perhaps the best place for me to go."

With the babe nestled in her arms, she haltingly told Sir Brian everything. He had not one word to say but sat through the entire story with an astounded expression on his face. When she finished all she had to tell, she asked, "What think you, Sir Brian?"

He looked into the fire and took a sip of his ale, his meal cold and long forgotten. "I'll take you to the Welsh, Milady," he finally said, "to the people who have killed your husband, who was also my closest friend."

The Kingdom of Deheubarth
Home of Prince Rhys ab Gruffydd and Keyna verch Aherne
Cantref Mawr, Southern Wales
November, 1164

Chapter Eighteen

He was not completely sure, but Prince Rhys ab Gruffydd was relatively certain that there was not one single solitary person who was pleased with him. Patting the fine piece of horse flesh he was examining, his mind wandered regarding the present circumstances of his life.

His fellow countryman, Owain of Gwynedd, was furious with him for his lack of complete support in the most recent battle with the *Saeson*. Because of Rhys' choices the *Cymry* were unable to annihilate the enemy army as they had wanted to do. Because of him *Cymry* numbers were too low to draw the hated *Saeson* out and eliminate them once and for all. Because of him the enemy had been allowed to retreat, which only meant that they would regroup and return to battle another day.

Rhys' son Hywel would not speak with him. Indignant for what Hywel claimed his dishonorable behavior – breaking his word to King Henry, the tenuous relationship they were only just beginning to rebuild had almost completely unraveled. How could you explain in simple words the thoughts and emotions that were the very essence of who you were, are, and strove to be? *Yes, my word is my bond, but my people are my soul.* He had tried and failed. Hywel, his own flesh and blood, had been too long from him to feel the connection, to know the passion. Hywel was *Cymry* on the outside, but *Saeson* on the inside. Mores the pity.

His clansmen eyed him with a concern that bordered on distrust, and were Rhys to be completely honest with himself he could hardly blame them. Could they trust all they held dear to a man who had paid homage and sworn fealty to the King of the English? Not bloody likely. In securing the freedom of his son and himself, he had set his leadership power back considerably. He knew that were it not for his past reputation and his present sword he would have even greater troubles. *By all that's holy, do not give me cause to have to fight Owain or Hywel,* he thought bitterly.

"Milord!"

Rhys turned to see his most senior and most trusted man, Glen, gesture towards the far courtyard. Striding towards him in full fury was his wife, Keyna. *God help him.*

Rhys nodded to the stable master who had been showing him the latest acquisition of horseflesh: twenty sturdy mounts all courtesy of the *Saeson* army, thank you very much. He turned and made his way purposefully toward Keyna, and by her expression he mentally added his wife to his growing list of critics. What had he done this time?

Keyna was the perfect wife. Strong, intelligent, independent, and outspoken. She did well with him or without him, which was excellent given the fact that he was rarely home. Oh, he had no doubt she loved him, with a passion that could drain him almost to death sometimes, but she didn't really need him. She was a complete package all to herself: a tiny, dark haired, dark eyed, spitfire who would just as soon punch you as kiss you. As she approached him, he tensed to duck.

"Hello, my *carried*," Rhys murmured with a grin, "to what do I owe this pleasure?"

"Don't you 'my love' me, you beast. There is a *very beautiful* woman who would like to have a word with you *now*."

Her eyes were flashing, but her cheeks were not flushed so he knew she wasn't as angry as she could get. He still had a chance with her. "All right, my *very beautiful woman*, you have my undivided attention. What do you wish to talk about?" Rhys grinned at her and touched her cheek.

Keyna slapped his hand away. "Not *me*, you fool, some *Saeson* woman with a babe and a military escort. She wears a Deheubarth pendant around her neck that she says *you gave her*."

Rhys looked towards the far courtyard. "Lady Rosamund is *here*?"

"Oh, aye, she's here alright. Brought in by one of the eastern patrols not moments ago. Do I need to loose my temper *now* or shall I wait until later?"

The strongest part of their relationship was the knowledge that they each shared; there was no one else that either wanted but the other, as they had pledged so many years before. Rhys grinned at her. "She's a beauty, is she not?"

"If you like that ginger coloring and that fair insipid skin tone."

"I do not."

Some of the anger slipped away and she grinned up at him. "I know." Keyna took his hand. "You'd best come. The hall is tense with their presence and I'll not have blood spilled on my clean floor today. We've just spent all morning making ready for Owain's arrival." She looked up at Rhys, her anger returning. "*I have not time for this, Husband.*"

He slipped his arm around her shoulder and whispered in her ear, "Might you have time for anything else?"

Dark eyes glanced up at him, accompanied by a sly grin, "You'll just have to wait and see." Rhys threw back his head and laughed.

It was Lady Rosamund, all right, escorted, to his surprise, by Sir Brian. He nodded to them both upon entering. "Lady Rosamund, Sir Brian."

Both looked tense and ill at ease, and Rhys took time to study them before he made any overtures to set their minds at ease. Sir Brian, though unarmed, assumed the air of battle readiness and had positioned himself near Rosamund, his back guarded by the wall. His eyes darted nervously, taking in the place and the people.

Rosamund looked ... *done*. That was the only word that would fit. She looked exhausted, with dark circles under her eyes. Her skin had a grayish pallor, and her expression was wane and hopeless.

The silence in the hall was profound. So many people, yet no one spoke and no one moved. "Cath," Rhys said to one of the serving girls, breaking the dangerous mood. "Bring some wine and bread and cheese for our guests." He looked at his soldiers standing alert and ready near Sir Brian. "My thanks to you men. Go see to your horses and your needs. Sir Brian is known to me and one of the men who saw to my protection while I was a *guest* of King Henry's." He looked at Sir Brian. "I am sure we have nothing to be wary of while he is here enjoying our hospitality."

Sir Brian hesitated and then bowed respectfully. "It is as you say, Prince Rhys."

Keyna followed Rhys' lead. "Please, you must be tired from your long journey. Come sit by the fire and enjoy the warmth." As she spoke, William began to fuss. "Do you have needs regarding the babe, Mistress?"

For the first time, Rosamund spoke. "Nay, he's just been fed and changed. I fear he grows impatient with the constant confinement required while we journeyed."

Rhys stepped forward. "May I?" and reached out for the child.

Rosamund hesitated for only a moment. "His name is William," she said quietly.

Rhys took the child from her and held him up high. "Hello, William," he said and the baby cooed delightedly. "Welcome to my home of Cantref Mawr." The baby burped and everyone laughed.

There were two chairs near the hearth. Keyna took one and Rosamund took the other. Colorful woven rugs lay on the hard stone floor, making the area welcoming and homey. Rhys settled on the rug nearest

Keyna and carefully laid William down next to him. The baby waved his arms and legs and cooed contentedly.

Rhys studied the babe intently, and then with a start of surprise looked at Rosamund and said with certainty, "This is Sir Thomas' son."

"Yes, we were handfasted almost a year past," Rosamund said in a whisper. "However, Sir Thomas is dead and I have been banished by the King." She managed a tremulous smile as she looked to Keyna and then said to Rhys, "T'would seem my predicament is even worse than when you last saw me, Sir."

"Sir Thomas is dead?" Rhys glanced at Keyna. "How do you know?" He asked Rosamund carefully.

It was Sir Brian who answered as Rosamund could not. As they sipped wine and ate bread and cheese, Sir Brian shared details with Prince Rhys and Lady Keyna that even Rosamund had not heard. Having been part of the scouting teams that had been sent out, he had first-hand knowledge of the circumstances that led up to Thomas' disappearance and subsequent death.

"So the King pulled the army out before they returned?" Rhys asked frowning in thought.

"He had little choice, Sir. Rations were exhausted, your people continued to attack, and more than five days had past. It was assumed that as neither the northern nor the western scouting party had found any signs of the Welsh army, that Thomas and Gavin had, to their own detriment. By that time it was too late for the army to act. It was agreed that it made more sense to retreat to save lives rather than attack and perish." At Rhys' frown, Sir Brian said, "Would you have done differently, Sir?"

Rhys snorted. "Absolutely."

"'Tis always easy to make suggestions after the fact," Sir Brian said bitterly. "I was there. Sir Thomas and Sir Gavin were my closest friends. I agreed with the withdrawal."

"I'm sure my husband did not mean to offend," Keyna said.

"Of course I did," Rhys said impatiently to Keyna. He looked at Sir Brian, "But by the time you were to Corwen, the outcome was already decided. Do you know that they call the path your army took 'The English

Road' because it is always the way in which you approach us?" Rhys shook his head at the folly of it. "You *Saeson* are always so damned predictable."

Rosamund had taken on a pallor close to death. Keyna noticed, rose and knelt before her. "Milady, we have a comfortable chamber where you could rest and refresh. Your things have already been carried up. Would you allow me to show it to you?"

"I would be most obliged," Rosamund said as she bent to pick up William and rose to follow Keyna.

Rhys watched the women leave and then looked at Sir Brian. "She looks like hell."

"She's been through hell," Sir Brian said, and relayed the story Rosamund had told him.

"Who's man are you?" Rhys asked him after moments of silence between them.

"King Henry's, have no doubt, Milord. But Thomas was my friend and would have done the same for me. I see no conflict in bringing her here to you. Hell, she had no other place to go. I was at a loss where to take her and what to do with her until she showed me your pendant. Had King Henry known, I doubt he would have banished her. He wanted her to die, I've no doubt of that."

"Nor do I, Sir Brian." Rhys said. He walked over and leaned against the fireplace. "Prince Owain arrives here tonight. We have many issues to settle amongst ourselves, most importantly as to whether we are truly friend or foe."

He looked at Sir Brian. "I did not fight in this last battle between us, but did allow my men to go if they wished. Many did, but not all. In doing so I have pleased no one; Prince Owain feels that I have betrayed him, and my son Hywel feels that I have broken my oath to the King." Rhys snorted. "King Henry is a sly fox, for he has caused me great consternation having forced me to give homage and swear fealty to him. My word is my bond and I have never forsworn an oath. Furthermore, he has returned to me a son who is more English than Welsh, yet he is my oldest son and I love him. I have caused my wife enough grief and worry to last a lifetime and I grow tired of the fight. Prince Owain senses this in me as do my people."

Rhys sighed. "I sense that King Henry is the opportunity I need to bring peace to my kingdom. Were I to continue the fight, my son would not carry on in my stead. He has told me so. He does not believe in the cause; he lacks the passionate hate required. Hywel will never command the respect nor the following that I have, so he will never be the strong leader needed to keep the peace. If I do not settle this thing between our countries once and for all, *now*, then at my death I fear there will be bloodshed as we have never known. History shows what happens when a leader does not leave a strong legacy. Your own King Henry the First left a legacy of civil war that you are still recovering from. I do not want that for my people.

"Owain comes tonight to try to convince me to throw all my efforts in for one last great battle with the *Saeson*." Rhys looked at Sir Brian. "I will anger and disappoint him for I will refuse. Openly, this time. While I will not fight with the *Saeson* against my *Cymry* brothers, I will also not fight alongside them any longer. I do not know for certain what path this will lead us on, but I have better hope of peace and prosperity than the one we have been traveling on for these many, many years.

"I am the last of the line of Gruffydd ab Rhys' sons. I have watched three older brothers die in a conflict they did not start and could not end. With me, perhaps things will be different. I desire that for myself, my family, and my people."

"Why do you tell me this?" Sir Brian said after a time.

"Because," Rhys said, "I've fought against you, traveled with you, eaten with you, been guarded by you, and quite frankly come to respect you, Sir Thomas, and Sir Gavin. My time in captivity showed me things I did not think possible," he grinned, "that *Saeson* can be fair and reasonable when given the opportunity. I seek to prove the same to you about the Welsh."

Sir Brian smiled and bowed. "I am at your disposal, Prince Rhys."

For Rosamund, it felt wonderful not to be moving, on a horse, or sleeping in the open. The simple pleasures of life: a pitcher of water, a chamber pot, and a straw and tic mattress, made her feel like she was in the lap of luxury. *Then* a bath arrived, and she thought she was in heaven. She bathed, napped, and tended to William. And prayed. She had much to be thankful for, and she made a point to acknowledge her blessings in her prayers.

Lady Keyna had gone out of her way to welcome Rosamund and make her feel at home. Rosamund liked her enormously for she spoke her mind, seemingly honest and forthright. After Lady Keyna's initial cool welcome it was a relief to know that Rosamund had not made a grave error. A young girl, Gwen, had been sent up to attend to her and the babe's needs. For the first time in months Rosamund felt the stress of the circumstances of her life lessen *just a bit.* Maybe, just maybe, she might survive after all.

Gwen pressed the only gown she had that was clean. Beatrice had packed for practicality and warmth, not to impress and dazzle. She had been thankful for that as they had traveled along the English roads and then through the dense Welsh forests. Now, as she gazed at herself in the peering glass, she wished for more glamour. She tied her hair in a ribbon and made sure that the *Deheubarth pendant,* as Lady Keyna called it, was displayed.

"Best go, Mistress, dinner was about to be served when I came up."

"Are you sure, Gwen, that you can stay and watch William?"

"Aye, Mistress, Lady Keyna told me to do such. She's instructed me to stay with you and sleep in the adjoining room. I am at your disposal."

"You'll call me if he cries? I've just fed him and he should be content for some hours but you never seem to know with him. Some days, he'll eat every chance he can get."

"*Go* Mistress. I've cared for six brothers and sisters, and though I have no babe of my own yet, I'm well and truly skilled. You have my word that I will come for you should he cry."

With one more hesitant glance at William and Gwen's hand firmly on the small of her back pushing her out the door, Rosamund headed down toward the hall.

Lady Keyna had told her about Prince Owain's imminent arrival, so she was not surprised to see him in the crowd of people being seated and getting ready to eat. A servant hurried to Rosamund's side and escorted her to the head table next to Lady Keyna. "You do me a great honor, Milady, seating me such. I am more than happy to sit at a lower table."

"Nonsense, my husband has told me much of you. I owe you a debt of gratitude that I can never repay."

"'Tis not true, Milady."

"Rhys also told me you were more modest than you were beautiful. I see he is correct."

Rosamund felt uneasy and looked up to see the penetrating stare of Prince Owain. He inclined his head. "Lady Rosamund, I did not think I would ever have the pleasure of your company again."

"Nor I yours, Prince Owain."

"You find the role of King Henry's mistress no longer to your liking?" he said conversationally as he plucked a pheasant leg from the platter in front of him.

The blush that she felt stain her cheeks made her almost as angry with herself as she was at him. She would not be embarrassed for something she had no control over. She was so terribly tired. "Since you seem so curious, let me set the record straight. I *never* found the role of the King's mistress to my liking." She made an effort to dismiss him.

"I am pleased to hear you say so."

Rosamund could not help herself. "Why?"

He shrugged. "You are an uncommon woman. I had a hard time attributing *common* behavior to you. Now I know the truth, and it better fits the image I had of you."

"And what image was that?"

Owain shrugged, all of a sudden appearing uncomfortable. "Intelligent, resilient, opinionated, independent - not the type of woman who would be easily swayed by Henry's flowery words and bought with his abundant gifts."

"My, my Owain, it seems you've done a fair bit of thinking about the lovely Fair Rosamund," Prince Rhys said with a smile and a hearty chuckle. "I never would have thought you would have a kind word to say about any *Sais.*"

Owain allowed a small smile. "I guess there is always a first time." He looked at Lady Rosamund. "Why are you here, Milady?"

"You will all think I am here because I have no other place to go and part of that is true. But a while ago, Prince Rhys invited me to come here and begin again, away from the troubles that were already consuming my life." She looked down at her hands, folded in her lap. "I would have gone then, for the opportunity of a new beginning had *great* appeal. But I could not risk the chance of bloodshed for such a selfish reason.

"I stayed, and consequently lived through the very greatest joy and the very greatest sorrow of my life. The heartbreak I have now would crush me but for the gift God has given me to balance out the sorrow. He seems to know exactly how much I can bear before I fall apart! I am greatly complimented by your description of me, Prince Owain, and yet a Woman of God is the quality most important to me."

"You no longer consider yourself a failure?" and she turned to see Prince Rhys' smiling eyes.

She blushed again. "No, Prince Rhys, on that subject I have proved capable after all."

Prince Owain looked well and truly puzzled. "What is the gift that God has given you?" he could not help but ask.

Rosamund gave Owain her first true smile of the night. "Why, did you not know? I have a son. A beautiful baby, healthy and strong."

Prince Owain's face registered absolute shock. "You bore King Henry a son, and he let you *leave*?"

"Nay, I bore my *husband* a son, Prince Owain, much to the King's fury."

"Her husband was Sir Thomas," Prince Rhys volunteered, looking pointedly at Prince Owain, "one of the King's most trusted knights. He was wounded and apparently killed in the most recent battle between our people."

"Your greatest sorrow," Prince Owain said now understanding.

Rosamund looked up at him, her eyes filled with unshed tears. She took a deep breath, held it, and let it out slowly. She lifted her chin. "My greatest joy was to find love and my greatest sorrow was to lose it so quickly. My son helps me face the sunrise *or* the rain each morning. Whatever comes I can handle. That is God's faithfulness to me.

"And I firmly believe that God's caring has extended to bringing me here to this place. I was born and raised in the Marches. I know the people and the land. I know that life here is harsh and unyielding, and that to succeed you must work and sweat and sometimes bleed. But whether it is Welsh blood or English blood or even Scottish or Irish blood, we all truly want the same thing, do we not? To love and be loved, to have a few moments of happiness, to have the opportunity to do a good day's work using the most of our talents, and to be able to look at oneself in a peering glass from time to time and be pleased with what we see."

Rosamund smiled at Prince Owain. "I can do that *anywhere* I am; I just need to find someone willing to give me the chance to do it." She looked at Prince Rhys. "This man has made me the offer, and I have accepted. He will have my undying gratitude for giving my son and I this opportunity, and I will make it my goal that he never, ever regrets his actions. With a little bit of persistence, *and much prayer*, I should be able to accomplish this."

Rosamund nodded her head most emphatically. "I will make the most of the opportunity God has given me and be ever grateful for it."

The meal was enjoyable. She realized it had been a full year since she had enjoyed the liveliness of a mixed group of people talking, laughing, and arguing. It was nice to feel, even vaguely, that she belonged again. She smiled occasionally, ate, listened and just sat and enjoyed the feeling of not having to worry. For now.

Gwen came and got her as the evening ebbed, carrying William who was furious with hunger. She excused herself and went back to her rooms intending to make it a night. But after William was asleep, she had no desire to stay. Perhaps it was the loss of tension. Maybe her body had so long adjusted to fear and anxiety that it would need time to familiarize with this new-found peace.

Peace. Yes, that was the feeling. She stood by the window, gazing at the clear night sky, brilliant with stars. Pacing about the room, she suddenly felt hemmed in, trapped. Gwen was more than happy to listen for the babe while she went for an evening walk. She grabbed her cloak and slipped out the door.

She went to the parapets, a favorite place for her before her life became unmanageable with dictatorial kings, imprisoning mazes, and suffocating stress and grief. She stood there, breathing the crisp night air, letting the wind blow through her hair. She closed her eyes, took a deep breath, held it, and then let it out slowly. She let her thoughts wander to Thomas, and for the first time she was not torn apart with grief. "He's lovely, Thomas, you should see him," she said quietly to the moon and the stars. "He has your eyes and your dark hair and," she choked back a sob and a laugh, "your appetite!"

The tears came again and she didn't fight them. "Not enough time," she whispered and took a shuddering breath, "not enough time." She closed her eyes and let the treasured scenes play through her head, reading, laughing, talking, kissing, loving. The memories were wonderful, but far too few.

She heard someone ascending the steps and quickly made an effort to dry her tears. She turned to look at the doorway and waited long moments; it seemed the person was in no hurry. The apparition that appeared at the top of the stairs was a vision, it must be she thought, for it was impossible that it was truly Thomas standing there before her. When she made a move toward him he put his hand up stopping her, seeming to catch his breath. He stood there leaning heavily on a walking stick, breathing deeply, looking thinner and older and ... *beautiful.*

The look of love and longing he gave her took her breath away. "I met a beautiful girl up on the parapets a lifetime ago," he said once he had caught his breath. "She had jewels in her hair and at her neck and sewn into her gown. I thought she might be a queen. When Prince Rhys told me that I might find the same beautiful girl in his own castle I thought I must surely be dreaming."

"*Are* you a dream?" she whispered finally, afraid to approach in case he vanished.

Thomas shook his head. "Nay, I'm just a captured *Saeson* soldier, wounded and broken beyond repair, unwanted by his King and country except for hanging. Worse off than when you last saw me." He walked slowly and stiffly toward her, "All because I loved a girl to the exclusion of all else." And then he touched her, just a finger to her lips, disbelieving what his eyes told him. "*How are you here?*" he said with wonder. "When Rhys came and told me, had it been anyone else but him I would have thought it was a cruel joke. But he told me that you had arrived, just today, with Brian as your escort. *How can this be?*"

He wanted her to explain how she had gotten from England to Wales, while she needed to know how he had gone from dead to living?! "They told me you were dead…," was all she could manage.

"Almost," he said wryly, "but not quite." He moved slowly to the corner and sat with his back against the wall. "I cannot stand on the leg for long, but it gets better each day." He made a face, "I half suspect that Rhys waited until you were up here just so I'd have to work the leg on all the damned steps." He looked at her. "We have much to say to each other, but come and let me taste and touch and smell you *please.* I've dreamed so long of you, I would see how good my memory serves. Come, let me see how well you have kept my heart for me and I will show you yours."

Rosamund ran to him then and threw her arms around him, laughing and crying and kissing him. He stilled her finally to give her a proper kiss, one that took her breath away. After a long while, she pulled away to speak. "More," he said and pulled her to him once again to get lost in the kissing.

He stopped kissing her long enough to say, "I feel like I have spent my entire life dreaming and wanting you, Rosamund. Always from a distance, always as an impossibility. Can it really be that you are here and we are safe and … free? *Can it be?* I fear that if I let you go, you will disappear and I will be alone and wanting once again. Let me tell you this, should it be so: *it would kill me.*" His arms tightened possessively around her. "I will *never* get enough of you, but I intend to have great fun trying."

She was lost in the moment, disbelieving of his arms and his kisses and his words. *It cannot be real,* her practical mind said to her, *it cannot.* Fear of awakening from this moment made the need to understand the whys and hows almost overwhelm her. Thomas must have felt the same. "How are you here, Rosamund, *how?* The King would never, ever let you go. He said that so many times and with such determination. *How?*"

"Oh, no," she shook her head, "you will tell me *first.*"

So he did. And all the while he talked he touched her, fingering her hair, her lips, her arms, her waist. Thomas shrugged. "I only know what they tell me, and they don't tell me much because they still don't really trust me. I was one of twelve soldiers captured and held hostage by Rhys' men. In those early weeks, I was overcome with fever and infection in my leg." He touched her cheek. "I know you never ceased praying for me, for all who saw me and cared for me said it was only by a miracle that I survived, let alone with both my legs." He looked at her with wonder. "Was I the man who doubted you when you told me about the power of your prayers?" And he took the time to kiss her again in the moonlight.

He smiled. "Never one to miss the opportunity to gain a coin, the Welsh ransomed us, contacting King Henry to let him know who and what they had. I had the highest credibility, for by my armor they knew me to be a knight, not just infantry. They read to me the letter, Rosamund, that they received from King Henry, and I made a point to remember every word they read. It said, '*For the lives of the eleven loyal infantrymen we gladly pay you fifty gold sovereigns, and for the head of the knight named Thomas we pay you one hundred.*' Rosamund gasped.

He looked at her with a haunted expression. "It was then I realized that the King knew of us, and I so feared for your life."

"How are you still alive then?" she said in awe.

He snorted. "I wonder that sometimes." He got a twinkle in his eye. "I suspect that as the King paid *in advance* for my head, perhaps, being the practical Welsh that they are, they thought, 'Why not keep the gold and further defy the King by keeping him alive?" Thomas couldn't resist and kissed her. *"God, I will kiss you forever.*

He continued. "Rhys also forbade my death. Said it was a waste. Told them all that I had a strong back and, if nothing else, I could be of good use to cleaning the cesspits. Privately he asked me why the King would want my head. When I refused to answer, he asked me if it had something to do with the spice vanilla." At her puzzled expression he said wryly, "We had a fight about that once before you see." He reached behind her neck to draw her close and inhaled deeply. "Were I well, we would have had another fight and well he knew it. That was the answer he needed."

Rosamund murmured, "Rhys told me, before he left, that there were not many *Saeson* he could call honorable, but you were one." At Thomas' surprised look, she smiled. "I agreed with him."

"That was before the King left and put you…"

"In the bower," she finished. "Yes, I know."

He touched the side of her face, *"How are you here?"*

"Beside telling me that he thought you were honorable, Prince Rhys also invited me to leave with him the night he departed."

"What?!"

She smiled. "He is not one to follow the way things are always done. He challenged me to go with him and start anew. *Not* as his mistress, just as a woman desperately in need of a new beginning." She looked directly at Thomas. "I would have gone but I feared that there would be renewed bloodshed over my disappearance. I could not have lived with that, so I stayed."

"We would not have…," but Thomas could not finish, the enormity of never finding and knowing her choking him.

"Yes, had I gone we would not have found this love we have between us. I have thought *many times* how very close you and I came to never meeting, never knowing each other. It only assures me that what we have between us is something God wanted almost more than we." She kissed him. "As hard as that is to believe," and grinned.

Rosamund took Thomas' hand and kissed it, then continued to hold it in both of hers. "I told the King of us and he delighted in telling me that you were dead. I realize now it was the start of his determination to seek revenge. I do not know the order of things between the truth and the lies. He banished me, Thomas. Bid Sir Brian to take us from his sight and from his holdings. Brian, loyal to you, saw no wrong in taking me to the Welsh when I asked him to."

She shrugged. "I thought in the end, why not? Prince Rhys bid me come and guaranteed my safety should I wear this," and she showed him the Deheubarth pendant. "He promised never to rescind the offer, and there was no place else for me to truly go."

Thomas studied it intently. "I saw this ... on our wedding night," he looked at her and grinned, "but got too caught up in *other things* to ask you what it was." He frowned, his mind figuring out the details of it all, "How did the King learn of us, Rosamund?"

She studied him in the moonlight, "I had no choice," watching for understanding but there was none. *He does not know of William!* "What has Rhys told you of my arrival?"

Thomas shrugged. "Not much. He never seems to tell me much. I was kept separate from the other hostages once the King's message was received. I never saw any of them again. I was too weak to pay much attention, really. When I realized they were not going to kill me, I made the most of a very bad situation. They seemed not to know what to do with me. They didn't trust me, Rhys wouldn't let them kill me, and they couldn't seem to get rid of me." Thomas smiled at the humor of it, "It was somewhat funny, really." He ran his fingers through his hair and looked out into the night. "I have been here before, Rosamund, prisoner in an unfamiliar place. I know to make myself useful and not to alienate anymore than I have to. If they will let me, I am willing to work and be of assistance. The Welsh are a practical people. When I offered to work to repay them for the food and lodging and care they had given me, they were more than willing. It helped make the time pass and kept me from getting lost in the hopelessness of my circumstances and going mad. Just recently, they've allowed me to attend some hunts. 'Tis good exercise for my leg, and better than sitting around feeling sorry for myself and worrying myself sick over you. I went on a hunt today and it fare killed me with this leg. When I returned late this evening, Rhys found me in the stables." Thomas snorted and shook his head. "I would not believe him at first. Rhys worked long and hard to convince me that he spoke the truth. I began to truly believe you were here when your maid told me you were not in your room but had gone for a walk. This was the first place I checked."

"He told you not of … what I brought with me?"

He frowned. "Yes, he said Sir Brian brought you, and I am anxious to see him."

Rosamund became tremendously agitated all of a sudden. "*Stay here. Do not move. I shall be right back. I must go get something to show you. Promise you will not move.*"

Thomas' face showed concern. "What? What is it? Tell me." When she stubbornly shook her head no and pursed her lips he nuzzled her neck. "Kiss me, and then I'll promise you I will not move." He received his kiss.

She returned minutes later and he was sitting on the parapet wall gazing at the moon in the same manner as when she had first met him. She stayed somewhat in the shadows and said, "I did not come alone, Thomas. Beside Sir Brian, I traveled with another." She stepped into the moonlight. "This is William." She stepped still closer and kissed Thomas on the mouth and breathed against his lips, "*Your son.*"

"*My son!?*"

Rosamund nodded, tears trickling down her cheeks. "It was a bit difficult to hide our time together considering…"

Thomas reached out and took the babe. Father and son stared at each other with identical expressions of intensity, with identical blue eyes and black hair. After a few moments, William gave Thomas a big, wet, toothless grin.

Thomas looked at her as tears made slow paths down his cheeks. "*Oh, my God,* Rosamund, look at what a magical thing you have done!"

Rhys was sitting in the hall before the fire with Keyna looking more than smug with himself when the three of them entered, Thomas' long hair was firmly gripped in one of William's chubby hands. "I knew you would show up sooner or later, and Keyna and I just couldn't wait until the morning." Rhys stood and offered his chair to Thomas. "Here you pitiful excuse for a soldier. Sit."

Thomas glared at him and remained standing. Rhys sighed. "He has *no* sense of humor, you know, Lady Rosamund." She merely smiled at him and continued to hold tightly to Thomas' arm – the arm that held their son.

Rhys tried again. He looked at Keyna. "What am I to do, wife, with this motley collection of displaced humanity? In my old age, am I to operate a poor house?"

"Sounds like a grand idea to me, husband," Keyna said with a smile, used to his provocative ways.

"I will not take handouts," Thomas said.

"I will not give them," Rhys shot back.

"I cannot, in good conscience, work against my country in word or deed," Thomas said.

"Is this the very same country that has offered me one hundred gold sovereigns for your head and banished your wife and son from its shores?"

"The very same and well you know it."

Rhys walked over to the hearth and tossed another log into the fire. "You have earned my respect, Thomas. *You need not fight for it.* You have chosen to love a fine woman, you have remained loyal to a King who does not deserve it, and you have let your conscience determine what is right or wrong despite what others insist." He walked over to Thomas and came within a hand's breath of him. Rosamund felt her husband tense beside her. "You have earned my respect, Thomas, because you are *just like me.* I look at you and I see myself. I watch you and I watch myself. I listen to you and I hear myself. I understand your struggles and your passions."

He walked over to his wife and extended his hand. She rose, walked short steps to him, and took it. Rhys spoke to Thomas but looked at Keyna, "I am done with fighting, Thomas. I seek to forge a new path between my people and yours. I will need men, *and women*, who are intelligent enough and forward thinking enough to question the ways in which things have always been done, and instead seek to find the path *that will succeed.*

"I want someone at my back whom I can trust, who does not fear to challenge or contradict me, and yet has these same goals in mind because he has loved ones to protect. Someone who will strive to succeed at *all costs.*"

Rhys turned to Thomas. "I ask you, Thomas, can you be that man? I have asked no other, for you are my first choice."

Thomas looked at Rosamund, and her smile was filled with love and pride and *hope.* He took William, untangled his fingers from his hair, kissed him, and handed him to Rosamund. Then he stepped forward toward Rhys and began to kneel.

"Nay!" Rhys shouted. *"Enough of this.* Stand, give me your hand and speak to me face to face so that I can look you in the eye and you can do the same to me. *You are not a better man than I, Thomas, and I am not a better man than you.*"

Thomas extended his right hand and Rhys took it. With his left hand, Thomas clasped Rhys' forearm and Rhys followed suit. "I join you on this new path," Thomas said, "with great pride and conviction. *I am your man, Rhys.* You are never to doubt it."

Keyna turned and looked at Rosamund. Their faces mirrored each other's expectations and happiness. She reached out and took Rosamund's hand, drew her to where their men stood, and placed their clasped hands on the men's. "And *we,*" she said in a loud clear voice, *"are proud to be your women.*"

When as king Henry rulde this land,
The second of that name,
Besides the queene, he dearly loved
A faire and comely dame.
The Ballad of Fair Rosamund, 17th Century A.D. [26]

Actual Facts

Yes, there really was a Rosamund Clifford, so beautiful that she was known as 'Fair Rosamund'. And her avaricious father, Walter FitzRichard (who changed his name to Walter Clifford) encouraged her to become mistress to King Henry II.

But it was the fictional Thomas whom I imagined first when I began to write the story. As his character developed, I just liked the person he was *so much* that I wanted him desperately to find everything he wanted *and more*. I wanted him, in the end, to have more than he had ever hoped or dreamed, because life *can be* that way. So often, the medieval times are romanticized with handsome knights and beautiful ladies who meet, fall in love, and live happily ever after. That was hardly the truth. As I searched through British monarchies, looking for a time and place to settle Thomas,

I happened upon the account of King Henry II and Fair Rosamond, and I thought *now here's something I just can't pass up.*

The facts surrounding Rosamund and the King segue into legend and folklore quickly, making it the perfect story for any historical fiction author to write. I enjoyed having the King say to Rosamund, *'Fair Rosamund will disappear. No one will every truly know the story of what became of her. You will simply be remembered as the woman who caught the eye of the King for the briefest of intervals and then vanished like so many others before you.'* Which is all too true today. No one knows the true story and never, ever will.

King Henry II, who ruled England from 1154 to 1189, was by most accounts an excellent king. He was organized, intelligent, and ruthlessly determined to reestablish England to the glory it had achieved under his grandfather, King Henry I. W.L. Warren, in his biography *King Henry II*, wrote, "Given the framework within which Henry II chose to operate, his achievement is remarkable. That any man should have tried to rule such wide and diverse dominions ... was an astonishing piece of impertinence. With no means of communication swifter than the horse, without the aid of maps and gazetteers, with, at first, only rudimentary means of enforcing his authority, and with no rational body of law or a corps of trained administrators, he set out to establish law and order."[27] Even those in power during his time thought highly of him. Wrote the Bishop of Lisieux in March of 1165, 'He is great, indeed the greatest of the monarchs, for he has no superior of whom he stands in awe, nor subject who may resist him."[28]

His reign was framed by the chaos of his country which had endured ten long years of civil war, the constantly problematic Welsh to the west, the ever difficult French to the east, the unpredictable Scots to the north, *and* the growing controversy between Henry and the Church which culminated with the brutal murder of Archbishop Thomas Becket in 1170. When King Henry bemoans the burdens of his obligations to Rosamund that night in the maze you could almost feel sorry for him ... as I have Rosamund do, albeit briefly.

Rhys ab Gruffydd was the leader of the southern kingdom of Wales during the reign of King Henry II. He was the last surviving one of four boys, all who died brutally in the constant Welsh/English battle that was the way of life at the time. He was captured in battle and brought back to Woodstocke as prisoner and his son – Hywel - was held for many years as hostage but was finally released by King Henry II as a show of good faith. Rhys did eventually become a trusted ally and agent of King Henry II and achieved such a favorable status that he was given the title 'Lord Rhys'. At the end of his life in 1197, he had been an active participant in war and politics for sixty years, and had been the dominate ruling prince in Wales for more than forty years.[29]

King Henry II was married to Eleanor of Aquitaine, the greatest heiress in Western Europe. Just eight weeks after her annulment from King Louis VII of France, she and Henry II married. She was thirty and he was nineteen. In the first six years of their marriage she had five healthy children, four of them boys. Eleanor was "a remarkable woman, surrounded all her life by an aura of romance and scandalous rumour."[30] I found numerous sonnets singing her praises. One of my favorites was by a German poet who wrote, *Were the world all mine, From the sea to the Rhine, I'd give all away, If the English Queen, Would be mine for a day.'*[31] She did indeed lead her own army of soldiers in the Second Crusade, intent on saving the Holy Land from the Saracens. She was only twenty-five at the time! In the later years of her marriage to Henry II, Eleanor sides with two of her sons (Richard and John) in a plot to overthrow Henry. She spends her remaining years of marriage imprisoned and only finds freedom once her sons begin to rule. Whether she and King Henry II ever found love with each other, they certainly were aptly suited in personality and temperament.

There were various speculations about the when and where in which King Henry II and Rosamund first met. Some felt that they met when she was just a child, while others firmly believed that they became involved after Eleanor ceased to bear Henry any more children. (Henry certainly made no effort to be faithful to Eleanor, as there are numerous known mistresses and bastard children. Why, by some accounts, Henry even saw fit to 'try out' son Richard's intended bride to assure that she would be tempting enough in bed.) Other sources definitively state that Rosamund bore the King two sons, Geoffrey, who became the Archbishop of York, and William, who became the Earl of Salisbury. But other sources, who argue different dates in which they were involved, strongly feel that there were no children from the relationship.

And then there was the maze. Supposedly located at Woodstocke Manor, now the home of Blenheim Palace near Woodstock, England, the only thing still remaining is 'Rosamund's Well'. Was there really a maze? It depends on what you read. The stories of one hundred and fifty doors, silver threads secretly trailing the way in and out, and Queen Eleanor forcing Rosamund to drink a bottle of poison in a jealous fit of rage makes for a wonderful ... story. But fact? Again, who knows?

But what if the entire legend of the maze were true? What if King Henry loved this beautiful young woman so very much that when he traveled (and he did extensively throughout his reign) he sought to keep her safe by placing her in the center of this complicated labyrinth so that no one could cause her harm. He would put her in her richly furnished and amply supplied bower garden and then go away. For months. Maybe Years. And leave her. Alone. Isolated. When I thought it through, my mind screamed *What kind of love would that be?!* Maybe King Henry would have been happy with that arrangement, but I find it hard to believe Rosamund would be.

The Ballad of Fair Rosamund has one stanza that has King Henry saying, "And you, Sir Thomas, whom I truste, To bee my loves defence; Be carefull of my gallant Rose, When I am parted hence." That's how Thomas got his name in the story (I started out liking the name 'Walt'). My fictional Thomas rose above and beyond all the adversity of his beginning. He's a bastard who doesn't know anything about his family or his heritage, and yet he has an intrinsic goodness that everyone seems to recognize. He's sincere, he's honest, he's honorable, he's loyal ... and yet it's those qualities that begin to weigh heavily on him when Rosamund comes on the scene. Not because his love overshadows them, but because he cannot justify what he sees his King doing given what he knows is right and wrong. He's the thinking man's good guy. In the end he has to realize, as he drags Rosamund out of the maze and is determined to take her away at the cost of probably everything including his life, that being honorable doesn't mean you follow blindly and never question, it means doing what's right even when the price is higher than you can truly pay. Rosamund, dealing with her own version of the very same issues, is his perfect soul mate, even though their love and any future together seems a complete impossibility.

Women of that day (as in many other days!) were by and large pawns in the political intrigues in which they lived. Marriages were *rarely* for love, especially among the nobility, but always to forge alliances and gain advancements. It was all about who you were, who you knew, where you planned to be, and how you were going to get there – no matter the cost. As I had Rosamund describe to Sir Thomas the terror that every bride and unmarried woman felt, the enormity of the plight most of these women faced overwhelmed me.

One of the saddest things I read in my research for the book was the declaration written by Marie, Countess of Champagne, *who was Eleanor of Aquitaine's daughter* by Louis VII, which said, *We declare and we hold as firmly established that love cannot exert its powers between two people who are married to each other, for lovers give each other everything freely, under no compulsion or necessity, but married people are in duty bound to give in to each other's desires and deny themselves to each other in nothing.*[32] There in a nutshell was the reality of married life in medieval times. It was not pretty.

Medieval women were tough. They had to be in order to survive. What means they used to survive, be it avarice, deception, benevolence, hatred, love, or faith was up to them. I gave Rosamund faith. A huge faith, set as a child by her beloved Aunt Helen, and then nurtured and tested and proved over the course of her life. Her faith made her honorable to her obligations as a young woman such that she was dutiful in following through on her first marriage, but it also made her principled when she was faced with the unsanctioned relationship with the King.

This story, mixing a little bit of fact and a lot of fiction, was meant to illustrate the reality of God's faithfulness and the rewards for us should we choose to follow in His directed path. In many ways, as it is in real life, Rosamund's faith made life more difficult at times. But in the end that faith made the rewards all that much greater. She stayed the honorable course, passed through the many fires unscathed, and ultimately had a glorious reward; Thomas, William, freedom, and hope. Was it all worth it?

Rosamund would say it is. And for those of us who walk daily in that spiritual realm, we would say it was all worth it, too.

> *And we know that God causes everything to work together*
> *for the good of those who love God and are called according to his purpose for them.33*
> Romans 8:28

Cast of Characters

Thomas

> Born 12 October 1133
> Page to Sir Richard FitzUrse, knight of King Stephen
> Squire to William FitzRobert of future Earl of Gloucester
> Knight of the Realm

Rosamund

> Born 16 September 1148
> Father is Walter FitzRichard, also known as Walter Clifford
> Mother is Margaret Isobel Tosney, sister of Earl Roger Tosney, owner of Castle Clifford

Marries on 14 August 1161

Humphrey de Vern, Earl of Hereford and Essex

> Born 20 June 1101
> Owner of Goodrich Castle in Herefordshire

Beatrice

> Rosamund's lady's maid

Brian

> Friend and fellow knight of Thomas

Gavin

> Friend and fellow knight of Thomas

Maxwell

> Rosamund's brother Nathan's tutor

Nathan

> Rosamund's brother
> Born 9 February 1140
> Father is Walter FitzRichard, also known as Walter Clifford
> Mother is Margaret Isobel Tosney, sister of Earl Roger Tosney, owner of Castle Clifford

Prince Rhys ab Gruffydd

> Known as Prince Rhys or Lord Rhys
> Leader of the southern tribes of Wales
> The Kingdom of Deheubarth, Cantref Mawr, near Carmarthen
> Married to Keyna verch Aherne
> Father is Gruffydd ab Rhys
> Brothers: Anarawd ab Gruffydd, Cadell ab Gruffydd, Maredudd ab Gruffydd (all died in conflict with England)

Owain of Gwynedd

> Known as Owain "Fawr" ab Gruffydd, Prince of Gwynedd
> Leader of the northern tribes of Wales
> The Kingdom of Gwynedd, Caernarvonshire, Wales
> Father is Gruffydd ab Cynan

King Henry II

    Known as Henry FitzEmpress, Henry Plantagenet, Count of
Anjou, Duke of Normandy, Duke of Aquitaine

    Born 5 March 1133.

    Mother is Empress Matilda, daughter of King Henry I.

    Father is Geoffrey Plantagenet, Count of Anjou.

Marries on 18 May 1152

Eleanor de Poitiers

Known as Eleanor of Aquitaine, Duchess of Aquitaine

Born 1 April 1122

    Father is William X, Duke of Aquitaine

    Mother is Aenor Aimery

    Eleanor's children by Louis VII, King of France: Mary of
Champagne, Alice Capet

    Eleanor's children by Henry II, King of England: William
Plantagenet (1153), Henry Plantagenet (1155), Matilda Plantagenet
(1156), King Richard I (1157), Geoffrey Plantagenet (1158),
Eleanor Plantagenet (1162), Joanna Plantagenet (1165), King John
(1166)

Book Timeline

Date	Historical and Story Events
1066	Clifford Castle built by the time of King Henry II. The Castle is owned by the Tosny Family.
1068	Henry, 4th son of William I, is born. (Henry I)
1087	King William I, also known as William The Conqueror, dies.
1087-1100	King William II, son of William I, also known as William Rufus, was King of England from 1087-1100. He was born in 1056 in Normandy, France and died on August 2, 1100 at age 45 of a hunting accident. He never married or had children.
1100-1135	Henry, fourth son of William the Conqueror ruled. His titles included King Henry I, King of England (1100-1135) and Duke of Normandy (1106-1135).
1118	Thomas Becket was born in London.
1122	Eleanor of Aquitaine is born.
1127	Matilda, Henry's daughter, marries Geoffrey, IV, Count of Anjou.. She is 26 and he is 14. They have three children: Henry II, Geoffrey de Gatinais, Count of Nantes, William de Gatinais, Count of Poitou.
1133	**Thomas is born.**
Dec. 1, 1135	King Henry I dies. As his only legitimate son William had died in 1120 (while crossing the Channel). He had insisted that the Barons swear allegiance to his daughter Matilda. Although the Barons bowed to his wishes they are not happy. They do not want a female ruler or a ruler from Anjou (her husband's country).
1135-1154	King Stephen Rules. Stephen, who's mother is William the Conqueror's daughter Adela, with the support of his brother the Bishop and therefore the English church, was crowned King at Westminster Abbey by the Archbishop of Canterbury. Matilda, Henry I's daughter, contests Stephen's succession to the throne. Another claimant, Robert,

	Earl of Gloucester (who was an illegitimate son of Henry I) eventually sides with Matilda in her claim to the throne. Civil War in England looms.
1137	*William X, duke of Aquitaine and count of Poitou, dies leaving his daughter Eleanor of Guienne, 15, as duchess of Aquitaine and countess of Poitou.* The orphaned Eleanor was the richest heiress in France, thus a marriage was arranged for her to its King, Louis VII (1121-1180)
1137	Gruffydd ab Rhys, ruler of the Kingdom of Deheubarth, dies and his four sons work closely together to defend and consolidate their territory. Each son, Anarawd, Cadell, Maredudd, and Rhys took the lead in succession, and there seems to have been no discord between them.
1139	**Thomas is made a page to Richard FitzUrse.**
1139-1154	The Civil War in England
12/1140-1/1141	The Battle of Lincoln – the Welsh side with Matilda. King Stephen is captured and taken prisoner.
January 1141	✸ **Chapter One**
1141	In April Matilda is elected Queen and moves to London for her coronation. But her treatment of the citizens of London is so poor they drive Matilda and her followers out before she can be crowned. King Stephen's wife raises and sends an army to assist her husband, who is still captive. During this siege Robert, Earl of Gloucester is captured. Eventually both captives are exchanged and Stephen resumed his position as King.
November 1141	✸ **Chapter Two**
1143	**Thomas begins serious knight training under William FitzRobert of Gloucester.**
1144	With the wars of Stephen and Matilda, the Tosny's hold on Clifford Castle weakened. Roger Tosny's steward, Walter FitzRichard, had for a long time been calling himself Walter Clifford and had married Margaret Isobel Tosny, Roger's sister.
1146	Eleanor of Aquitaine, age 24, announces at Vezelay on Easter Sunday, that she is turning over her thousands of vassals to the Abbe Bernard of Clairvaux for a Second Crusade, which she vows to lead herself.
1147	Robert Earl of Gloucester dies and Matilda, having

	lost her most powerful ally, returns to Normandy never to see England again. William FitzRobert becomes the 2nd Earl of Gloucester.
1147 and 1149	Matilda's son Henry (Henry II) like his mother is unhappy with Stephen as king. He attempts to invade England twice but fails both times (when he is 14 and 16). He returns to Normandy where he concentrates on building a future for himself.
1148	**Rosamund is born.**
1151-1153	The Welsh capitalize on the civil war raging in England and begin to attack previously Norman strongholds. Led by Rhys ab Gruffydd, they began extending their control in every direction and soon dominated all of southwest Wales.
1151	Henry and an unknown mistress have a son, Geoffrey Plantagenet. Becomes Archbishop of York. Not to be confused with legitimate son Geoffrey with Eleanor of Aquitaine.
1152	*France's Louis VII has his marriage to Eleanor of Aquitaine annulled on grounds of consanguinity and returns her land and titles. Eleanor, now 30, has produced two daughters in 15 years but no male heir.* Within two months of her divorce Henry marries Eleanor of Aquitaine and adds through marriage the territories of Aquitaine. He is 19; she is 30. He is now Count of Anjou, Maine, and Touraine, and Duke of Normandy. With the marriage he gains domains that make him master of more than half of France.
1153	Henry and Eleanor have a son, William Plantagenet. (lives to 1156)
1/1153	Henry invades England again. It is his first time back in England since 1149 when he was knighted by the King of Scotland. During that same year, Stephen's son Eustace dies and Stephen agrees to Henry's wishes. Stephen lives out the rest of his life as King of England.
1153	**Thomas is knighted.**
1154	Henry becomes king. His empire now stretches from Scotland all the way through England, Normandy, Anjou to Aquitaine. The heart of his empire is Anjou, not England. Henry's early years as king find him controlling the rebellious Barons who had used the chaos of the civil

	war to fortify their homes and illegally control their territories. The castles they built are now known as "adulterine castles".
1154	Thomas a Becket is recommended by Theobald the Norman monk-archbishop of Canterbury to the new King Henry for the position of chancellor. Perhaps Theobald wanted someone reliable to report to him on the actions of the throne. Thomas and Henry become fast friends.
1154	**Thomas is involved with controlling the rebellious Barons along the Marches bordering England and Wales.**
1155	Henry and Eleanor have a son, Henry Plantagenet (lives to 1189, The Young King)
1156	Henry and Eleanor have a daughter, Matilda Plantagenet (lives to 1189)
1156	**Rosamund is sent to the nunnery of Godstowe in Stowe, Gloucestershire.**
1157	Henry and Eleanor have a son, Richard Plantagenet (lives to 1199) King Richard I
1158	Henry and Eleanor have a son, Geoffrey Plantagenet (lives to 1186) Duke of Brittany
1160	Rhys ab Gruffydd seeks an alliance with Owain Gwynedd, the leader of North Wales, as well as lesser chieftains, which quickly becomes a coalition. A Welsh alliance of unprecedented proportions marks the end of the peace the King had enforced in Wales.
1161	**Rosamund returns to Castle Clifford to prepare for her marriage.**
August 14, 1161	✪ Chapter Three
1161	**Rosamund marries at 13. The wedding is at Warwick Castle. She marries Humphrey de Vern, Earl of Hereford and Essex. He is 55. She resides with her husband at his Herefordshire holdings – Goodrich Castle. Humphrey swears allegiance to King Henry but his holdings are near the disputed Welsh borders.**
1162	Henry and Eleanor have a daughter, Eleanor Plantagenet. She lives to 1214
1162	Prince Rhys captures the royal castle of Llandovery.
August 1162	✪ Chapter Four
November 1162	✪ Chapter Five
November 1162	✪ Chapter Six

December 1162	✤ Chapter Seven
December 1162	✤ Chapter Eight
1162	**Castle Goodrich is attacked and taken by the Welsh. King Henry II is informed.**
1163	Henry returns to England and stays until 1166
1163	Henry marches into Carmarthen, captures Rhys in his lair of Cantref Mawr, and brings him back to England as his prisoner.
April, 1163	✤ Chapter Nine
May, 1163	✤ Chapter Ten
1163	Archbishop of Canterbury Theobald dies. Henry makes Becket archbishop the day after he is hastily ordained as a priest. Perhaps Henry thought he could better control the church with his friend in power even though Thomas warned him he might regret the choice.
June, 1163	✤ Chapter Eleven
June, 1163	✤ Chapter Twelve
July, 1163	✤ Chapter Thirteen
July 1, 1163	Henry summons all the leaders of the Welsh together with the king of Scots – King Malcolm to attend his court at Woodstocke on July 1 and requires them to perform homage as his vassals. They apparently found the experience humiliating, for thereafter King Malcolm's relations with Henry became frigid, and the Welsh immediately break into a massive uprising against Anglo/Norman occupation. Also at this council, Archbishop Becket publicly unfurls the banner of defiance, loudly condemning a not unreasonable proposal by the King to divert a larger proportion of sheriffs' profits into the royal treasury. The issue is not of major importance and Becket seems simply to be seizing an opportunity to declare to the world that he is no longer the king's lackey.
10/1163	The Council Meeting of Westminster.
November, 1163	✤ Chapter Fourteen
1163	**Henry II builds a bower in the gardens of Woodstocke Manor that is a maze of such difficulty that no one can get in or out without knowing the key.**
January, 1164	✤ Chapter Fifteen
July, 1164	✤ Chapter Sixteen

October, 1164	✦ Chapter Seventeen
November, 1164	✦ Chapter Eighteen
1164	Henry begins his famous quarrel with his friend Thomas Becket, the Archbishop of Canterbury.
1165	Henry and Eleanor have a daughter, Joanna Plantagenet. She lives to 1199
1166	Henry and Eleanor have a son, John Plantagenet, He lives to 1216. King John
1170	Becket returns to England and an outburst of anger by Henry "Who will rid me of this meddlesome priest?" leads to four magnates murdering Becket at Canterbury on December 29th. The four knights names were Richard Brito, Hugh de Moreville, Reginald FitzUrse, and William de Tracy.
1171	Eleanor of Aquitaine and her daughter Marie establish a "court of Love" at Poitiers to teach concepts of courtly love.
1171	Henry confirms Rhys' tenure of the lands he had conquered: Ceredigion, Cantref Bychan, Emlyn, and two others near Carmarthen. Confirms his right as justicular for south Wales, gives him an English title which carries clear delegation of royal authority over Welsh leaders and communities which look to Rhys from the lordships of Gwynllwg, Usk, Caerleon, Glamorgan, Elfael and Maelienydd. He is known as Lord Rhys, one of the greater lords of the southern March. He dies in 1197, and was the dominate ruling prince in Wales for more than 40 years.
1172	Eleanor of Aquitaine raises Aquitaine against her faithless husband, Henry II, and he is forced to reconcile his differences with the Pope.
1173	The English princes Richard and Geoffrey lead a rebellion against their father, Henry II with support from Eleanor of Aquitaine and many of Henry II's barons. But the House of Commons gives hearty support to the king.
1174-1189	Queen Eleanor is imprisoned by Henry for supporting the rebellion of two of her sons against their father. She in imprisoned in Winchester.
1174	Marie, countess of Champagne, daughter of Eleanor of Aquitaine by Louis VII, issues a proclamation: "We declare and we hold as firmly established that love cannot exert its powers between two people who are married to each other, for lovers give each other

	everything freely, under no compulsion or necessity, but married people are in duty bound to give in to each other's desires and deny themselves to each other in nothing."
1176	Henry and an unknown mistress have a son, William Longsword, (lives to 1226), becomes Earl of Salisbury
1189	Henry II dies.
1189-1199	Richard Plantagenet, The Lionheart, is crowned King of England.

About The Author

usan McGeown is a wife, mother, daughter, sister, aunt, uncle (don't ask), friend, teacher, author ... but, most importantly, a "woman after God's own heart." Living in Bridgewater, New Jersey, with her husband of over fifteen years and their three children, writing stories is just about the best way she can imagine spending her free time. Each of Sue's stories champions those emotions nearest and dearest to her: faith, joy, hope and love.

Philippians 1:20-21

For I fully expect and hope that I will never be ashamed, but that I will continue to be bold for Christ, as I have been in the past. And I trust that my life will bring honor to Christ, whether I live or die. For to me, living means living for Christ, and dying is even better.

Footnotes

[1]Marie, Countess of Champagne, daughter of Eleanor of Aquitaine by Louis VII, proclamation issued by her in 1174, <u>The Women's Chronology</u>, By James Trager, Henry Holt and Company, New York, 1994, ISBN 0-08050-2975-3, pg. 66

[2] Demosthenes, (?385-?322 B.C.), Greek Orator, <u>GenderBabble</u>, By David Olive, Perigee Books, New York, 1993, ISBN 0-399-51821-5, pg. 19

[3]Aristotle (384-322 B.C.), Greek philosopher, 4th Century, B.C. <u>A Woman's Place</u>, Quotations about Women, Edited by Anne Stibbs, Avon Books, New York, 1992, ISBN: 0-380-71850-2, pg. 6

[4] Pythagoras, (?532-?500 B.C.), Greek Philosopher, <u>GenderBabble</u>, By David Olive, Perigee Books, New York, 1993, ISBN 0-399-51821-5, pg. 17

[5] Plutarch,(?46 - ?120 A.D.) Greek biographer and philosopher, 2nd Century, <u>A Woman's Place</u>, Quotations about Women, Edited by Anne Stibbs, Avon Books, New York, 1992, ISBN: 0-380-71850-2, pg. 9

[6] Gottfried von Strassburg (1210 A.D.), German poet, <u>A Woman's Place</u>, Quotations about Women, Edited by Anne Stibbs, Avon Books, New York, 1992, ISBN: 0-380-71850-2, pg. 15

[7] Juvenal (Decimus Junius Juvenalis, 60-130 A.D.) Roman satirist, 1st century A.D., <u>A Woman's Place</u>, Quotations about Women, Edited by Anne Stibbs, Avon Books, New York, 1992, ISBN: 0-380-71850-2, pg. 9

[8] Aristotle (384-322 B.C.) Greek philosopher, <u>GenderBabble</u>, By David Olive, Perigee Books, New York, 1993, ISBN 0-399-51821-5, pg. 17

[9] Herodotus, (5th Century B.C.), Greek historian, <u>GenderBabble</u>, By David Olive, Perigee Books, New York, 1993, ISBN 0-399-51821-5, pg. 17

[10]German poet who wrote about Eleanor of Aquitaine, <u>The Middle Ages</u>, By John Gillingham and Peter Earle, Edited by Antonia Fraser, University of California Press, Los Angeles, CA, 1998, ISBN 0-520-22799-9, pg. 44

[11] Epicurus, 341-270 B.C., http://www.quotationspage.com/search.php3?Search=&x=40&y=16&Author=Epicurus&C=mgm&C=motivate&C=classic&C=coles&C=lindsly&C=poorc

[12] Andreas Capellanus, 12th Century, A Treatise on Courtly Love, 1184-1186 A.D., From "The Rules of Love", Number 9,

http://historymedren.about.com/gi/dynamic/offsite.htm?site=http://icg.harvard.edu/%7Echaucer/special/authors/andreas/index.html

[13] The ballad of *Fair Rosamond* appears to have been first published in "Strange Histories, or Songs and Sonnets, of Kinges, Princes, Dukes, Lords, Ladyes, Knights, and Gentlemen, &c. By Thomas Delone. Lond. 1607." 12mo. http://www.english.vt.edu/~drad/Courses/ENGL3034/Percy/Rosamond.html
[14] The Adventures of Beowulf an Adaptation from the Old English by Dr. David Breeden, The Adventures of Beowulf, Episode 11, Beowulf Fights the Dragon, http://www.lone-star.net/literature/beowulf/beowulf11.htm

[15] Exeter Book, Manuscript volume of Old English religious and secular poetry, compiled 975, Exeter Cathedral by Bishop Leofric (died 1072) http://www2.kenyon.edu/AngloSaxonRiddles/texts.htm

[16] Verse sung by Bernart de Ventadour, a famous troubadour said to be in love with Queen Eleanor, http://www.womeninworldhistory.com/EofAreturns.html

[17] George Gascoigne, 1539-1578, The Complete Works of George Gascoigne, 1587, http://www.sourcetext.com/sourcebook/Star/appendix.html#anchor265263

[18] Heraclitus, 540-480 B.C., On the Universe, http://www.quotationspage.com/subjects/character/

[19] 2 Timothy 1:7, KJV

[20] Valerie Worth, 1933-1994

[21] Aristotle, 384-322 B.C., http://www.quotationspage.com/subjects/happiness/

[22] Sophocles, 496 B.C.-406 B.C. http://www.quotationspage.com/subjects/love/31.html

[23] From Divina Commedia "Paradiso", Dante's Alighieri's third canticle, (1265-1321) http://mr_sedivy.tripod.com/quotes4.html

[24] Deuteronomy 31:8, King James Version

[25] Bill Watkin's favorite Welsh sayings. http://wildbillwatkins.com/songs/sayings.html

[26] The ballad of *Fair Rosamond* appears to have been first published in "Strange Histories, or Songs and Sonnets, of Kinges, Princes, Dukes, Lords, Ladyes, Knights, and Gentlemen, &c. By Thomas Delone. London. 1607." 12mo. http://www.english.vt.edu/~drad/Courses/ENGL3034/Percy/Rosamond.html

[27] Henry II, by W. L. Warren, University of California Press, 1973, ISBN: 0-520-03494-5, pg. 628.

[28] Arnulf of Lisieux, *Letters*, no. 42, 73, Henry II, by W. L. Warren, University of California Press, 1973, ISBN: 0-520-03494-5, pg. 628.

[29] Medieval Wales, By David Walker, Cambridge University Press, 1990, http://www.castlewales.com/lrdrhys.html

[30] The Middle Ages, By John Gillingham and Peter Earle, Edited by Antonia Fraser, University of California Press, Berkeley, 2000, ISBN 0-520-22799-9, pg. 44

[31] The Middle Ages, By John Gillingham and Peter Earle, Edited by Antonia Fraser, University of California Press, Berkeley, 2000, ISBN 0-520-22799-9, pg. 44

[32] Marie, Countess of Champagne, daughter of Eleanor of Aquitaine by Louis VII, proclamation issued by her in 1174, The Women's Chronology, By James Trager, Henry Holt and Company, New York, 1994, ISBN 0-08050-2975-3, pg. 66

[33] Romans 8:28, New Living Translation